Sorting Out Billy

Jo Brand

review

First published in 2004
by HEADLINE BOOK PUBLISHING

First published in paperback in 2005
by HEADLINE BOOK PUBLISHING

A REVIEW paperback

10 9 8 7 6 5 4 3 2 1

ISBN 0 7553 2030 1

Typeset in Caslon 540 Regular
by Palimpsest Book Production Limited, Polmont, Stirlingshire

Printed and bound in Great Britain by
Mackays of Chatham plc, Chatham, Kent

Headline's policy is to use papers that are natural, renewable and
recycleable products and made from wood grown in
sustainable forests. The logging and manufacturing processes
are expected to conform to the environmental
regulations of the country of origin.

HEADLINE BOOK PUBLISHING
A division of Hodder Headline
338 Euston Road
London NW1 3BH
www.reviewbooks.co.uk
www.hodderheadline.com

'There isn't a dull passage. You could open the book at random, throw a dart and find something droll, well-observed and hard to forget' *Sunday Express*

'Fans of Brand's take-no-prisoners wit should find plenty to enjoy' *Marie Claire*

'A laugh-a-page tale of three girls, their friendship, their blokes and their living arrangements; highly readable and genuinely funny' Alan Davies

'It gives great insight into what life is like on the comedy circuit (shit); what new motherhood amounts to (shit); families (shit); south London (double shit). But what the hell, pass me one of life's cream cakes – that new book by Jo Brand will do' *Guardian*

'Rude, crude and crammed full of brilliant one-liners' *Scottish Daily Record*

'This no-holds barred, no language spared, and no behaviour too bad tale of our times packs as much punch as any Jo Brand show and is guaranteed to leave you rolling with laughter' *Northern Echo*

'Jo Brand's fiction debut shows her to be a smart stylist with a confident narrative voice . . . [an] accomplished comedy of romantic bad manners' *Observer*

To Bernie, Maisie and Eliza

My thanks to everyone who has helped me put together this novel . . . they know who they are. I am particularly grateful to my family for leaving me to get on with it and to my editor Martin Fletcher whose enthusiastic and friendly manner got far more out of me than any homicidal drama queen would have managed. Thanks to Vivienne for reading it all in one go and for making encouraging noises. Thanks to all the poor sods who had to drag through this, ferreting out inconsistencies and correcting my terrible punctuation. My progress from novel virgin to woman of limited experience wasn't nearly as painful as I might have imagined. Cheers.

Prologue

Martha could remember exactly when it was that she had first started hating her father. She was four years old. Before that, she had simply felt a sense of unease about the harshness of his voice, his unpleasantly smelling hands and the way her mother Pat spent most of the day looking like a rabbit that has been taken out of its cage by some schoolboys and is about to be tortured.

The Day of Hate should have been a very joyous occasion because it was her sister Mary's seventh birthday, and in an uncharacteristically generous gesture, the Rev Brian had decided to throw a party for her. He had asked some friends and family round, but very few of either group had responded to the offer because his family didn't like him and most of his friends were in the process of becoming unfriends.

As the Harris family so rarely entertained, the Rev Brian was in a state of advanced anxiety, manifested as a mixture of bad temper and mild hysteria. This worried Martha. Some children from Mary's class in the small Suffolk village school had been roped in – under duress as none of them, despite the fact that they quite liked Mary, actually wanted to spend any time in the house of 'Reverend Smelly Belly' because he scared them. His nasal hair had been allowed to get out of control and as he always spoke to people – even small children – by shoving his face only a few inches away from theirs, it was enough to make a seven year old cry. Besides, he was a vicar.

So Rev Brian did his best to be an entertaining host, but after a couple of hours, the strain of marshalling ten grubby village children in what he considered to be his beautiful home and seeing dirty fingers travel up and down the curtains, pictures and wallpaper, his thin veneer of amiability was beginning to slip away.

Mary copped it first during a game of Pass the Parcel when she screamed a little too delightedly for the Reverend Brian's fragile state. He hauled her into a room out of earshot and smacked her with the words, 'Keep-the-noise-down-you-silly-girl-and-don't-show-me-up.' Mary had no idea what this last bit meant and was so shocked she almost forgot to cry.

Pat Harris, oblivious to the changing moods of her sulky husband, was in the kitchen humming and putting candles on the cake when the Rev Brian stamped in and said he had had enough of the little shits ruining the place, and that he was going to entertain the marauding gang of plebs in the garden, where they couldn't do any damage.

'Oh, come on, Brian,' said Pat, 'it's only once in a blue moon and they're having such fun. It's nice to hear them laughing and see their little faces looking so happy. Please don't ruin it, dear.'

This was too much for the Reverend, who had been bubbling under since that little Jim Baker from the village had cried when he discovered that the prize for winning Pass the Parcel was a Bible and since Kim Meades had wet her pants over the Persian rug in the hall when he shouted at her. He finally blew a gasket and marched Pat, holding her by the ear, through the party room, announcing as he passed that one thing he couldn't abide was a cocky woman and the only way to deal with her was to discipline her.

Under the fixed gazes of Martha and Mary and to the confusion of the guests, he pushed Pat, who was desperately trying to make a joke out of the whole thing, into the cupboard under the stairs and locked it.

'And stay there until you've learned some manners,' he said.

Even at the age of four, Martha was mortified. Pat could be heard, pleading in her gentle voice to be let out, but Rev Brian wasn't having any of it. He led everyone out into the garden, dismissing any protests and proving once again that people will pretty much do what they are told as long as someone is enough of a bully.

Martha could not contain her anger, and marching up to her father with all the sophistication and language control a four year old could manage, gave it to him right between

3

the eyes. 'I hate you, I hate you,' she said. 'You are a . . .' she hesitated. 'You are a wanker, Dad.'

Time stood still as the Rev Brian bore down upon her like a musty avalanche, scooped her up and carried her into the house. He took Martha to the bathroom where he pushed a lump of soap into her mouth. Then he hung her out of the bathroom window in as jokey a way as he could manage and shouted, 'Here she is, we're only having a bit of fun!' His voice sounded as if his testicles had recently been removed and made the word 'fun' sound as if it meant murder.

This was too much for the ordinary village families, who filed out of the vicarage garden and as soon as they were out, quickened their pace, giggling and whispering, eager to tell whoever they could as fast as they could.

It was many months before the Rev Brian was given absolution by the village for his behaviour that day, and Mary, Pat and Martha were punished for all that period, as naturally it was *their fault*.

As time passed on, things didn't get any better between Martha and her dad because Martha had decided to fight him at every opportunity. Mary, on the other hand, had decided she would submit and that would make life a lot easier. It was. The Reverend pretty much ignored her from then on, apart from the occasional scathing comment about her looks, domestic competence or choice of husband.

Both Martha and Mary had to be confirmed despite the fact that Martha had chosen, at around the age of six, to be an atheist, because she felt if God existed He wouldn't ever allow the sort of behaviour the Rev indulged in. It was on this occasion that her father took the opportunity to give a little talk to the congregation about the nature of God, illustrating it with some stories from family life, the dénouement of which was the relating of an incident which had happened the week before.

'Now my daughter Martha is a difficult little cuss at the best of times,' said the Reverend Brian, 'and not only that, she is quite greedy. Last week, for example, my wife Pat made some homemade lemonade which Martha loves and despite us urging moderation she drank gallons of the stuff. Consequently that night she wet her bed – can you believe it of a girl of eight?'

The children in the congregation sniggered and the parents looked embarrassed.

'I am only telling you this because my wife and I kept warning Martha not to have so much lemonade or there'd be an accident,' said the Reverend. 'Now we adults are a bit like Martha as far as God is concerned: we don't always heed His advice but He knows better.'

Martha felt as if all eyes were turned on her and wondered how she would survive school on Monday. Pat and Mary both burned with indignation and shame on her behalf, but neither would say anything, because Mary was now almost mute and Pat didn't want to wind the Rev up.

After that incident, despite the number of times Martha prayed desperately in the little church, she couldn't get God to admit that her dad was doing a crap PR job for Him or even give her a clue that He could see what she meant.

The Rev Brian haunted Martha's nightmares for the rest of her childhood and popped into her adult dreams with alarming frequency as well. He was tolerated by the villagers who all knew he was a bit of a bastard to his family but they found him good at his job, efficient and businesslike, and therefore were prepared to accept the slightly Dickensian attitude he took towards the three women in his life.

By the time she was a teenager, Martha's relationship with her father was constantly stirred to boiling point by the added ingredient of hormonal changes. Martha had thought the Rev Brian couldn't get any worse but then he showed a side to his nature she wasn't prepared for: he became a bit of a lech. After one evening when the Reverend, sweating and embarrassingly over-attentive, clingily waited hand and foot on Martha and her friend Joelle whose bosoms were enormous, Martha decided to size up friends on the basis of how much they would sexually arouse the Rev and hence a series of spotty, unattractive teenage girls could often be seen trudging in and out of the vicarage as if all beauty and animation had been banned. Boyfriends were recruited solely on the basis of their unsuitablility, Martha bussing in drug-users and working-class boys to wind up her father and becoming sexually active at the age of fourteen.

She lost her virginity to a local farmworker who was nineteen and she fantasised about a shotgun wedding ceremony conducted by her father, head in his cheesy hands.

Mary was neither help nor hindrance in the battle against

the Reverend Brian and like a great sulking bat withdrew to her bedroom for most of her teenage years and surrounded herself with Gothic paraphernalia and dressed herself in the manner of a Victorian widow with a penchant for erotica.

Pat, who had been an innocent, cheerful farmer's daughter attracted by the brooding bad temper of Brian as a young man, constantly berated herself for allowing her husband to treat her two daughters as if they were dangerous dogs that needed to be taught who was boss.

And despite the fact that she knew her husband was a pathetic bully, she could not quite bring herself to administer the coup-de-grace of a divorce because she wanted to feel that underneath the sulking, bad-tempered surface there was an intellectual and an idealist who still loved her very much. Unfortunately he had been replaced by this malodorous, labile old fart within a very short time of them having married, and it seemed unlikely that pre-marriage Brian would ever resurface. So Pat sat through many humiliations, both public and private, about which she was enormously ashamed and the little whispers she always seemed to hear behind her when she went to the village for some shopping or to borrow books from the library always seemed to say, 'Pat you are pathetic, Pat you are weak, Pat you deserve what you get.' Eventually she believed it.

The Reverend Brian did go through a period in Martha's twenties of temporarily being struck by the teaching of Christianity as a true force for good and he thought he'd better try and win back the respect of his daughters.

Mary wasn't too difficult. By that time she had married Derek the skull and anything which interrupted the tedium of their ordered life was welcome even if it was her irritable father attempting to slime his way back into her affections.

In contrast Martha stood firm and continued to notch up a series of coronary-inducing firsts for the Reverend Brian, including having a tattoo which said *Jesus Sucks* on her bum and flashing it on the odd occasion in the village when she was pissed, dropping out of college, becoming a Muslim for a while and getting a job as a waitress in a strip club in Soho.

Her three ambitions were to be a single mother, to see her mum happy, and to have her father on his knees begging for forgiveness. If he was naked and covered in the contents of a rubbish bin, all the better.

Chapter 1

The telephone rang in Martha Harris's twelfth-floor council flat in South London, interrupting the fantasy she was having about killing her father with a steel knitting needle thereby terminating one of his usual lectures on any subject about which he deemed himself knowledgeable, which was Everything-In-The-World-Ever-Written-Thought-Or-Said.

She picked up the phone and the image melted away. There was a silence at the other end of the line, punctuated by the occasional almost inaudible squeak, the sound you make when you are trying not to cry.

The squeak was replaced by a faltering voice. 'It's me . . . Sarah,' it said.

'What's up, mate?' said Martha.

'I can't tell you on the phone. Meet me in the pub in half an hour,' said Sarah. 'I'll call Flower.'

Martha wanted to light up a fag, but looking down at her huge, alive tummy, she thought better of it. A potential crisis warranted a cigarette but this wasn't a real emergency yet, although she had lost sight of what was: nowadays, getting a bad picture on Channel Four would merit at least two packs of Silk Cut. She wished she'd been brought up in a happy, hippy home which had left her serene and content, not addicted to anything and everything that staved off her anxiety, and she often thought about wreaking a terrible revenge for a lifetime of disinterest and humiliation on her father, the Reverend Brian Harris. For over thirty years now, Martha had carried around in her head a list which condemned her dad to death and it grew with almost every encounter they had.

Reasons To Kill My Dad
He is responsible for me being called 'Martha'.
He smells like an old cheese sandwich.
He's horrible to Mum and has made her believe she
    deserves it.
He's cruel, despite the fact he's supposed to be a
    representative of Jesus.

This is a random selection from hundreds of resentments nurtured during her childhood, adolescence and adult life. As soon as she could, Martha escaped from the disapproving gaze of the tiny village in Suffolk and took emotional potshots at the Rev from long distance, her latest involving living in this really grim council flat in South London and getting pregnant by someone she hardly knew.

Even though she relished the thought of being a single

mother, Martha had genuinely made a mistake with contraception, something she was too ashamed even to tell her friends. She'd arranged a termination but hadn't been able to go through with it – the curse of the Rev Brian's moral values was too deeply instilled. And now 'Lump' was seven months old in her womb and really starting to make his or her presence felt. Nobody knew the identity of the father and Martha was determined not to tell them. Her friends thought it was because the father was someone hideous or right wing; her father thought it was because he was black; and her sister Mary thought it was because it was her husband Keith. Little did Mary know that if some enormous, bloated, syphilitic dictator and Mary's husband Keith were the last two men left on earth, and Martha *had* to have sex with one of them to continue the human race, she would have tackled the north face of the Dictator, ignored the squirting, and got on with it.

Martha enjoyed telling her father about Lump and also took particular pleasure in revealing that she wasn't sure who the father of the baby was. The news was delivered during tea one weekend at the vicarage.

'You're *what*?' screamed the Rev Brian.

'Pregnant,' said Martha calmly.

'Not married,' spluttered the Rev Brian, disgorging biscuit crumbs onto the cat's back. 'What will the Parish think?'

'That I'm an old slapper?' suggested Martha.

At this point the Rev used some inappropriate language for a man of God and Martha left. The Reverend Brian would have liked to give his daughter a slap but as she was thirty-seven he realised this was not on, so instead he fumed to Pat, and bemoaned the fact that he hadn't had a son who undoubtedly would have turned out more like him. Given that he had named his two daughters Martha and Mary, that meant he would, if he was being faithful to familial relationships in the Bible, have had to call his son Lazarus, and Lazarus loomed large as a figure of hate in Martha and Mary's consciousness. Lazarus certainly would not have said 'fuck' to Mrs Avedon at the 1979 summer fete. Martha's defence – that it was in response to a very boring story about the woman's runner beans and that at least she didn't say 'Fuck off' – did not impress the Rev and he went into one of his long, grim silences which really cheered Martha and her mum up, briefly.

Martha's friends wanted to tell her that this lifelong battle against the Rev had something of the 'cutting off her nose' about it, and ask why she didn't just relax and enjoy herself, but they never got round to it. There were quite enough drunken parties at which they could have told her. Flower had had a stab at it once, a couple of years ago, when they were all a bit pissed on New Year's Eve, but Martha, who didn't drink vodka very often, had turned nasty and threatened to punch Flower who, being of hippy stock, as evidenced by her name, withdrew swiftly and tried to persuade Sarah to tell her instead. Sarah, however, was too timid and even if she had attempted it, she possessed the subtlety of a smack in the gob, so she would just have made things worse.

Sarah was an enthusiastic consumer of modern life (except food) and all its demonic trappings, from her regular order in the newsagents for celebrity magazines to her frequent trips to Oxford Street in a tidal wave of purchasing reminiscent of the feeding frenzy of a lottery winner shortly before buying a helicopter. Flower often berated her about her rampant gobbling up of the capitalist ethos, but Sarah had no idea what capitalism was, and Flower's frequent attempts to get Sarah on the odd protest march always elicited the sort of horrified face that Sarah reserved for someone who had borrowed her new top without asking. Sarah was the sort of person who made a cup of tea when a brilliant TV programme was on and lapped up the adverts. Along with her acceptance of the status quo, she, much more than the others, had been on a long-term pilgrimage to find a man to validate her existence in the starring role of husband and sperm provider for the future production of children. She had already worked out the kids' names (Nathan and Emily), what they would wear at their Christenings and she wanted an elective Caesarean because this involved fewer unpleasant fluids cascading over her nightie. (No one had told Sarah yet that in the birthing process, a pretty nightie tends to metamorphose into a butcher's apron.) Sarah found herself somewhat miffed when Martha announced her forthcoming event, in the pub, to her and Flower.

'Are you sure you're pregnant?' she said.

'Well, I've done a test,' said Martha.

'Oh, I'd do another one – they don't always work, you know,' said Sarah.

'Bollocks! Yes, they do,' said Martha, sensing something in Sarah's voice. 'Don't worry Sar. It is written that you will produce some little buggers. And Connie begat Sarah begat Nathan and Emily,' she announced in biblical tones to the pub, whilst Sarah looked nonplussed and wondered if her friend had gone bonkers.

The three always met at the same pub, the King's Head near the Oval cricket ground. It stood, Victorian, scarred and lonely, surrounded by 1950s estates, like the sole survivor of a bombing raid, and glowed at night like a dying ember amongst the harsher neon lights of a threatening, scarier age.

Martha set off for the pub at seven and was pleased to see it was raining. She felt safer in the rain. She assumed that burglars and rapists didn't go out when it was raining because at heart, they were lazy, pathetic bastards who were reluctant to get wet.

Sarah was heading to the pub from a different direction. She hated the rain. It made her make-up run, her clothes look shite, and meant she turned up at places where potential husbands might be lurking looking bedraggled and unmarriageable. Martha, Flower and Sarah were all in their mid- to late-thirties and Sarah rather regretted the fact that she'd missed out on being a ladette because she was too old. Had she been able to run around drinking beer and swearing she thought that would have given her life so much more meaning.

Being six foot tall, the rain always hit Flower before

everybody else and she would happily raise her head and let it run over the make-up-free zone that was her face. Sarah was appalled by Flower's refusal to wear make-up. To her it was like going without pants. Flower hadn't actually told Sarah she was knickerless too!

Although she didn't like to admit it because people thought she was a ballsy feminist, Martha was absolutely terrified of negotiating the rubbish-cluttered street round where she lived at night, because of the gangs of what would have been considered ten years ago, relatively young lads. Now, with the benefit of better diets, they were testosterone-soaked, huge, grown-up men in the bodies of fourteen year olds whose vocabulary of swearwords and sexist abuse was precisely targeted, if not vast. They could also smell fear, and its presence in their nostrils led them to track Martha along the road, trying to make her cry. It didn't take much, given that her hormone content was running at about 97 per cent of her body mass, so even if someone shouted something as harmless as, 'Up the duff!' at her, she would be reduced to tears. And these were South London boys. They weren't going to stop at something as Ealing Comedy as 'Up the duff!' Oh no. Poor old Martha was regaled with everything their poor starved imaginations could come up with, and with her head down, she marched on wishing that the cane was still used in school and that capital punishment existed for the extra special crime of calling someone 'a fat slag'.

'Fuck off!' she retorted, wishing she didn't sound quite so much like a language coach from Surrey.

Flower, because of her height, her bicycle and her social-workeresque appearance, also suffered the harsh verbal slings and arrows of the public, but it tended to be more amused banter than vitriolic abuse, until one day, a car full of lads had passed and one of them leaned out to pull her plait.

'Oi!' he shouted. 'It's a fucking giraffe on a bike!'

Flower had discovered in herself a rage she did not know she was capable of. She followed them to the next set of lights, pulled off their windscreen wipers and kicked the side of the car, oblivious to the fact that they could kill her if they wanted to. Lucky for her, they were more bemused than angry to see this angular girl lay into their car, and she escaped without injury.

Sarah, on the other hand, was the sort of person who got a bit miffed if some medieval sex offender on a building site *didn't* comment on her appearance.

The unlikely trio of friends had met some ten years before at a charity Christmas function aiming to feed and water London's homeless. Sarah had thought there might be some nice blokes there, Martha had thought there might be some horrible ones she could introduce to the Rev Brian, and Flower hadn't fancied Christmas dinner at home. They were the last of the single hold-outs as all their separate groups of friends gradually met people, got married and moved to somewhere with fewer asthma-inducing agents in the air.

The King's Head was its normal scruffy self, the sort of place where the last bloke to clean the ceiling had got nicotine poisoning. Martha liked its dingy corners, which hid her imperfections even in the daytime and, as she sat there nursing a mineral water and no fag, she speculated on the possible reasons for Sarah's phone call. Given Sarah and her foibles, it had occurred to Martha that it might be due to a bad decision in a shoe shop in Covent Garden at the weekend, or perhaps a haircut that made her look three weeks older than she was, but there had been something about the call that suggested otherwise. She looked up to see Flower, flushed and wet, heading towards her.

'Drink?' said Flower.

'No thanks,' said Martha. 'Just the one water always does me.'

Flower purchased some hideous concoction involving tomato juice, lime cordial and soda water, and sat down next to Martha.

'Well, what do you reckon?' she said.

'I expect it's something to do with Billy,' said Martha, who had only met the man a few times and had taken an instant dislike to him; even with her limited knowledge of psychiatry, she had pronounced him to have a personality disorder.

'Multiple personality disorder?' Flower had enquired, having watched a film once about some woman in America who had loads of personalities.

'A "no personality" disorder from what I can see,' said Martha.

'Man-hater,' teased Flower, which caused Martha to launch into her usual speech about why being a feminist didn't mean you had to hate all men, accompanied by Flower slumping ever lower under the table with the whites of her eyes showing and a slight trail of dribble coming from the corner of her mouth, until Martha eventually noticed and shut up.

Then Sarah was blown in through the door looking almost human compared to her usual immaculate self. Sarah was one of those people who could wear a white suit in a coal mine and come out looking exactly as she did when she went in, as opposed to Martha, who seemed to attract flying lumps of curry onto her clothes wherever she went. Sarah, it seemed, had seriously let herself go, an indication that a huge crisis was occurring. To Martha and Flower's horror, she hadn't even put on any make-up, a disaster to rank in Sarah's book along with pet bereavement.

Flower had already got Sarah her bottle of fizzy lemon mixed with vodka and called something like 'Tropical Shag', a drink in Martha's opinion that was responsible for more teenage pregnancies and venereal diseases than anything else. Still, Martha couldn't talk. She, at the great age of thirty-seven, wasn't exactly setting a good example to local spinsters.

'So,' said Flower, 'what's the matter, Sarah?'

A tear began to make its way out of their friend's left eye and down her unmade-up cheek.

'It's Billy,' she said in a weary voice especially reserved for telling Flower and Martha that her latest relationship had failed in some oh-so-predictable way again.

'Has he finished with you, disappeared without trace,

stolen your watch or sat on the cat when he was pissed?'
enquired Martha, recalling Sarah's last four relationships
and hoping to lift the gloom somewhat.

'He's hit me,' said Sarah.

Martha and Flower were stunned. Neither of them had
expected this. True, they both treated poor Sarah's increasingly desperate search for a man and subsequent failure as
a bit of a joke, but they hadn't prepared for this eventu-
ality and there followed a very long pause.

Finally, at exactly the same time, Martha said, 'The
bastard,' and Flower said, 'Are you all right?' Sarah
responded to the question. 'Yes,' she said. 'I'm all right
physically. He didn't hit me very hard, but I'm not all right
up here.' She pointed to her head.

Flower, who unfortunately for her had done a bit of
supply teaching and had had to wise up very quickly at a
local comprehensive, not having realised that if fourteen-
year-old boys were bored, they had wanking competitions
in class, remembered a study she had read in which teenage
boys said it was perfectly all right to hit girls if they nagged
you and went into overdrive.

'Have you called the pigs?' she asked, an enquiry which
because of its seventies' protest angle made Martha laugh
very inappropriately.

'Flower,' she said, 'you can't call them pigs any more.
That's so . . . so . . . Greenham Common.'

Flower looked at her with irritation. 'I don't think now's
the time to discuss my use of language,' she said and turned
again to Sarah. 'Have you called . . . *them*?'

'God, no,' said Sarah. 'That would be well over the top.'

'What about Rape Crisis?' continued Flower.

'Flower,' said Martha, 'I'm all in favour of these organisations in their rightful role, but Rape Crisis – that would be bonkers!'

'What about a refuge of some sort?' said Flower, leading Sarah and Martha to believe she really had lost it big time.

'Shall we all calm down,' said Martha. 'Come on, Sar. Tell us what happened.'

'Well,' said Sarah, 'last night I was working late and when I got in about nine, Billy was watching telly and drinking beer, and he was in a really foul mood. When I asked him how he was, he just ignored me, so I asked him again and he told me to shut up.'

Had he been studying at the Academy of the Reverend Brian? Martha wondered.

Sarah continued, 'Well, I went into the kitchen to make some food and called out to him to see if he wanted any, at which point he came storming into the kitchen telling me to leave him alone, to shut the fuck up, hadn't he told me enough times already, was I a fucking moron . . .'

At this point she began to cry again, and Flower, who was nearest, put her arm round her, somewhat awkwardly it has to be said, for despite the fact that Flower's mum and dad were good, old-school hippies, they'd been quite uncomfortable about the whole physical thing.

'So, then what happened?' said Martha who, subconsciously, had started to treat the incident as an omnibus version of a soap opera. Flower threw her a look which said,

'Can't you be more sensitive?' and Martha lowered her eyes demurely.

'I said to Billy, "I don't know what I've done, but I'm sorry",' said Sarah, 'and then he hit me round the face and walked out.'

'So what did you do then?' said Flower.

'Went to the toilet,' said Sarah, who was very regular and faithful in her reporting of the incident.

'And then?' said Flower.

'I watched telly, cried and went to bed,' replied Sarah. 'He came back in about midnight and—'

'Oh, I bet he was all over you, wasn't he,' interrupted Martha, 'saying how sorry he was, how he couldn't believe what he'd done, he'd never done it before, he'd never do it again, he loves you, he was so ashamed, he'd get help, he couldn't understand how it had happened . . .'

'Well, no,' said Sarah. 'He got into bed and went to sleep.'

'Yeh, but you're going to throw the wanker out today, aren't you?' said Martha.

Sarah's mobile rang. It was one of those ring tones you can buy from a magazine that is supposed to sound like a violent rap song, but in reality sounds like the tuneless musical accompaniment to some toy from the Early Learning Centre, so you find yourself humming 'Fuck the L.A.P.D' like a drama-school desperado on *Playbus* who hasn't moved onto grown-up stuff.

Martha could tell it was Billy calling, because poor old Sarah blushed and tried to sound businesslike and strict with him, when in fact Martha could tell that she desperately wanted to pretend the whole thing had never happened. After the call finished, Sarah, rather embarrassed, said, 'I've got to be going.'

Comments like 'Got to make his tea for him, have you?' or 'Does *he* need comforting, poor little bastard?' lay unsaid on Martha and Flower's lips, and they nodded semi-sympathetically. They'd both been there, not with violence, but with moody men who made them feel like pieces of shite, and felt that they should cover up to their friends and pretend they weren't that bad. Sarah was walking home now, wishing she had never mentioned 'the incident' to Martha and Flower. It would make life so much easier not being torn between Seemingly Proud Woman Who Doesn't Take Any Shit From Men In An Unacknowledged Yet Fundamentally Feminist Way and . . . Woman Who Loves Bloke So Much She Puts Up With Unspeakable Acts Of Abuse.

Martha and Flower sat morosely in the pub.

'She'll tell us if she wants some help, won't she?' said Flower. 'I get the feeling she doesn't want us to interfere. Maybe we should just keep an eye on things from a distance.'

Martha, who had been about to suggest they went round to Sarah's flat mob-handed, dragged Billy out, tortured him and left him for the crows to peck out his eyes, was somewhat taken aback.

'Do you want another of those weird drinks?' she said.

Chapter 2

A week or so later, Martha emerged from the reeking lift and walked heavily towards her front door. Martha always felt relieved when she finally got into her flat after work. At the moment she was a waitress in a club in Soho, some twelve steps down the social ladder from the Geography teacher her dad had hoped she would be. Getting around was an assault course for Martha, not only because she was frightened, but because she was hypersensitive to the comments of everyone she passed on her way. It was more to do with the fear of abuse rather than the reality. The combination of the Rev Brian as a father, an overactive imagination, and a life spent watching rather too many films in which women got stabbed, burned, slashed, decapitated, strangled, garrotted, de-entrailed and generally not treated very respectfully, had given her an ultra-developed sense of vulnerability. She was the one at whom the presenter's reassuring comments were aimed at the end of crime programmes and on whom, like most other anxious people, they had absolutely no effect whatsoever.

Therefore, a knock at the door past seven o'clock at night in Martha's block didn't bode well. It was unlikely to be someone selling organic vegetables or a Jehovah's Witness, who risked crucifixion if they ventured onto the estate. Martha thought that the organic vegetable-seller would have stood up to the test of crucifixion much more steadfastly because they were healthy and full of stamina, whereas the poor old Jehovah's Witness wouldn't even have been able to have a blood transfusion.

But somehow the apologetic tap at the door wasn't menacing and although Martha put the chain across, she opened the door with some confidence.

It was a shock. Her mother, Pat, was standing there, having made it alive and proud through the middle of a South London estate with a terrible reputation. She, who couldn't even manage a night's sleep in the tiny Suffolk village without a light on and a cheese knife under the pillow. Somehow, this intrepid woman had made it past some scary, scary obstacles, not least the gang of McDonald's-fuelled, ill-educated hecklers.

'Mum,' Martha managed to say, with as little panic and surprise as possible in her voice. 'What are you doing here?'

'I've left your father,' said Pat, as triumphantly as a timid, sixty-one-year-old vicar's wife could manage, 'and I couldn't think of anywhere else to go.'

'What about Mary in Sevenoaks?' said Martha automatically, thinking less than fondly of her bad-tempered sister married to a shrunken, spotty collection of bones and skin minus a personality.

'Oh, Mary would just send me straight back,' said her mother, 'and she can't make a decent cup of tea.' (Vicars' wives' lives are punctuated with many very bad cups of tea.) 'By the way, what's an "effing minger"?'

'Never mind,' said Martha, touched that her mother still couldn't manage the 'F' word, and taking her very small case from her. 'Come in.'

She could sense Pat's fragile good spirits sliding out of her body as she came into the flat. Yes, it was grim. Yes, it was neglected, and thanks to a curry last night, yes it smelled. Martha didn't believe in covering up smells with commercially produced different smells. After all, there's nothing worse than going into a toilet impregnated with some entrail-shifting floral scent. Martha suddenly foresaw an evening, nay a week, full of horror, as she tried to entertain her poor mother while Pat made up her mind about her future. Martha almost found herself wishing that her mum had stayed with the Rev.

She knew, first of all, she would have to put up with a bout of spring cleaning in which her mother would do a passable impression of someone with St Vitus's Dance, accompanied by minute questioning of the validity of every single item in the bathroom cabinet, a thorough excavation of her washing basket, and a laundry session the like of which had not been seen since Flower's netball team all got diarrhoea after a night out at a local Italian and Flower brought their kit round because the washing machine in the squat had a sculpture of some pants in it.

'Sit down, Mum,' said Martha, 'and tell me what's happened.' Martha had an eye on the clock, because one of her favourite programmes was on in five minutes.

'Turn the television off, dear,' said her mother.

Martha turned the sound down, but continued to sneak a look at the screen, and when the titles of the programme came up and her mother had only got as far as the incident outside the bathroom this very morning, when the Rev Brian, according to him, driven insane by her quiet incessant knocking, had appeared at the door, dignity dispensed with, various bits of himself flailing around, and landed a blow on her arm with a wet flannel, she found herself ever so slightly irritated.

'Oh, that's awful,' Martha said every few seconds while her mother continued the sorry tale, waltzing through what sounded like a comedy row conducted in every room of the house, before the dénouement in the garden with the woman next door threatening to call her husband and her mother's eventual flight from the vicarage with the vengeful words of the Rev Brian ringing in her ears. 'Don't come back here until you can stop behaving like a mouse!'

Martha had been at her mum and dad's a few weeks before to impart the news of her soon-to-be-visible illegitimate child, so her cushion-shaped tummy wasn't a surprise to her mother, but Pat Harris chose to tackle difficult situations by pretending they didn't exist, so she hadn't even mentioned it yet. Martha wasn't too bothered about this huge abyss in mother-daughter communication, because the sort of upbringing she'd had precluded mentioning periods without someone fainting. So, the two of them sat there for the evening talking politely like ladies at a church coffee morning, until Martha made up a bed for her mother with the cleanest-looking sheets she could find and heaved a sigh of relief as her mother disappeared for the night into the room she used as an office. It was only nine thirty. Martha still hadn't got over that teenage wonderment of people who can go to bed before midnight and consider it normal.

Sarah phoned at about ten, having got rid of Billy either in the bath or down the off-licence. It was a couple of weeks since the incident of the slap. Given the current crisis, it was of course impossible for Sarah to phone while he was in earshot in case she had to relate, second by nail-biting second, some recent incident between the two of them. Martha found her calmer and more back to her old self and under-exaggerating like a holiday rep.

'Yep,' said Sarah, 'I think I overreacted the other day. I mean, it wasn't really even a slap. It was a tap. Don't hold it against him, will you, Mart?'

'I'm not sure I could help it,' said Martha.

'Oh, please. For me?' There was a desperate girliness in Sarah's voice.

'I'll try,' said Martha, unconvincingly.

Martha wished she'd talked Sarah into ditching Billy and his flying fists, but instead she dialled Flower's number to compare notes.

'What do you reckon?' she asked Flower.

'Dunno, really,' said Flower, who was tired, irritable and not a little unsympathetic and temporarily floating outside her stereotype of a nice friendly hippy. There was the minutest of throat-clearings during a pause.

'Charlie!' said Flower. 'Get off the fucking extension.'

Charlie was Flower's bloke, a library assistant at the LSE who spent his spare time protesting about what an incredible mess the planet is in and how horrible most people are. Unfortunately, more by chance than design, because he was always in the thick of some sweaty, angry protest, he tended to meet quite a lot of horrible people, namely policemen who wanted to take their frustrations out on his unwashed head and assorted anarchists who saw every protest as an opportunity to rearrange a policeman's face into the shape of a piece of steak . . . unusual for vegetarians. Charlie, despite his laidback nature, was insanely jealous of Flower's every contact with the world and he attempted to monitor calls . . . as if Flower would phone her lover while Charlie was at home wandering about. Flower wanted to ask him who on earth would be interested in a six-foot-tall, vulture-nosed, failed stand-up comic and part-time social worker, but was aware that if he cottoned onto her sense of low self-esteem, he might bugger off too. One thing Flower had learned was that if you pretended you thought you were great and normal, nine times out of ten, people believed it. So that was what she tried to do. She often thought of Princess Diana and Marilyn Monroe and marvelled at how these women could hate themselves, although she knew intellectually that it was possible, despite the fact that Sarah maintained steadfastly that all the reports about low self-esteem were a mistake and someone who could shop like Diana couldn't possibly be unhappy in any way.

Another knock on the door startled Martha just as she was telling Flower about her day at work, and Flower agreed, as a safety measure, to stay on the phone while Martha went to the door, and then call the police if she didn't come back or heard blood-curdling screams. Martha herself knew that as the walls in the estate were fag-paper thin, any noises of violence would be heard, but ignored. In order to attract someone's attention, you had to put on a record really loud, as that would bring the neighbours down on you like big, badly-dressed locusts.

Just before Martha put the receiver down on the table, Flower said she didn't think she could stand to hear her being murdered, as if it was almost certain to happen, and then Charlie chipped in and said he'd listen for her, and Flower screeched at him and an argument started. So as the knocking got louder and more insistent, Martha left them at it, thinking they wouldn't even notice if a twenty-minute excavation of her innards took place. She put the chain across the door and opened it.

The two-inch crack revealed a snarling Rev Brian with what looked like some dog poo on his face. Still, it made a change from the snuff that dribbled out of his nose and went unnoticed only by him.

'Is your mother here?' he shouted.

'No,' Martha experimented. This didn't wash, of course.

'Don't lie, Martha,' he said. 'I've been to Mary's, she wasn't there, and let's be honest, the silly cow hasn't got the gumption to go anywhere else.'

Martha wondered, as she had on numerous occasions, if men of the cloth were allowed to behave like this, and resolved to grass her father up with an impassioned speech at the General Synod. Something she'd read recently in the Sunday paper came back to her, a simplistic analysis of Freudian theory in one sentence, which proposed that men spend their lives trying to escape from their mother and women spend their lives trying to attract their father's attention.

Christ, how wrong can they be, she thought. She sensed someone behind her. It was her mum in her favourite dressing-gown.

'Pat,' said the Rev Brian, through the crack in the door. 'Come home with me at once.'

'I will not,' retorted Pat, quite defiantly Martha thought. But just as she turned to congratulate her mother on her stand, the words, 'Oh all right then,' sailed past her towards her father.

'Mum,' she said, as imploringly as she could without the Rev Brian cracking on that she was trying to take her mother's side.

'No, dear, I've made up my mind,' said her mother.

And five minutes later, she was dressed, with her travelling case packed. The Reverend Brian looked smug. Martha felt depressed.

Then Pat Harris walked out of the flat door, banged the Rev on the nose with a spoon, and went straight back in. It was a dessert spoon, Martha noticed. Perhaps the only piece of information she had retained from domestic science lessons.

The Rev Brian yelped, backed off and disappeared into the gloom. He walked towards his car with a thunderous expression which should have told the *Big Issue* seller on his way home to give him a wide berth, but no. A man with a dog collar was too hard to resist; at which point the seller felt and smelled a huge, slightly cheesy hand being pushed into his face and found himself sitting down in the gutter. So much for the Good Samaritan, he thought.

Arriving at his fifteen-year-old Rover, the Rev Brian found it daubed with words which, when witnessed the next morning in the village, gave some of the residents quite a turn. The Rev Brian had presided over the parish for some thirty years now, although 'scared the shit out of it' might have been more accurate, and no one was surprised to see those sort of feelings expressed towards him.

Martha congratulated her mum and wondered whether she had found the little bottle of vodka she kept in her desk. Being a mother, Pat had naturally honed her ability to dig up drugs, sexual paraphernalia and booze. When she sobered up, things might be very different.

'We won't talk any more tonight,' said Martha. 'I'll see you tomorrow.'

Her mother padded off again. Martha cursorily flicked through the TV channels and, finding only the suicide-inducing crap that passed for late-night telly, flicked it off and sat thinking in the semi-darkness. She always left the big light off in her sitting room, as she only had lace curtains which became see-through at night and fuelled her fantasies about being watched by an army of self-abusing, frustrated old sex-offenders.

Gradually, she became aware of a tiny, yet angry noise, like a mosquito, and realised it was coming from the phone receiver. It was Flower, nearly hoarse with screaming. It was difficult to make out what she was trying to say, and Martha didn't need to bother because that very second, an over-ambitious, slightly hyped-up and very irritable rookie policeman kicked her door in.

Chapter 3

Flower had always wanted to express herself artistically in some way, and being a grungy old hippy had originally intended to do juggling or stilt-walking, until it began to dawn on her how brain-fragmentingly dull it was and she had a vision of the future in which an audience tried to gnaw off its own toes while sitting through her routine.

In the end, she had plumped for stand-up comedy, her reckoning being that it involved the least amount of work for the most amount of money. She also thought it was crap that people considered stand-ups brave in some way. All right, so verbal humiliation from a sadistic member of the audience was always a possibility, but Flower thought there were far worse things. Her approach was pragmatic. She knew, given her height and general oddness, that she would be heckled by people in the audience and so she had attempted to anticipate every type of heckle she could possibly receive and have an answer ready for it.

Unfortunately, this was not as easy as she had first thought. So, in her book of anticipatory put-downs, there ranged such possible replies as, 'Please don't be horrible to me, I've got a medical condition,' or, 'Why don't you fuck off,' both of which she knew she needed to improve on. The problem with humanity in all its glorious unpredictability, was that it kept coming up with heckles that she *couldn't* anticipate and which crumbled her comic resolve.

Flower was at the stage where she had maybe ten unpaid five-minute slots under her belt and was trying to persuade a number of equally frustrated male comics, who had decided the only way they could make it in comedy was to run their own clubs, to give her a paid gig. Many of the problems she had were associated with Charlie sitting at the back of every gig and threatening to assault the heckler before Flower even had a chance to try out her put-down.

Flower had tried to redirect Charlie's energies in a more fruitful way by asking him to help her write put-downs, and there hadn't been an incident for some weeks now. An additional string to Flower's comedy bow was that she was a social worker. Social workers are desperately unpopular, because the decisions they make can never be tested, unlike doctors who, if someone dies, just get all their mates to say it wasn't their fault. Flower worked in a residential home for people with learning difficulties, although the children who lived in the street in which the home was situated still preferred to address them as 'mongs', assuming that this word shouted very loudly at the group when they walked down the street was extremely funny.

Flower had begun to hone her put-down technique on these little bastards without even realising it, and her latest sharp-tongued assault, she believed proudly, had left a twelve year old in tears. This was less to do with 'How would you like it if someone in your family had learning difficulties, tosser?' and more to do with Charlie's surreptitious clip round the ear as he walked past him.

Flower had received an irate phone call from Martha after the police raid débâcle and had had to apologise several times in five minutes for calling in the Old Bill. She couldn't help herself, she explained, as the Rev Brian's voice sounded very frightening relayed down a phone line and when she heard his reaction to being hit on the nose by his wife, she decided to call the police, who were constantly on the alert as far as Martha's estate was concerned because there was often trouble there.

According to Martha, a group of hyped-up young policemen had destroyed her door and been pretty pissed off when they discovered there was only Martha and her mum inside. Martha had offered them a cup of tea, but taking in the state of her flat and Pat in a dressing-gown with the Ten Commandments printed on it, they withdrew swiftly, making a mental note that any trouble there in the future was likely to be a false alarm.

Coincidentally, earlier in the week, Flower had taken the liberty of contacting the police anonymously to find out what would happen if she called upon them in the future to sort out the Billy and Sarah situation.

Police operator: 'Yes?'

Flower: 'Um.'

Police operator (more impatiently and more unpleasantly than the first time, which had been quite unpleasant to start with): '*Yes?*'

Flower: 'I'm phoning for some advice.'

Police operator: 'About what?'

Flower: 'I'd like to speak to someone about domestic violence.'

Police operator (with a sigh): 'Hold on please, caller.'

There is silence on the line – thankfully, thinks Flower. At least we've not got 'The Four Seasons' or something grim out of the charts. Just good old wholesome silence for a change. In fact, come to think of it, the police could show themselves to be the possessors of a good bit of irony if they played something along the lines of 'Fuck the Police'. Eventually, a gruff male voice containing as much empathy as that of Travis Bickle came on the line and immediately wound up Flower by saying, 'Yeh?'

Flower: 'I've got a friend who's been hit by her boyfriend. Is there anything I can do?'

Gruff male voice: 'Does she want to press charges?'

Flower: 'No.'

Gruff male voice: 'No?'

Flower: 'Yes.'

Gruff male voice: 'Eh?'

Flower: 'Yes.'

Gruff male voice: 'Yes what?'

Flower: 'I can't remember.'

Gruff male voice: 'Call me when you can, love.'
Flower: 'Oh right. Thank you for your help.'

This last sentence was spoken into dead air, although of course Charlie was on the extension, but he couldn't say anything to Flower because he wasn't meant to be there. He wondered whether Flower was talking about herself. He tried to approach the topic several times after the call, but Flower's mind was elsewhere as she had a booking coming up. She was doing another five minutes at a small comedy club in East London which offered a try-out night for all new acts and was known by the other more experienced comics on the circuit as Death Valley, because you couldn't make that audience laugh if you paid them. And so a succession of unsuspecting baby comics flayed themselves, totally unaware that they were pissing in the wind in front of an audience who wouldn't have been out of place at a gangland funeral.

That night, Martha, Sarah and Billy had come down to give Flower 'some support', although what support a girlfriend-beater who had a closer relationship with his computer than his girlfriend could give Flower it was difficult to say.

That night on the bill there were the normal no-hopers and budding comic geniuses who hadn't yet descended into the pondlife where they would naturally settle in five years' time.

On the bill was 'Muff Diva', a cheerful lesbian who mixed great opera arias with rants about castrating men:

'Evening, women and complete fucking arseholes . . .'

Then there was 'Edie Azzard', a female version of a certain very successful stand-up:

'Hi, hi! What would it be like if a horse could open a bank account . . . ?'

And finally 'Dick Knob', whose comedy heroes included various sex-offenders and murderers. Dick Knob was quite a scary character whose friends had evaporated, given his propensity for trying out his act on them, since it involved a lot of spitting and occasional physical violence:

'I was holding this girl down on the floor earlier tonight . . .'

Five years later, an interested observer would have found Muff Diva in a steady relationship with a male school-teacher in Sussex and working as a sports mistress; Edie Azzard married with three kids to the timpanist in an orchestra and going slightly insane at home while her husband toured the world; and Dick Knob presenting his own TV show in Australia and being fêted by his peers.

Flower was on third, and the audience was thin. Her supporters included a couple of girls from her netball team who never went out in the week and therefore were quite excited. There was a group of blokes who looked much worse than they were, as groups of blokes invariably do, a couple of friends who had wandered in looking for a drink, Muff Diva's mum and Edie Azzard's boyfriend, who was the only person in the world who had any faith in Edie's comedy.

Charlie was stalking round the back of the room waiting for someone to start on Flower as she stepped onto the stage. The smattering of applause she received wasn't encouraging and although the group of lads weren't child-killers, they had had a few bevvies and felt it was their duty to start on her.

'What's the weather like up there?' ventured the group wag, as Charlie pulled him backwards off his chair.

'Charlie, for Christ's sake!' shouted Flower. 'Leave him alone, will you.' She took advantage of the moment to launch into her longest speech ever.

'Lookatyouyoulooklikeabloodyrescuedogwhothehelldo-youthinkyouaretryingtoprotectmelikesomewankymedieval-knightwithaweirdsenseofloyaltyletmestandonmyowntwo-feetorwe'refinishedandstoplisteningtomycallsyouarse-holeand . . .'

This was a bit of a departure from Flower's normal material which was about recycling and the ozone layer, and the audience loved it because it seemed so 'real'. Charlie was taken aback by the applause and cheering which accompanied Flower's rant and, rather than taking in what she said, started to plan her new act.

In the dressing-room afterwards – well, not so much a dressing-room, more a small kitchen which smelled of rotting vegetables and dirty tights – Charlie went through a brief list with Flower. Then he went off to the toilet and as Flower, all alone for a moment, turned to walk out and rejoin her group of friends, she found her face about two inches away from Billy's, which had transformed itself from its normal resting expression of bad temper into snarling aggression with a side dish of spittle.

'Keep your very big nose out of mine and Sarah's business, you overgrown piece of hippy scum,' he snarled, 'or you'll regret it.'

Typically, the one time that Flower was really threatened, Charlie wasn't there.

'I don't know what you mean,' said Flower, sounding like Celia Johnson in *Brief Encounter*.

Billy sneered like a bad actor, but with some real menace thrown in. 'I know you've been thinking, you and that pregnant cow, of getting involved in what doesn't concern you, but just forget it, or there'll be a lot more violence.'

Suddenly his face broke into a warm smile. 'Hiya, Charlie mate,' he said, as Charlie came back into the room. 'Better find Sarah, get her home. She's got a long day tomorrow.'

He led Sarah away from the table as if she was five years old and Martha thought of suggesting he might like to get her some reins for those difficult times when his hands were full, but didn't.

Flower hadn't told Charlie about Sarah and Billy's bit of domestic so she didn't know how she could bring it up, considering it had moved onto a more serious level. And Charlie shouldn't have been listening in to her conversation, so he couldn't mention it to her. Flower grabbed Martha and took her aside.

'Billy just threatened me,' she said.

'Don't be ridiculous,' said Martha. 'Threatened you about what?'

'Well, I'm not really sure,' said Flower, whose reporting skills weren't terribly sharp. 'He said that we shouldn't poke our noses into his and Sarah's business, but how could he know? I haven't even told you yet!'

'Told me what?' said Martha.

'Well,' said Flower, 'I phoned the police recently, because I just wanted to know where Sarah stood if Billy decided to cut up even rougher than he has done already.'

'And?' said Martha.

'Well, they were totally unhelpful. I don't know what I expected, but since they've got rape suites and all that sort of thing I somehow hoped that I might get some nice, floaty woman who sounded like a therapist and would listen patiently to my problems then give me a considered and useful answer.'

'And you got the usual.'

'Exactly. But how could Billy have known I was doing that?'

'Lucky guess?' said Martha.

Chapter 4

Sarah and Billy had walked about half a mile towards the river before a cab went past and they managed to stop it. As they crossed Tower Bridge heading for Sarah's flat, the argument, which had flared up like a small fire in a wastepaper bin, had become a raging house-destroying inferno by the time they got home.

'Give us a fag,' said Billy.

'I haven't got any,' said Sarah. 'We'd better stop at the garage.'

'Why didn't you get any earlier?' said Billy. 'It's not like they're something we don't get very often.'

'I don't know. I'm sorry,' she said, but thought, Well, why didn't you get any, arsehole?

'Sorry's no good, is it? Can't you just remember in future?'

Sarah giggled nervously and her thoughts started to escape from her head. 'Perhaps you should remember,' she said.

'Oh, I'm *so* sorry,' said Billy. 'I didn't realise that I had to do all the fucking shopping as well as working all day.'

'I work all day too.'

'Oh, that's a proper job, sitting at a desk saying "Hello, can I help you?" like some stupid parrot all day long, is it?'

Sarah calculated that Billy had had eight pints, so it probably wasn't safe to push him any further. But she'd had six vodkas.

'Yeh, but you could make a bit more effort to do . . . stuff.' Her voice trailed off as she felt the almost palpable change in Billy's mood and knew she should have just kept quiet. Billy looked tight-lipped out of the window and Sarah wished:

She was anywhere else except in a cab with him.

She didn't love Billy.

She had done a karate course.

She still lived at home with her mum.

She had a gun.

Alcohol had never been invented.

She could be more like Martha.

She'd had her nails done today.

Billy could be more like Charlie and hit other people instead.

They stopped at the late-night garage to get cigarettes. Outside London, many garages stay open in the normal way all night, but Londoners are too criminal to be trusted with an actual open door; they have to use grilles like they do in New York. Tonight, every kind of person was queuing at the grille. Dope heads after Rizlas; young single mothers bored out of their skulls craving chocolate, having left their babies alone; a great big fat person who only ventured out at night and got enough of a hard time then from the group of clubbers buying water; and two boys on their way to burgle a house. Sarah joined the queue, while Billy sat like a thin, sulking Buddha in the cab. Normally, Sarah would have been too frightened to join this queue to hell, but given the mood Billy was in, she thought it might be safer.

The harassed Asian guy behind the counter was struggling under the weight of the single mother's chocolate demands, going backwards and forwards with each new request rather than taking the whole order. Consequently, the mob outside became restive like a post-office queue on pension day, and started to shuffle and grumble. One of the burglar boys happened to have a personality that was constantly at boiling point. Londoners are familiar with these characters and give them a wide berth. The queue parted for him as he sauntered up to the counter to purchase his bits and pieces. Sarah, two vodkas short of a challenge, kept her mouth shut, but desperately wanted to kick him up the arse. She was soon back in the cab.

'Did you get any chocolate?' said Billy.

'You didn't ask,' said Sarah.

'Oh, for fuck's sake. Do I have to actually bloody say everything I fucking want?' shouted Billy, as though non-verbal communication was perfectly natural between them.

The cab driver, who had been listening to all this thought, Poor cow. Why doesn't she find herself a decent fella? but didn't say anything. It was something he regretted, along with the many other missed interventions into lives whose inevitable progress he had left untouched, because that's what's expected. The most he could do when the cab pulled up was try and communicate his fatherly concern in a look, which unfortunately came across to Sarah as a slightly pervy leer and made her recoil.

Once inside the flat, what passed for Billy's public social niceties evaporated into thin air and his true face, the one only his mum had ever seen and which Sarah was getting to know rather too well these days, was revealed. Billy and Sarah had been together for two years now, and the protective veneer of romance which keeps bad behaviour at bay had long been scoured away. Normally this just causes the odd row or ongoing irritability, but sadly, in Billy's case, it had opened a Pandora's box of flying demons.

Much of Billy's bad behaviour could be laid at the feet of his mother, who had brought him up to be a right little bastard. He was the only child of a couple in their thirties who had tried for many years to conceive and had eventually, to their disbelief, produced Billy. His mother wasn't a bad person, but she was a big softie who found it impossible to deny her son anything because she couldn't bear to see him upset. Billy's father tried to assert some authority but he had failed. By Billy's third birthday, a tantrum got him anything he wanted. Attempts by his father to intervene were rebuffed with such screaming that psychologists were consulted but their advice was rejected on the grounds that they were all weirdos who made perfectly normal children into miniature weirdos.

Billy didn't like women. Even his mother got on his nerves. A quarter of the children in this country have fathers who are not actually their real fathers, but unfortunately, Billy's dad could not even claim this privilege. Billy's mum had hardly ever had sex with him, let alone anyone else.

Billy's violence was unpredictable. Sarah had assumed that it would happen tonight but it didn't. He shouted at her a lot, called her a stupid cunt, and said her friends were a nightmare and she should find some decent people, although he wouldn't mind giving Martha one if she wasn't quite so bloated. Sarah listened to all this in a resigned fashion, knowing her response could either soothe or agitate Billy's troubled waters.

One of the problems that occurs when boy meets girl is that we are not called upon to give a truthful relationship CV to each other. Although our real personalities eventually will out, it can be some time before we have a sense of what our partner is holding back. The problems surrounding the history of a new partner are tackled in magazines for teenage girls and women under the heading 'previous partners'. Leaving aside a certain section of gay men who seem to have an inexhaustible appetite for sexual encounters, men don't want to hear they are not taking on a virgin, and women don't want to hear that they are. Apart from that, we explore very little of our partners' previous. Computer dating is a very good example of how utterly shallow we are in terms of matching people up and it is luck rather than judgement that puts the occasional fortuitous pair together. It doesn't actually matter a stuff that one person likes Country and Western and the other likes Easy Listening. Those sorts of differences can be ignored. But it does matter if one person is a bully and the other a winder-upper. If Winder-Upper is constantly niggling at Bully, Bully will explode and a pattern is set. The CV Billy never revealed to Sarah went something like this:

I never liked the opposite sex much, thinking they were a bit silly and stupid, but I liked having sex. I first hit a girl at school who was screeching and getting on my nerves. Her dad battered me to a pulp, which just made me more angry. My first serious girlfriend went off with another bloke, my second finished it when I pushed her and my third put up with me hitting her for three years before she left. I like Sarah, but she's stupid like a lot of them, and if she steps out of line, I try to behave, but I can't help myself.

I was fairly bright at school; my parents sent me to a private one where I always felt like the poor relation and never invited anyone back to my inadequate home. I got friendly with a group of boys whose trademark was defiance and I didn't want to seem like a creep. So I failed most of my exams and' ended up working in computers because it was not very demanding and I could sit back and do the minimum amount required. Also there weren't too many women around to get on my tits and I could have a laugh with the blokes there.

If Sarah ever kept a diary, she might have seen a pattern revealed of Billy's true nature, and could probably have worked out, with the use of a computer programme, when the optimum time to get out would have been.

24 January
Meets Billy in a pub when out with Flower and Martha. Chatting to him. Flower and Martha making 'He's a wanker' signs behind his head.

23 February
Bumps into Billy in same pub a month later. He'd been in there once in that time. Sarah had dragged either Martha or Flower in there a total of eleven times. Billy asks for Sarah's phone number.

2 March
Billy phones Sarah and arranges to meet her. Sarah proudly points out to Flower and Martha that she hasn't sat by the phone all this time like a wimp but has led a 'normal' life. She doesn't tell them that when she is out she has diverted all calls from her land line to her mobile.

8 March
Billy and Sarah go out to the pub. He puts extra vodkas in her drink when he goes to the bar. She pours her drinks into a plant when he's at the bar because she knows if she gets pissed, she'll end up having sex with him.

She ends up having sex with him.

9 March to 10 September
Billy and Sarah conduct the initial stage of their relationship in a blur of happy feelings, laughing at daft things, playing games they will never play again, washing much more often and spraying themselves with a selection of chemicals, having uninhibited alcohol-fuelled sex a lot smattered with many orgasms and both Sarah's anxieties and Billy's grumpiness are kept at bay for many months.

10 September
Billy, irritable because he's had a bad day, is tired and has had a row with someone on the Tube, pushes Sarah out of the way when she tries to show him a picture in a magazine of a sofa they might buy. Sarah bursts into tears and Billy walks out of the flat.

14 December
Billy has been at the firm's Christmas party and comes home very drunk. He breaks two cups in the kitchen and kicks Sarah's cat by accident. When she remonstrates with him, he slaps her round the face with a wet tea towel. She cries because it hurts and he laughs because he is so drunk and it's a wet tea towel.

15 December
Billy cannot apologise enough; hung-over as hell he drags himself out to get flowers. Sarah is touched and forgives him. But when she tells him she has buggered up the video

and taped *Morse* instead of a programme about the Jam, he tells her to shut the fuck up and leave him alone.

One spring day two years after they first met
Billy slaps Sarah harder than last time and she phones Martha and Flower. He isn't drunk.

Sarah crept round Billy for the night and things calmed down a bit. She was aware that in a breathy way, she was being a geisha, running round making him drinks and food, moving stuff nearer for him, finding the telly pages and keeping the peace. She could almost visualise herself in a basque, boop-boop-pe-doo-ing in and out of the room with a selection of tempting snacks and drinks. She kept quiet because she was in love with him in the psychotic sort of way that means you'll put up with almost anything, and as she lay in bed that night, she tried to work out what being in love with him actually meant in her case. Did it mean she couldn't envisage being with anyone else ever? No, it meant that he was nice *most of the time*, so that would have to bloody do. Martha had been sarcastic about her previous failed relationships – but were she and Flower laughing at her?

She woke up and realised Billy wasn't there. She put on an old T-shirt and went out into the hall. She could see him silhouetted against the window.

'What's the matter, Billy?'

Chapter 5

Martha to Flower 11.30 a.m.:

Martha: Have you spoken to Sarah today?

Flower: Yes, she sounded weird.

Martha: In what way?

Flower: Sort of stilted . . . a bit low.

Martha: It's probably that dungeon she works in . . . they even have to write down when they go for a piss. They'll be measuring the volume next and setting a minimum level.

Flower: It's like when Charlie got arrested in Newbury. He had to piss in a pot in the cell.

Martha: Still, at least he had a pot to piss in. Sorry.

Flower: Call her tonight when she gets home. She's got a half-hour window before Bolshie Bollocks gets in.

Martha: Why can't you call her?

Flower: Netball practice.

Martha: Speak to you later. Hello, Charlie.

Flower: No, he's out . . . something in Suffolk coming up. They're meeting in the park. How's Lump?

Martha: Fine, moving about a lot.

Flower: Give Lump a kiss for me.

Martha: If I was that agile I'd get a job at the club blowing ping pong balls out of my . . . Bye.

Charlie to Flower 12.03 p.m.:

Charlie: Hello! Can you hear me? I'm on Dumbo's mobile. Are you all right? Some fucking bastard farmer's kicked me in the bollocks.

Flower: I can't hear you . . . love you . . . talk to you later.

Martha to Sarah:

Martha: It's me, are you all right?

Sarah: I don't know really, yes I'm fine.

Martha: Is Billy being all right?

Sarah: Martha, he's being absolutely fine, please don't worry. Please, let's just leave it . . . we're all right now.

Martha: Are you sure?

Sarah: Yes, really. I'd tell you if there was a problem.

Martha: All right. Are you OK for Thursday night down the King's Head?

Sarah: I don't know . . . I'll call you tomorrow, OK?

Martha: OK. Look after yourself, don't let him—

Sarah: Yeh, all right, bye.

Flower to Com Club 5.54 p.m.:

Flower: Hello, is that Martin?

Martin: Yeh.

Flower: I did your club recently and I just wondered whether you're going to give me a booking.

Martin: Which one were you?

Flower: Tall, hippy-ish I suppose . . . Oh hang on, I've got a call waiting.

Charlie: Who are you talking to?

Flower: Get off the phone, Charlie, I'm talking to someone about work. Hello? Martin? That was Tim from Jesters in Croydon offering me a twenty-minute spot.

Martin: Oh well, all right then. Twenty-sixth of April.

Flower: Thank you.

Flower to Jesters in Croydon:

Ansaphone: Hello, this is the ansaphone for Jesters', Croydon. There's no one here right now. Please leave your name, phone number and the number of tickets you require. This weekend's bill includes Dick Knob and Terry Hunter.

Flower: Hello, it's Flower Gardener here. I did your new act night, three weeks ago. Please, please can I have a gig, It's really important.

Billy to Ambulance Service 7.31 p.m.:

Billy: Can I have an ambulance, quick.

Operator: What's the problem?

Billy: My girlfriend's unconscious. She fell over, tripped
. . . hit her head. Quick!

Operator: Address?

Billy: 17, Denbigh Mansions, Denbigh Road, SE17.

Operator: On its way.

Charge Nurse, A & E to Martha, 10.23 p.m.:

Charge Nurse: Hello, can I speak to Martha Harris please.

Martha: Speaking.

Charge Nurse: Hello, I'm Lesley Griffin, Charge Nurse
at King's A and E. We've got a Sarah McBride here.

Martha: Oh Jesus, is she all right?

Charge Nurse: She'll be fine, just a bit concussed.

Martha: Concussed! Christ, what happened?

Charge Nurse: Well, we're not really sure . . . I think
she fell down some stairs. She says can you ring work
for her and . . . something about a flower.

Martha: Yes, that's our friend, I'll talk to her.

Charge Nurse: She doesn't want to worry her mum.

Martha: OK. Can I come in and see her?

Charge Nurse: Tomorrow.

Martha: Thanks, bye.

Martha to Flower 10.24 p.m.:

Charlie: Hello?

Martha: Hello, Charlie, it's Martha. Can I talk to Flower?

Charlie: Hold on.

Flower: Hello?

Martha: It's me, Sarah's in hospital.

Flower: Oh God, what's happened to her?

Martha: Concussed, apparently. Fell down some stairs.

Flower: Oh yeh? That's quite hard in a flat. Billy?

Martha: I wouldn't be surprised, but there's nothing we can do tonight.

Flower: Has she got her mobile? I might text her.

Martha: That'd be nice . . . I'll go up in the morning and see how things are.

Flower: How long's she been with Billy now? About two years . . . I remember that with Charlie, that was when he stopped following me to work. Two years – that's when you're so familiar with each other, you start to let things slip a little on the mystery of romance front.

Martha: Hitting someone's hardly categorised as letting the romance slip.

Flower: You know what I mean though.

Martha: 'Spose so, not that I'm the expert recently.

Flower: How's Lump?

Martha: Lump's fine.

Flower: What are we going to do about this Sarah and Billy situation? Do you think she might give him the push now? I don't think it's going to happen on its own. She's that kind of mad about him that she'll let him do this for years. I think we should help him.

Martha looked down at her pad on which she'd been doodling and surveyed her list.

Hang him and make it look like suicide.

Contract killing.

Push him in the river.

Tinker with the brakes on his car.

Giant kebab skewer.

Martha: I think we should encourage him to fuck off.

Chapter 6

A faint whiff of urine, jumble-sale clothes and the sickly-sweet smell which clings to illness and death and has probably been commercially produced as a perfume by Joan Collins, greeted Martha as she entered the main door of the local general hospital. Being located in SE5 it found itself at the very centre of shabby scabbiness and witnessed a daily showing of stabbing, maiming and other acts of random violence. Martha felt like she'd smoked a whole packet of fags passing, as she did, through the collection of wraiths and strays that hang about outside hospitals wringing that final drag out of whatever's-on-offer-this-week-at-the-newsagents, before retiring back to the oncology ward to nurse their scalded lungs. However, their lungs hadn't been so shot that they couldn't manage a few cursory comments about Martha's appearance.

'Fat cow,' attempted a fat red-faced bloke. Martha had long ago given up on pointing out the fundamental inequity of this exchange from fat bloke to fat woman. The other smokers, including two women, cackled phlegmily. Martha's face burned and it annoyed her so much that after years of this sort of verbal public assessment, she still couldn't just let it wash over her. She was tempted to try, 'Well, at least I haven't got a terminal illness,' but that seemed way out of proportion. Instead she contented herself with a 'Go fuck yourselves,' at a volume not even a dog could hear, and walked on.

A sign on the wall pointed the way to a series of 'Wars', the Ds having been scratched off during a drunken rampage by some Casualty visitors who, not content with tormenting the staff in A and E, had done a quick tour of the hospital, pissing in the window boxes, writing 'knob' all over the walls and making the surprisingly astute observation that the founder of the hospital was 'a wanker'.

Graffiti of this nature always turned Martha into a rabid, big-bosomed Tory MP and she often imagined herself strangling those responsible with one hand whilst scrubbing with the other at the offending words with a huge Brillo pad. She believed that a decent environment begets decent behaviour – yet more evidence, Flower thought, of a lurking unreconstructed reactionary in her soul.

Ward 7, in which Sarah was stranded, was at the end of a long corridor peppered with soiled dressings, bits of fluff and the odd human blob lying groaning on a trolley. This scene would not have been out of place in Scutari, thought Martha as she and the Lump humped their way along, and suddenly her plans to eject the Lump in this very institu-

tion seemed mad and a home birth even in the dust reposi-
tory she called home, seemed preferable.

One positive side to bad hospital care, she mused, is that
at least it discourages the malingerers because one has to
be really ill to want to stay. This technique, Martha thought,
was also employed by teenage sales staff in the West End,
who rely on people's desperation to buy because they always
looked at her as if she'd just shat in their sandwiches whenever she made the first of many polite enquiries about
whether they had any clothes that fitted people without an
eating disorder.

Sarah's ward was a sort of grey colour, as were the people
in it. The staple occupant of these wards, the elderly,
allegedly confused woman, was much in evidence and
amongst them Sarah looked like a child who has spent too
long at her grandma's.

Sarah had two black eyes and some bruising round her
neck. Apart from that, she looked great, thought Martha
enviously, who in a similar position would look like a Balkan
peasant who had not had access to 'facilities' for some
years.

The woman in the next bed, who looked like Miss
Havisham's mum, appeared to be blind and had been sat
at the end of her bed for a better view of the ward for no
apparent reason, was shouting continuously, 'Please kill
me! Please kill me!'

'I fucking well will if she doesn't shut up,' said Sarah
grimly as Martha drew up a chair to the bed.

'What's the matter with her?' whispered Martha.

'You don't need to whisper,' said Sarah. 'She's deaf as well, you know.'

Martha started to cry.

'Your bloody hormones,' Sarah sighed. 'Come on, it takes more than this normally to set you off.'

'Sorry,' said Martha. 'Poor woman though.' She sensed Sarah wanted to talk about Sarah. 'So how did this happen?' she asked, feeling like a detective.

'Fell down the stairs outside the flat,' said Sarah, feeling like a suspect.

'Oh, come on,' said Martha.

'No, really, I swear,' said Sarah.

'Did Billy push you?'

'No.'

'Trip you?'

'No.'

'Swing you round by your hair several times until you had gathered enough momentum to clear the balcony, then let you fly?'

'No,' laughed Sarah. 'Look, it really was an accident.'

'I believe you,' said Martha. She didn't.

'Thanks,' said Sarah, who knew she didn't. 'Well, Bill and I had a bit of a set-to last night – no, no fisticuffs or anything like that – but we had a row and he stormed off. I assumed he'd gone out for fags so I went on to the landing to see if he was coming back and fell over a pile of new *Yellow Pages* some idiot had dumped there. I could have broken my fucking neck! Bill found me on his way back from the shop.'

Martha realised the woman in the bed opposite was listening to every word and conspiratorially shaking her head to indicate she thought Sarah's story wasn't true either. Martha tried to summon up a look on her face which conveyed the message, 'Yes, I'm sure you're right,' but the look in fact just conveyed constipation.

'So,' she said to Sarah, 'how long are they keeping you in for?'

'Only tonight.'

'Do you want a lift home tomorrow?' asked Martha, even though she didn't have a car.

'No, it's all right, Bill will collect me,' said Sarah.

'Oh, that's good of him.' Martha was trying to sound genuine.

Sarah began gingerly to pull herself out of bed and reached for her handbag, a purchase which had cost her three hundred quid, but made her feel good as she swung it down Oxford Street on a Saturday morning while elderly people and weaker children were plunged by the never-ending bustle of shoppers into the path of oncoming vehicles.

As Sarah passed the end of the blind woman's bed, her swinging handbag caught the woman's head a glancing blow and set off another stream of entreaties. Sarah looked embarrassed, muttered sorry rather pointlessly and moved off quickly. Martha went over and held the woman's hands and patted them as if to try and convey she was sorry that she'd received a knock on the head.

'Who's that?' said the woman. 'Jack, is that you?' making

63

Martha doubt Jack's positive qualities if his arrival was heralded by a bang on the head.

'That's her son,' said the woman opposite. 'Never bothers to come in and see her. She'd be better off dead, the poor cow, the way her family treat her. We've often discussed bumping her off late at night, you know, when the volume of her shouting gets too much and the night staff just leave her to get on with it. Maybe we could get *her* boyfriend to do it,' she said with a wink, looking in the direction of Sarah's bed.

Martha rather liked the idea of a murderous coterie of seventy-year-old ladies in a medical ward, applying a spontaneous form of euthanasia.

'Anyway,' said another woman two beds up, 'what are you going to do about her bloke? You've got to teach 'im a lesson. We all think so, don't we, gels?'

South-East London's hardened elite of grey-haired working-class women was in an unforgiving mood and nodded its head as one.

Martha found herself slightly on the defensive, much to her surprise. 'He might not have done it, you know,' she said.

'Oh, pull the other one, love,' said a woman on Sarah's side who looked like a drag act. 'We saw the shifty-looking bastard last night. He done it all right.'

Were these women victims themselves? wondered Martha. She had a sudden vision of all their husbands as skinny little henpecked anorexics quivering against the wall protecting their testicles as these huge women ran riot round their kitchens. She tried to substitute it for a picture of bullying thugs but couldn't manage it.

Sarah appeared at the door of the ward having managed a quickie makeover in the toilets, bringing colour to her cheeks and sparkle to her eyes.

'Oh darling, you shouldn't have bothered just for little old me,' said Martha.

'She didn't,' said a voice behind her and she turned round to see Billy smiling and holding what she considered to be a rather aggressive bunch of flowers. Why would you want to buy anyone red-hot pokers?

The eyes of Ward 7's women were immediately boring into him and urging him to do the decent thing, something unspeakable using a blender and his testicles, she thought. Martha half-expected pantomime booing to start or a pelting of Billy with used dressings and wondered why they hadn't warned her about Billy's presence with a timely 'Behind you!'

'Evening, ladies,' said Billy, and suddenly they turned from an elderly death squad to fluttery, girly girls.

'Evening,' they chorused, several semitones higher than five minutes ago and turned with great interest to their *Woman's Own*s.

Billy looked towards the shouting woman in the next bed who seemed to have slumped over backwards with her mouth open. 'Is she all right?' he said with such a lack of concern that he might have been looking at a friend's pet rabbit's eczema.

'Oh God,' said Sarah. 'Call a nurse.'

Before Martha could stop herself or even think about what she was saying, she turned to Sarah and said, 'You've killed her with your handbag,' and then she started to laugh.

The nursing staff arrived and drew the curtain round the bed affording poor Miss Lucas the only dignity she'd ever had in that place, but they could still be heard trying cursorily to revive her, not making much of an effort because of her age and the amount of irritation she caused. Martha made her excuses and left, aware of the strange looks she was getting as she and the Lump tried to suppress their laughter.

When she got home, she phoned Flower and related the details of her visit. In a way, the death of poor old Miss Lucas, ancient as she was and expected as it may have been, had totally overshadowed the presence of Sarah in hospital and the reasons why she was there. Eventually though, Flower got round to it.

'How did Billy seem?' she said.

'Well, very cool really,' said Martha.

'What, not womanbeaterish?' said Flower.

'What is womanbeaterish?' said Martha.

'Dunno,' said Flower. 'So did he do it?'

'Oh, I think so,' said Martha, 'but Sarah doesn't want to say.'

'So what can we do?' said Flower. 'Perhaps my brothers could go round.'

'We're not the Mafia. That sort of thing only works in *The Godfather*,' Martha said sensibly. Besides, she wanted to add, your brothers are about as scary as some frailer members of the Women's Institute.

'Well, let's work on Sarah first then while we think what to do about Billy,' Flower said, sounding bright. 'How about self-defence classes?'

Martha had visions of a lot of emotionally needy women clustered round a muscle-bound knucklehead. She looked down at Lump and thought she'd better just watch.

'Let's all go,' said Flower, as though it was a nice day out.

Chapter 7

'State of you, love. Walked into a door, did you?'

Another cheerily executed gem emanated from the fag-bearing lips of Mr Cancer the fat, red-faced champion smoker, as Sarah slunk out of the hospital clutching the handbag that allegedly killed Miss Lucas and a carrier bag of belongings bearing the logo of a very expensive shop in Bond Street because Sarah still felt this sort of thing mattered.

'Go fuck yourself,' she said, loud enough even for the poor dear departed Miss Lucas to hear.

Billy was waiting on a double yellow, his foot idly accelerating in time to some music. 'All right?' he asked tenderly as Sarah got in the car and she wished she could have videoed this moment and played it to Flower and Martha who, she was convinced, were beginning to build up a profile of Billy, not dissimilar from that of a serial killer.

'Yep, fine,' she answered.

Billy squeezed her hand and accelerated away. 'I'll drop you off home,' he said, 'and see you after work. Is there anything you need?'

'No thanks,' said Sarah, thinking friends with very poor short-term memories would be helpful and save her from having to pay lip-service to Martha and Flower and the idea of sorting out Billy.

Billy pulled up outside the flat, gave Sarah one of those kisses your grandparents give one another which would be considered obscene if their tongues ever got involved. As Billy drove off and checked his rearview mirror, he saw Martha and Flower rise like a couple of bedraggled phoenixes from behind two large pot plants by the front entrance. He smiled.

'Oh God, I think he saw us,' said Flower.

'Oh, so what?' said Martha, who once she had hit the deck in her condition had begun to believe she wouldn't get up again without the help of a first-aid team.

'What are you two doing here? Come to talk me into self-defence classes or some piss-awful women's group, I suppose?' said Sarah sarcastically.

Martha and Flower looked at each other, embarrassed.

'Oh you wankers,' said Sarah, who didn't believe the paltry array of English words available for abuse should be confined to just the one gender.

'You can't be a wanker if you're a girl,' said Flower.

There then ensued a pointless argument about whether

women look as ridiculous as men when they are wanking and whether someone's a wanker because they haven't got anyone to have sex with or because of their appearance during the aforementioned act.

Flower refused to believe women indulged at all at which Martha laughed uproariously and then, seeing the expression on Sarah's face, changed the subject.

'I have booked us in for self-defence classes this evening,' said Flower.

'Well, that won't look obvious at all, will it?' said Sarah.

'Don't tell him,' said Martha, whose way out of a tight spot always involved a badly conceived lie. 'This is all for you, Sarah. I mean, why someone who is eight months' pregnant is indulging in any form of rigorous exercise along with someone who's just been thrown down the stairs by their boyfriend . . .'

'I've told you loads of times,' said Sarah crossly. 'I tripped.'

'Methinks the lady doth protest too much.'

'Oh, not pissing Shakespeare now as well,' said Sarah.

'Look,' said Flower, 'I've found these really good self-defence classes on the net, Sar, and I'm not saying Billy did push you down the stairs, but he did whack you one the other day, so it's probably sensible . . . and besides, it might come in useful somewhere else.'

'Cancer patients maybe,' mused Sarah.

'Why is that bloke so fat when he's got cancer?' said Martha.

Flower didn't know what they were talking about and assumed it was someone from a celebrity magazine.

'So when are the classes?' said Sarah.

'Tonight,' said Flower.

'And what am I going to tell Billy about where I'm going?' said Sarah.

'Just tell him we're going down the pub and if he kicks up a fuss tell him to wait five hours and then you can come home and knock him out with the new skills you've acquired,' said Martha.

Some people, depending on how much of a personality disorder they have, are very good at lying and others are useless. Sarah fell into the useless category and therefore had to have the radio on and be turned towards the window when she told Billy of her plans for the evening so he couldn't hear her voice falter or see the reddened condition of her face.

'OK,' he said, not taking his eyes off the telly.

Sarah felt as if she was betraying him in some way and wanted to say, 'Look, I'm going to self-defence classes to learn some ways of dealing with you if you get arsey, because you have got a bit of a temper, not that I expect you to hit me again, but it's as well to be on the safe side because you wouldn't want to accidentally kill me and go to prison for life, would you?'

Instead she said, 'Shall I put the kettle on?'

Michael Randall, who ran the self-defence classes at the college in Vauxhall, was a genuinely decent bloke with two daughters in their early twenties, both of whom had been scared half to death by unlicensed minicab drivers at one time or another and had arrived home in a state of jelly-like paralysis and despair at not having been able to respond, despite the general 'bollock-kicking-I'm-up-for-anything-me' nature of the female zeitgeist.

Despite being a nice guy, Michael knew how the minds of not-so-nice guys worked and therefore knew that most men who assault or flash at women, rely on the victims being so terrified that very little coercion is required. So all Michael wanted to do with his self-defence classes was teach these young women a few simple responses to get themselves out of trouble and allow them to get away. However, this would only have taken him twenty minutes, so he had to drag this twenty minutes out into a rather tedious seven-week course accompanied by more tedium in the form of aggression theory.

The huge disadvantage in life for Michael Randall was that he looked like a photofit for your local paedophile ring-leader – sallow, wiry with thick glasses and greasy hair. Both his daughters were extraordinarily beautiful and if ever he and they were out together, people assumed he was stalking them.

The classes started at seven thirty and Martha, Flower and Sarah were in the pub by seven for a quick drink before what they all assumed would be karate-chopping dummies in the throat for two hours.

Flower, as usual, had been dropped off by Charlie who had temporarily acquired a van which smelled of dogs and cabbage, and she was dressed totally inappropriately for the weather, a cold, wet night perfect for a Jack the Ripper walking tour round Whitechapel. She wore a T-shirt, cardigan, jeans and flip-flops. Sarah looked like a minor turn-of-the-century Russian aristocrat on the outside and an American rapper underneath, and Martha who, because of her pregnancy was permanently boiling, wore a billowing diaphanous thing which was dark coloured, and some big, blokeish, boots.

The class was sparsely populated, a source of disquiet for Michael Randall who every day looked through his local paper with growing despair as a catalogue of rapes, assaults and murders floated in front of his eyes. He knew canvassing for business wouldn't work: half the women would take one look at him and call the police.

Tonight eight women looked at him expectantly as he came into the gym which had been furnished with some of those rubber mats that are supposed to break your fall but don't. Martha, Flower and Sarah were the only new faces at the class and they introduced themselves to the other five, two teenage friends, someone writing a PhD on violence against women, a posh middle-aged woman who had been threatened at a cashpoint and a young Asian woman in her twenties who worked in a newsagents and had seen her father and brothers suffer the most appalling verbal and physical abuse.

'Right,' said Michael Randall, fixing his paternal gaze onto the trio of new arrivals, 'and what brings you here?'

Martha wanted to say, 'We want to know how we can all give her boyfriend a good kicking,' but instead said something very neutral, like, 'Well, the streets are so dangerous these days, we want to defend ourselves and our sisters.

'I realise that sounded totally wanky,' she whispered to the others.

It had not escaped Michael Randall's notice that Martha was heavily pregnant, Sarah looked like she had recently been battered and the third one appeared incapable of responding aggressively to anything.

He said kindly to Martha, 'Obviously you'll have to take it easy with any of the physical stuff, dear.'

'Oh, don't worry about me,' said Martha. 'I'll make sure the Lump doesn't get in the way.'

'And you,' he said, turning to Sarah and trying a very sympathetic voice, 'have you been the victim of some appalling assault?'

'I fell down the stairs,' said Sarah flatly, knowing that the likelihood of that statement being believed in a women's self-defence class was about as likely as Billy plugging in and using the Hoover.

'Well, let's get on,' said Michael. 'Last week at the first session I talked about my daughters' bad experiences and we discussed some scenarios we'd like to deal with and this week perhaps we can come up with some possible situations and discuss how we might handle them.'

'How about a group of teenage boys calling you horrible names?' said Martha.

'What do you mean?' said Michael, looking puzzled.

'Well, fucking slag . . . lard arse . . .' said Martha.

Michael interrupted, 'No, I'm sorry, I meant what exactly is the self-defence issue in that scenario?'

Martha admitted that there wasn't one, but she would

still like some advice on how to physically assault the offenders and get away unscathed herself.

All the other women empathised with this but were not surprised when Michael pointed out that it is an offence to assault someone who has not touched you and a rather foolish one at that if that someone is a group of ten teenage boys.

Flower then intervened with a story about a demonstration she had been on with Charlie and described how a policeman had kicked her. She wondered whether there was anything legal she could have done to protect herself without getting into trouble. Once again Michael had to admit that assaulting the police wasn't really part of his session either.

'How about you?' he said, turning towards Sarah.

'Dunno, really,' said Sarah, whose reluctance to attend had metamorphosed into a growing resentment towards this rather strange-looking little man.

'All right,' said Michael. 'Let's look at what happened to Diana and see if we can come up with some ideas as to how she could have tackled things better. Just remind us Diana, would you?'

'Well,' said the posh middle-aged woman, 'I was at the cashpoint a couple of months ago at seven o'clock in the evening and I'd just got my money when I felt something sticking in my back and I heard a voice say – I'll leave out the swearing if you don't mind, "Give me your effing money".'

'And what happened then?' said Martha, always fascinated by all things violent.

'Well,' said Diana, 'I told him in no uncertain terms to bugger orf.'

'And did that work?' said Martha.

'Not exactly. He stabbed me. Oh Christ, it was awful!'

'Can you tell us about it?' said Martha.

'Well, my husband hadn't paid our private health subscription and I ended up at the local general hospital on a ward with a load of smelly old ladies and one awful old harridan who just kept shouting "Kill me!" all the time. The place was a filthy pit. The nurses were lazy and foreign, most of them. Couldn't understand what half of them were saying.'

Martha was beginning to be quite pleased Diana had been stabbed.

'So,' said Michael. 'How could Diana have avoided injury?'

'Just given the man her money?' suggested Flower. 'After all, he was probably desperate if he needed to do something like that.'

'Desperate to inject crack cocaine more like,' said the ever-charitable Diana.

Flower wanted to explain that you normally smoked crack but thought better of it.

'In a life-threatening situation like that,' said Michael, 'I would hand over the money.'

'I'm disappointed in you,' said Diana. 'I'd have thought, given what your daughters went through, you might have more spunk.'

'The teenagers giggled and Michael said, 'In this day and

age you have to be realistic if someone has a knife, particularly if it's in your back.'

'I'm wasting my bloody time then,' said Diana and she was, because as she got up, put her coat on and flounced out, not one single person tried to persuade her to stay.

The session continued more amicably with Michael suggesting a few ways in which they could improve their chances of staying safe, one of which was simply to be prepared for trouble at all times.

Martha's favourite self-defence move culled from Michael Randall's repertoire that evening was a punch in the throat, much more effective apparently than a kick in the testicles. She resolved to try it on the next groper.

The group of women had a good laugh that night and left very cheerful and optimistic about a future in which they talked, punched and twisted their way out of danger. Even Sarah, who had talked herself into a terrible mood, outside the college visualised a scene in which her toughness conquered Billy's violence and strengthened their love. For Sarah, though, tonight was going to be dirty and depressing. Billy had just happened to drive past and had seen her and her friends come out of the college gates.

Charlie, who had come to pick Flower up, was also there. Billy could see them all having a laugh and, like he so often did, wondered whether it was at his expense. He stopped the car, parked it badly, and walked back towards the group. In the twilight he didn't catch Sarah freezing up with fear. They all looked at him like an outcast.

'Hello, thought you were going down the pub,' he said, eyes narrowing at Sarah.

The four were struck dumb. No one knew who should lie first. Martha thought honesty was the best policy.

'We decided on the spur of the moment to go to this new self-defence class. You know, 'cause it's getting bad round here, and well . . .' she tailed off.

Billy's eyes narrowed further and he grabbed Sarah's arm rather roughly and pulled her towards him. 'Come on,' he said. 'We're going home.'

'Hey,' said Sarah, trying to struggle out of his grip.

Flower was more surprised than anyone to find that her body seemed to be in charge of her brain and before she could stop it, she had punched Billy in the throat. Well, that was the intention. What actually happened was that she rather soggily aimed a not very well screwed-up fist in the general direction of his throat and ended up scratching the side of his face with a ring she'd bought at an eclipse some years ago. So, Flower thought she'd have another bash. Billy thought otherwise, put his hand up to stop her and grabbed her wrist which, as she twisted away from him, gave way with a crack. Flower fell to the ground, sobbing hysterically, 'He's broken it, he's broken it!' Flower was not one of life's troupers.

Charlie leaped into action in his rather over-relaxed fashion. 'Hey man,' he said to Billy, 'what are you doing?'

Billy thought, Christ, I can't believe this is happening . . . they've all got me down as a woman-beater and now I've broken the hippie's wrist. 'I'm sorry,' he said. 'I didn't mean to.'

'And I'm sure Hitler didn't mean to kill millions of Jews,' said Charlie.

'Well, he did actually,' said Martha, irritating Charlie like she always did.

'Just call a fucking ambulance,' shouted Flower, the adrenaline enabling her to add swearing to her repertoire of newly acquired skills.

Chapter 8

The nicotine-stained gang outside the hospital vaguely recognised some combination of Martha, Sarah and Billy, but they
had not chanced upon the grungy flung-togetherness that
was Flower yet. Fat Wheezing Bloke thought her nose
deserved some of his urban poetry and then thought better
of it as he spotted the face of Billy grimacing just behind
Flower and almost felt the headbutt he would receive if he
said anything.

The group spilled into Accident and Emergency
expecting, as one always does, to be seen immediately,
despite the illuminated digital sign which said it would be
more like five hours.

Charlie had had half an hour to work himself up into a
righteous mood of indignation about the evening's events
and while Billy was humiliating himself, but only in his
own eyes, getting the teas, Charlie took out his frustration

on a wall in the corridor and bent his finger back in the process, breaking it.

Martha registered him at the desk where the clerk didn't bat an eyelid. In fact, had a troop of GIs come through the roof and napalmed the maroon crimplene jacket resting on the back of her chair, she would still have retained that fish-eyed expression that denoted compassion or interest had died long before her first anniversary in the place.

Billy, meanwhile, was rehearsing a few speeches in his head to counter the increasing tendency of Sarah's friends to classify him as existing down the worm end of the evolutionary scale. After a brief period of resolving to sort himself out, he decided he'd probably been condemned already and what was the point of trying to impress these two silly women and the hippy's boyfriend. Once again the nice person trying to get out of Billy got on the first rung of the ladder and then couldn't be arsed to climb any further.

Flower had broken her wrist and as she had fallen too, and knocked her head on the pavement, losing consciousness for a few seconds, the junior doctor who'd had a couple of patients die on him in the last hour was very anxious and instructed the charge nurse to find a bed in which Flower could be observed overnight. As per usual, beds were short but one was found and Flower was wheeled into the same ward on which Sarah had spent such a joyous night with the posse of elderly sheriff's deputies, who could not quite believe it when they saw Billy shuffling along behind yet another injured woman.

'Christ, Ivy,' said one to the woman next door to her,

'he's only gone and done another and look' (pointing at Martha), 'do you think he got that one up the duff an' all?'

'Wouldn't be surprised, Glad,' said Ivy. 'Some blokes these days have hundreds of women.'

They tried to muster up some dirty looks while Flower puzzled over this and thought it must be disapproval at the way she was dressed.

Charlie was still in X-ray at this point which supported the misapprehension of the ladies that Billy was the boyfriend of Flower too. Billy felt the rheumy eyes boring into his back and made his escape as quickly as he could when he realised where they were. Sarah had already realised and waited outside the ward, not mentioning this to Billy whom she wanted punished even if it was only by the disapproval of some grey-haired old ladies.

This then left Martha by Flower's bedside holding the hand attached to the unbroken wrist.

'He's a fucking menace,' she said as Billy left the ward. 'We've got to do something.'

'It was an accident,' said Flower, who had been thoroughly shaken up by the whole thing. Her peace-loving parents had never smacked her or even seemed in the slightest bit angry, ever, so any physical or verbal aggression really disturbed her, although London was teaching her very fast that everyone is a little pressure cooker waiting to spew all manner of nastiness over their fellow citizens.

Charlie stumbled into view grinning and holding up his finger which had what looked like a comedy dressing on it, inexpertly applied by an unsupervised student nurse who, having missed that module in the School of Nursing, appeared to be relying instead on cartoon characters she had seen as a child. If Charlie had had a toothache she would have tied a bandage round his head with a big bow on top.

Charlie's trousers were soaked. He had used a toilet which had needed repairing for months and had finally gone to the great urinal in the sky. It had attacked him by squirting urine back at him in a watery pattern on his less than pristine jeans. Still, at least it's my own, thought Charlie, who wasn't a contender for obsessional cleanliness but drew the line at being covered in piss.

Martha decided she'd better leave once Charlie had arrived as she was sure there was plenty for him and Flower to talk about.

'Look,' she said to Flower, 'we need to discuss various things. Can you come round mine tomorrow?'

'All right,' said Flower. 'I'll take the day off work, I expect, so I'll come about two, OK?'

'Fine,' said Martha. 'See you.'

Martha knew the smokers would be lying in wait, so she tried to sneak out the back way, but finding all other exits barred because of the late hour, she prepared a riposte.

Sure enough as she tried to sneak past, someone cleared their throat and mumbled something. Martha turned and with as much venom as she could muster managed to spit out, 'At least my lungs don't look like a phlegmy Christmas pudding, arsehole,' leaving a rather confused visitor who had just wondered how far the car park was.

As a smoker, Martha's lungs probably looked like that too. Martha, however, was blessed with the optimism of most smokers that they have a built-in cancer escape clause in their chest and that the lung lottery will be kind to them only.

The grey posse had by now decided that Charlie was Flower's brother and he had been injured in his valiant attempt to prevent his sister being beaten by the multiple-partnered Billy, who was a gangster and former jailbird. This was more exciting than the truth, but not much.

Flower had rejected the animal sandwich offered to her by a student nurse and resisted the further offer of another animal in a bun with some chips from a carnivorous porter who was on his way to get one from the outlet recently opened in the hospital providing good bowel-paralysing fare and extremely rare glimpses of anything that could be described as a vegetable.

Charlie had said he'd go home and get her something sproutish, but she declined and prepared to give her speech about Charlie's problem of controlling his temper.

Charlie knew what was coming and opened with, 'Well, at least I hit inanimate objects and not women.'

'Yes, I know,' said Flower, 'but you'll end up gradually breaking every bone in your body. Why not sort it out?'

'Forget it,' said Charlie. 'It's well under control.'

Flower then moved on to Billy. 'What shall we do?'

'Well, *that* man needs his anger controlled,' said Charlie.

'Look,' said Flower, 'I'm sure there are these groups you can go to where you discuss stuff like that and sort out your temper. How about going to one for me and finding out if it would be any good for Billy? We've got to do something.'

'Oh bloody hell,' said Charlie.

'Oh please,' said Flower. 'He's hit me now, and Sarah; that only leaves Martha who's not really in a fit state to be hit at the moment – well, not in the stomach anyway.'

'The size her bump is, that kid's going to be a human bouncy castle anyway,' said Charlie. He realised Flower's eyes were continuing to plead. 'Oh all right,' he said.

The next day, despite her bandaged wrist, Flower decided she could and would ride her bike round to Martha's as it was a bit too far to walk and the bus route went past a young offenders' institution, which meant the bus always contained some spotty mini-psychopath who had just had his fags confiscated and was on his way, in a fit of pique, to piss up a bus shelter or rob a pensioner, after having given Flower a mouthful of abuse.

This particular day Flower escaped relatively unscathed on her bike until she was turning into Martha's road, when two blokes in a van drew alongside.

'Fancy a jump, Conky?' said the greasy-haired occupant of the passenger seat whose breath could have been used to kill off garden pests.

Flower kept her head down and continued cycling determinedly along.

'Oi, nozzer!' added his mate, a worthy contender for the Unhealthy Pallor with Fetid Cardigan Oscar. 'Don't ignore us!'

Flower turned off at this point and could feel another layer of her equanimity being peeled away by the London Experience.

I must learn to drive, she thought. At least I can wind the window up then.

She arrived at Martha's in a bad mood and didn't mention the encounter because she was slightly ashamed of the number of times her nose was alluded to by the citizens of London, little realising that Martha minimised her quota of fat abuse for the very same reason.

Martha let Flower into her very untidy smelly flat with an apology. 'I'm so tired, you know, because of Lump. I can't even be bothered to clean.'

Flower knew Lump had nothing to do with it and that Martha's laziness and general lack of hygiene were her oldest friends.

'When's Lump due?'

'Three weeks.'

'Do you want me to help clean the place and try to create some sort of environment for a baby out of this landfill site?'

'Yeh, that'd be great.'

'Well, let's do it and while we're at it we can make a list of the options for sorting Billy out.'

Martha grabbed an old envelope and put her hand under the settee where several pens lay and headed the page *Billy*.

'Contract out on him?' she said. 'Or shall we just nail his bollocks to a convent wall ourselves?'

Flower laughed in a slightly restrained way. 'I think we should talk to him,' she shouted over the hoover as it rattled and spat out some dangerous-looking smoke, indignant at being asked to suck up the debris of a good month's worth of crap.

'What, tell him to stop it and see if he does so like a good little boy?' shouted back Martha, who was down on her hands and knees with the Lump pressed rather uncomfortably against the carpet scooping up newspapers, cups with varying degrees of penicillin-like growth in them and a couple of pairs of very unattractive knickers that would get her stoned to death in a lap-dancing club.

'No need to be sarky,' said Flower. 'I'm sure we could get somewhere if we talked to him – correction, *I* could get somewhere. You'd probably make him go out and spray some puppies with automatic fire you wind him up so much.'

'All right then,' said Martha, 'you have a nice little chat with him, put him bang to rights and if it cures him of his violent tendencies, I'll clean the bath.'

Flower's resolve to sort Billy out strengthened.

'What do you think Sarah will think of us interfering?' she asked.

'We won't tell her,' said Martha, whose inclination was always towards the cloak and dagger.

'Really?' said Flower, who nearly had a mental breakdown if she had to tell a lie.

'Look, she won't thank us. He won't tell her we've talked to him because he'll be too embarrassed. It's better all round to keep it quiet.'

'Oh my God!' said Flower.

'What?' said Martha and turned to see Flower gagging on account of an elderly plate of half-eaten dinner she'd discovered under a pile of mother and baby magazines.

'Look, shall we go down the caff and call it a day here?' Martha suggested, surveying the barely touched flat.

'Please,' said Flower.

They sat in Martha's local caff which surprisingly for the area was run by two very healthy people who served very healthy food – which meant that no one went in there very much.

The Sorting Out Billy list grew and moved from Flower and then Martha chatting to Billy to some slightly more duplicitous and then downright mad suggestions.

'How about trying to split them up?' offered Martha.

'But they love each other,' said Flower.

'What, in a Henry the Eighth-Anne Boleyn sort of a way, do you mean? Look, he's popped her one twice now and it's not going to stop, so if the gentle approach doesn't work we need some stand-by ideas.'

'Well, how could we split them up? I don't see,' said Flower.

'Easy peasy,' said Martha. 'You or I could sleep with him.'

'But Sarah would never talk to us again,' Flower objected.

'Yeh, but at least she would be able to talk . . . because she'd be alive.'

'Oh, don't be so melodramatic,' said Flower. 'He won't kill her, this is real life.'

'Yes, and ordinary people do things like this to each other,' said Martha grimly.

'What about just finding Sarah a new bloke?' said Flower.

'Sarah doesn't want a new bloke, she wants Billy.'

'OK, how about getting someone to threaten him?' This was an unusual and somewhat daring suggestion from a natural peacekeeper like Flower.

'Mmm, not a bad idea,' said Martha, 'but we'd have to get someone decent to really scare the shit out of him.'

'As opposed to . . . ?'

'Well, Charlie, or my dad,' said Martha. 'How about if we just go and buy a gun, get him in a room, point it at him and say, "Leave our friend alone or you lose your fucking crown jewels".'

They looked at each other and laughed uproariously.

Chapter 9

In the end it was decided that both Flower and Martha would start the process of sorting things out for Sarah by talking to Billy and it fell to Flower as the natural conciliator to have the first attempt. She decided she would phone Billy at work so Sarah didn't find out what they were up to and then realised she had no idea where Billy worked.

She got straight on the phone to Martha.

'Oh, it's some firm up in Whitechapel,' said Martha. 'Where all the killers come from.'

'Eh?' said Flower.

'Oh, a spurious reference to Jack the Ripper,' said Martha.

'No, he *killed* in Whitechapel, he didn't *come* from there.'

'How do you know?'

'Well, first of all, no one knows who he is so how would they know where he came from, and secondly—'

'Don't bother with secondly,' said Martha. 'I'm not that entertained by stories of prostitute murderers.'

'Ooh, you big fat feminist rebel,' said Flower.

'Anyway, I've got Billy's number,' said Martha. 'Got a pen?'

Flower gritted her teeth and dialled. She was hoping to get Billy's voicemail, but he picked it up.

'Hello, Bill Taylor speaking.'

'Bill, it's Flower,' said Flower.

There was a small pause during which Billy took in the information that one of his girlfriend's friends had called him at work. Within a split second he had speculated that she either wanted to sleep with him or shop him.

'And what can I do for you?' said Billy.

Flower hated that phrase. In her head she said, 'You can't do anything, you bad fucker, it's what I can do for you in terms of transforming you into a decent member of society.' She actually said, 'I want to have a chat with you about something. Can you meet me?'

'Very mysterious,' said Billy.

'I'm doing a gig on Wednesday at Frogs Wine Bar,' said Flower. 'Can you meet me there before it starts, about seven?'

'Give us a clue,' said Billy.

'No, I'll tell you when I see you,' said Flower and hung up.

'Who was that?' said Charlie, his radar bringing him prematurely from the bathroom.

'Oh, no one,' said Flower. 'Wrong number.'

Charlie wondered why Flower was even bothering with that lie because nobody ever believes that 'wrong number' line, but for once he let it go and sauntered into the kitchen to make some evil-looking, evil-smelling and evil-tasting tea.

Flower was slightly put out that he didn't give her the third degree. *Perhaps he's saving it for the anger management group*, she thought, which was where he was going the night she was meeting Billy.

Flower's heart thumped at the thought of it all going wrong with Billy, the gig falling apart and Charlie going mad when he found out that she had met Billy and talked to him on her own.

Why was life always such a worry? Why couldn't it be relaxing, fun and unchallenging? It was so much easier to do nothing than get involved in other people's problems. Flower thought of a saying her father was constantly trumpeting at her as a child, as she was dragged on yet another demonstration heading towards Hyde Park. He used to say, 'For evil to triumph it is necessary only for good men to do nothing.' Well, what a pain *that* was! Why couldn't it be, 'For goodness to triumph it is necessary only for good men to sit on their arses and get pissed'? Why was poking your nose into other people's problems always at such a high emotional cost?

Wednesday arrived with the unsettling speed of a teenage mugger, as do all days which engender apprehension of some sort, and Flower found herself walking towards Frogs Wine Bar going through her lines for her guest spot.

The man behind the Frogs empire of one sad lonely

club had decided to jump on the comedy bandwagon with very little idea of where he was going; the facilities, as usual, were not at their best. There was no changing room and Flower couldn't believe it when the choice put to her was the women's toilet – one smelly cubicle – or standing on the pavement outside.

Flower clocked Marty Mavers in the women's toilet, a highly ambitious Australian comic who kept a record of hers and everyone else's earnings and had her nose so far up the arses of the relevant TV people that, had her nose been the size of Flower's, their livers and kidneys would have been shredded. So Flower decided she'd stand out on the pavement with Dunk, a Cambridge university graduate who believed there was far more danger and excitement to be had amongst the comedy clubs of London than on some adventure trail in South America, much to his parents' disappointment as they had very little else to do with their money, their imaginations being inversely proportional to their wealth.

Billy found Dunk and Flower chatting just as it started to rain so he and Flower escaped inside to the relative warmth of the bar although she was to discover later that the audience was several degrees below freezing.

'So,' said Billy, 'come to ask me out?'

'In your dreams,' said Flower, whose boldness increased the nearer she got to a stage.

'Well, what then?'

'I want to talk to you about Sarah,' said Flower.

'Me and Sarah is none of your fucking business,' said Billy.

Aware of the fact she was already sounding like some really irritating unreconstructed seventies feminist, Flower said, 'Look, Sarah is a really good friend of mine and I wouldn't like to see any harm come to her.'

She waited for the eruption.

Instead, Billy just laughed.

'What are you on about?' he said. 'You ridiculous woman! How would any harm come to her?'

'Well,' said Flower, 'there was that night . . .' She trailed off not wanting to actually say the words.

'When I caught her accidentally with my hand, when I was trying to . . .' Billy trailed off too, searching for the right words.

Come on, thought Flower. This'll be good.

'. . . smack the cat?'

Oh, the cat that flies through the air at head height, thought Flower, but didn't say anything.

'Look,' said Billy, 'I've apologised about your wrist. I wasn't doing anything to Sarah that night, I was just having a laugh and you got it all wrong.'

Flower, as she had many hundreds of times, began to doubt herself. She felt silly – and felt silly that she felt so silly. Her chummy speech about whether Billy needed help working through his anger stuck two fingers up at her and flew out the window.

'Is that all?' said Billy. ''Cause I've got to get home.'

'Yes, I suppose so,' said Flower, now feeling pissed off and deflated and not in the mood for comedy. She hoped that the hideous Marty Mavers had vacated the Ladies and headed inside the club. Flower was on in the middle of the show. She didn't like to watch the show because it put her off and made her feel she wasn't funny.

Marty Mavers opened with a treatise on the size of her vagina and what particular makes of truck could be backed up into it. The repressed and depressed British crowd loved her and failed to notice her eagerly scanning the audience for anyone more influential than the compère with whom she had slept a couple of years ago.

While Marty was on, the final act of the night Des Plumpton turned up. He was a trouper from the old days who'd decided he had to get in with the kids and had swapped his racist, sexist act for one which included lots of swearing and jokes about adverts, although in the last few years he'd found his old set increasingly acceptable in the ever-shifting field of comedy. Flower and Dunk were the guest spots and had Flower not liked Dunk so much she would have been quite pleased that he struggled as this usually meant that the next act on would have an easier time.

Dunk was a nice unassuming aristocrat who was rather embarrassed about his family's wealth and had made a half-hearted attempt to separate himself from the bosom of his family, live in a squat and be an anti-hunt protester. He met his parents at a few fox-hunts and had pulled his dad off his horse once before he realised who it was.

The audience wasn't going for Dunk's gentle public-school brand of humour.

'Why don't you fuck off, you posh twat?' was a question

Dunk had been asked rather too many times by audience members and he retired hurt, having been unable to come up with the killer put-down.

Flower always timed her pre-performance piss very badly and heard her name called as she was reaching for the toilet paper. There then ensued a wild scramble while she tried to sort herself out, check everything was pulled up and secrete her set list in her pocket as she made her way to the stage. Flower vowed she would sort this problem out but always had to pee right at the last minute. It was preferable to incontinence on stage, which she felt was only one false move away. The memory of the time she went on with some toilet paper tucked in her waistband and a vast expanse of gruesome Christmas present knicker on show burned into her making her, even now, blush with shame. Too new in the game to turn it to her advantage or pretend she'd done it on purpose, she allowed the crowd to satiate their laughter lust and then quietly left the stage.

'Hello everyone,' said Flower, as she stepped onto the makeshift stage. 'I really do—'

'Cor, I'd like to sit on *your* face,' came a heckle.

The crowd laughed.

Flower floundered. 'Er . . .' she said.

'But I'd get my bollocks slashed to bits by that nose,' continued the voice.

The crowd laughed again.

Shit, I should have said that, thought Flower, not realising the simple act of repeating that out loud would have got her some sympathy and a round of applause in a parallel universe.

'Nice tits too,' said the heckler.

The crowd laughed again.

Where's Germaine Greer when you need her? thought Flower, yet again failing to capitalise on her thoughts. I hope Charlie's having a better time at anger management.

Charlie wasn't.

The anger management group seemed to Charlie to be an excuse to gather as many cartoon psychopaths into one room as possible and he was shaking with fear. His only ally, he felt, from the world of relatively stable non-homicidal people was a comic, Matt Vicious, who had broken the nose of an over-enthusiastic heckler, thus prompting his agent to send him here as he fast saw his percentage drying up if Matt began laying waste to audience members. Apart from Matt, the rest of the room consisted of convicted felons, wife-beaters and a bloke who always thumped bus drivers if, as they normally did, they arrived at his bus stop accompanied by two other buses of the same number. Unfortunately, this guy had been seen by many as the Robin Hood of South Norwood and many passengers often cheered as he took a swing at a series of unfortunate men whose only crime was to linger too long outside the local café stop.

The anger management group leader was a tiny psychologist called Sian who looked like she couldn't have held her own against an angry squirrel let alone these bruisers.

Therefore she had to rely on their ability to control themselves, the support of the other group members should an incident occur or, at the very least, the ability to run out of the room as fast as her tiny little legs would carry her. Group membership was fluid as some came and went, while others had a spell in prison or just couldn't be arsed to return because they considered their problem to be an advantage rather than a treatable symptom of a personality disorder.

Charlie was the only new member of the group that week and the other men had to look twice when they saw this rather bedraggled scruff slouch into the room.

'I could take that nonce out with my little finger,' mused Dave, a career criminal from Balham who knocked his wife about as a sideline and had no idea that she was a regular visitor to Michael Randall's self-defence classes just waiting to pick up enough knowledge to give her husband the biggest shock of his life. Dave's neighbour, at whom the remark was aimed, nodded and snarled a bit which tended to be his only form of communication. He didn't like hippies and this one had better not be a wanker into the bargain.

'Right,' said Sian brightly in a high-pitched voice which matched her appearance, 'I see we have a new member this week. If everyone would like to introduce themselves to Charlie, then he can tell us a bit about why he's here.'

One by one, this gene pool of lack of impulse control mumbled their names and within seconds they were back at Charlie who had been dreading this moment.

'Hi.' He raised a hand, realised he looked like a social worker and put it down immediately.

'I'm Charlie,' he said, and much to his surprise began to talk about himself, how he was a jealous character who found it hard to let Flower live her life, how he didn't use violence on her but couldn't wait until he was at some sort of march and could get his hands on a policeman. To his even greater surprise, this roomful of assorted terrifying blokes began nodding sagely at his words and a discussion ensued about jealousy, insecurity and their long-term effects, and whether they'd inherited it from their families.

Charlie was amazed. He'd assumed there would just be a short interlude before he was battered to a pulp and then taken to hospital, but he could see how these guys were really trying to tackle their problems. He was sitting there with a slightly soppy grin on his face when a chair hit him on the head.

Chapter 10

The chair that hit Charlie on the head had been lobbed from some distance by Dave's wife, Dawn, who had left a friend looking after the kids and made her way up on the bus determined to make an impact and a statement, given that Dave had been attending this wretched group for weeks and yet his behaviour had shown very little improvement. It wasn't so much Dave's violence, which to be honest was like their sex-life – infrequent and swift – it was more the incessant carping about her appearance/cooking/household-management skills/talent as a mother and human being that wore Dawn down. Once Dave had failed to come home for his dinner and in a fit of rage Dawn had gone to the pub with it on a tray, walked up to a table containing a very surprised Dave and three amused mates and dumped it in front of him and walked out. The reaction was not what she'd hoped. Dave got some salt and pepper from the bar and happily tucked in while the conversation about sport continued.

Unfortunately, it's not easy to aim a chair with any accuracy and therefore the chances of it hitting Dave were minimal, as soon as it left Dawn's hands.

Dave didn't help the situation by laughing out loud when he realised that the chair intended for him had hit the dopey hippy, and this incensed Dawn and interestingly Dave's neighbour Phil, who was quite happy to beat the crap out of blokes, but had sat there for weeks with his blood pressure slowly rising as he listened to tales of Dave's wife being battered in different rooms of the house and thought of his mum. Phil didn't realise Dave had exaggerated his violence for theatrical effect. Therefore he and Dawn between them leaped onto Dave and began battering him as best they could.

Sian had not encountered a brawl before, and finding her voice could not be heard above the din of Dawn's screaming and Phil's snarling, she thumped someone on the head with a hardback copy of *Psychiatry in Dissent* to try and break it up. Unfortunately this was Charlie, who was beginning to feel picked on and he turned and lashed out, catching Sian on the side of the cheek. At this point Phil, seeing this tiny childlike woman being assaulted, went mental and threw Charlie to the ground, banging his head on the floorboards as poor Charlie tried desperately to apologise to Sian and explain to Phil.

This was when the other members of the group – most of whom, to be honest, had missed the squirty adrenaline sensation of a bloody good ruck – got stuck in, and the anger management class became a seething Loony Toon mass of arms and legs and noise.

The fight was only stopped when a security guard, aged ninety if he was a day and almost transparent in his frailty, stuck his head round the door and hobbled towards the group to see what he could do, cherishing memories of bare-knuckle fighting for money as a teenager in the East End.

Even I could knock this one out, thought Sian as she saw him approaching, and if she was honest with herself, she decided to have a crack as she had never hit anyone in her life and wanted to see how it felt. When it came to it though, she just could not bring herself to stick one on that veiny nose planted in the middle of that pinched face and so the fight stopped even more abruptly than it had started.

Everybody got up and brushed themselves off in a matter-of-fact fashion, apart from Charlie who had been at the bottom of the pile of fighters and was winded and worried that he'd broken another one of his fingers.

Meanwhile, Flower's heart had been broken as she'd been forced off the stage by the heckler and there was nowhere to run except the ladies' toilets where Marty Mavers stood, combining the incongruity of a smug grin and a tragic voice full of empathy about Flower's demise.

'It all takes time,' she said, sounding like some teacher Flower had hated at school and Flower felt a rising inclination to thump her silly face. Instead she said, 'Thanks, Marty,' flatly and turned to leave.

As she did so, an audience member appeared in the doorway and said, 'I thought you were great!'

'Thanks,' said Marty, extending a hand.

'I'm sorry,' said the punter, 'I didn't mean you, I meant her.'

Flower was so grateful she could have cried and with her head held high she left the toilet, somewhat repaired, leaving a foolish-looking Marty Mavers wondering why the only punter in the whole room who could possibly prefer Flower's act to hers, had walked into their toilet.

On her way out, the club-owner Tom stopped Flower and for one joyful moment Flower thought he would offer her a booking. It wasn't to be. He handed her a note.

'Someone likes you,' he said.

Flower opened the note. It was from the heckler, she deduced cleverly as it was signed *The Heckler*, and it said:

This time the victory is mine but if you are very, very, very nice to me, I'll leave you alone. More instructions to follow.

Flower shivered. Oh great, she thought. This is just what I need. She chucked the note away thinking that if Charlie saw it, it might set back all the good work done by anger management.

If only.

All the good work done by anger management consisted of a bloody nose, bruised spine and torn trousers for Charlie. As he and Flower limped home from opposite points of the compass, each damaged in different ways, both feeling utterly defeated, Martha's voice was flying over their heads along a wire to Sarah who, revelling in the luxury of a night in on her own with no fear of saying the wrong thing or being clumsy or burning the dinner, was chatting happily on the phone with her, about the mess that was their romantic lives.

'Look, Marth, I love him so I'm hardly going to walk away, am I?' said Sarah, sounding like a girl band.

'But Sar, you've got to think of yourself in this,' said Martha. 'I know you underplay it 'cause you're embarrassed, but be honest, are you scared of him?'

'Sometimes,' Sarah said, underplaying 'almost all the time' to something more palatable.

'Well, is that a good basis for a relationship?' said Martha.

'It's better than not having one at all,' said Sarah, touching on one of life's great questions for many women who feel like a spare part-cum-leper if they are not accompanied by a penis-owner at all times.

'Oh thanks,' said Martha. 'Thanks for reminding me.'

'You've got the Lump,' said Sarah, who truly believed that it was possible for a baby to fill a relationship-sized gap.

'I can't fuck the baby,' said Martha crossly and then thought how lucky it was that her father couldn't listen in to her conversations any more.

'Marth, what a terrible thing to say,' said Sarah.

'Sorry,' said Martha grudgingly. She had got so used to winding up her dad, it leaked into other parts of her life too.

Tentatively, Sarah said, 'Look, Marth, you haven't told anyone who the father of Lump is yet. We want to help, you know. Why won't you tell us?'

Martha had been caught at a rather hormonal time by Sarah and her resolve, like some tuberculosis-ridden

Victorian heroine, to keep schtumm about the origins of the Lump, caved in and she started to weep great big hiccuppy sobs down the phone.

'Oh, I'm sorry,' said Sarah. 'I didn't mean to set you off.'

'I don't know!' wailed Martha through a wall of snot.

'Don't know what?' said Sarah. 'Don't know what to do?'

'No, don't know who the father is,' lied Martha.

'Well, how many possibles are there?' said Sarah.

'Three,' said Martha.

'Bloody hell!' said Sarah. 'I never realised.'

'I'm so embarrassed,' said Martha as she sobbed on.

'Can't you do one of them tests?' said Sarah. 'Who are they, anyway?'

'Look, I can't talk now,' said Martha. 'I'm dying for a piss. I'll meet you and Flower in the pub and tell you all about it.'

'Don't worry,' said Sarah. 'It'll be all right,' although she had no more idea whether it would be than whether Flower would make it on the comedy circuit, something she had assured her of many times.

'I'd better go,' said Martha. 'See you tomorrow night?'

Sarah didn't want to say, 'If it's all right with Billy,' but Martha sensed that this was an issue and said, 'If not then, Friday eh?' knowing Billy went out with workmates on Friday nights.

Sarah went to bed that night with a list of names in her head about who the most likely candidates could be and found herself, strangely, to be somewhat envious of Martha's predicament.

As she dropped off, she narrowed the list down to four and was eager to see if any of them were right. There was Martha's ex-boyfriend Alan the Planet, so named because his head contained many more facts than most people's. He'd moved away and the relationship had lost impetus as his visits got less frequent. Or could it be Martha's next-door neighbour, fourteen-year-old Junior, with whom she flirted outrageously whenever she got the chance? Perhaps it was Ted, her boss from work, whose unattractiveness was negated by a large wallet and a wicked sense of humour, or maybe that bloke whose name she couldn't remember whom they'd met in a club in East London.

Her money was on Ted.

Chapter 11

Charlie and Flower sat miserably at home like a pair of pensioners who'd just discovered rationing was back. They were hunched over a small electric fire because the central heating had broken down and the weatherman had been excitable to the point of idiocy as he described the coming cold snap. Charlie, as is common in enough men for women to comment on, was hypochondriacal to the point of having cheated death many times in his head and was swathed in hot towels with a Lemsip and Marijuana Sprinkle, as he called it, to dull the physical pain brought on by the anger management group. Flower, on the other hand, was suffering a higher form of pain, the emotional humiliation of the heckled-off comic which makes one feel like one's insides have been taken out and auctioned off outside the local newsagent for enemies to use as table decorations.

At that moment, Hitler ('so we never forget the evil bastard existed' . . . Charlie Knapp 1992), their black and white cat, entered the room, limping, with one of his back legs in plaster completing the sad trio of damaged creatures in the house. Had Charlie and Flower been a little less depressed the cat would have offered the possibility of a good laugh at themselves, a route untravelled by too many politicians and celebrities.

Charlie had related his tale of woe from anger management and was trying to explain to Flower that with such a volatile group he didn't think it was the best idea to send Billy along quite yet. Flower then related the tragic tale of her evening, leaving out the Billy and heckler elements because they would have upset Charlie, which meant he found it difficult to understand why it had been such a bad evening.

'Oh, let's do it,' said Charlie, which was his answer to pretty much any traumatic situation and Flower thought fondly of the times she had been pinned to the ground by him in the midst of some chaos – a demo that went wrong at Stonehenge, under a police van, round at her parents' just after an emotional dinner and their most unusual perhaps, a quick one in Sainsburys at two in the morning over the organic frozen section. It was quite difficult to make it look like they were taking a long time to decide whether to go for veggie sausage rolls or a turkey that had had a damn good run round a bit of mud in Essex before it was pulverised. Normally in a relationship the sexual urge cools unevenly, but in Flower and Charlie's case even after many years together there was an equal appetite not only for the long slow encounter but also the race against Big Ben's bongs for the midday news.

This time it was on the floor in their scruffy living room, and if either of them had been interested they would have spotted the flash of binoculars as their neighbour opposite, a long-time silent participator in their sex-life, thanked his lucky stars for a grandstand view and put the phone down rather abruptly on the local radio station before his voice rose too highly. Another skill Flower and Charlie possessed was the ability to discuss any aspect of their life, however trivial, during fucking – so the conversation about Billy's suit-ability for the anger management group continued accom-panied by a few squeaks and low-pitched grunts, making it sound to someone on the other side of the wall as though the news and a porn film were being played simultaneously. And there *was* someone on the other side of the wall listening – their next-door neighbour, a dried-up old misery of a woman who had made it her life's dedication to get Flower and Charlie out of the place by logging every sound above a whisper and plaguing the Environmental Health Office with a catalogue of the bangs, squawks, thumps, boings and sighs of Charlie and Flower's life. The fact that she had to use an old-fashioned ear trumpet to do it was not something she revealed to the authorities, however.

Charlie and Flower were aware she was trying to get them out and in their hippy Christian sort of way had tried to be nice. This elicited completely the opposite reaction and the woman, Mrs Edith Challoner, was so unpleasant to them that they had no option but to hate her in as uncharitable a way as possible. They called her 'Grandma PMT' because of her thoroughly ill-tempered behaviour, which was matched once a month by Flower, who possessed the genuine article: she had offered several times to pop in and stuff a pillow over Mrs Challoner's face, prompting Charlie to ladle an extra helping of Evening Primrose into her mug of tea at breakfast.

'Fucking hell,' said Charlie, ejaculating and seamlessly segueing into, 'We'll leave the anger management suggestion to Billy for a while, shall we?'

'OK,' said Flower squeakily as she dropped off, the one of the pair who always went out like a light.

Billy, meanwhile, was totally unaware of all this mental activity being directed towards his life as he sat with his feet up on a chair in a pub mulling over the conversation he had had with Flower earlier in the evening and wondering how much these bloody girls would interfere in his life. He supposed another approach would be forthcoming from Martha and quite looked forward to what the pregnant old sow would have to say to him. He also wondered whether Sarah was in on this and had sanctioned the approaches, but he presumed, rightly, that she would be absolutely devastated if she knew, because he recognised in Sarah the self-esteem level of a minnow and knew that she would plug any emotional outburst that might elicit a show of concern from friends or family. Family of course wasn't very likely as Sarah hadn't seen her mum for five or so years and had never even known her dad, so it was down to her friends to offer her the support a family would have provided.

Flower was having an affair with a car. She had booked driving lessons. She hadn't told Charlie about it, because he hated cars and thought that they both managed perfectly well on their bikes and with the odd lift in some hideous smelly van. But Flower was fed up with being on a bike. It felt like being on a conveyor belt that ran through a country of hecklers, and the anticipation of abuse made her anxious every time she mounted the bloody thing. This made her make silly mistakes, and so far she had ridden into a lamppost in front of some teenage boys who had predictably pissed themselves, broadsided an old lady on a zebra crossing (regrettably not Mrs Challoner) and run over their own cat, thus necessitating its leg in plaster.

Flower's driving instructor had the Sergeant Major air of someone who had been responsible for the suicide of several squaddies. He was possessed of a voice so gratingly loud that being stuck in a car with him was torturous. Flower would have changed to another instructor but hated to offend anyone, although to offend a creature with skin this thick would have required placing an explosive device in his Y-fronts. You could not have slipped even a fag paper in between Ernie Bolland's arse and the plastic seat in the tiny car. He parped out orders, which made Flower nervous, and she kept making a mess of things each time they had a lesson.

Mr Bolland always picked Flower up from work so

Charlie wouldn't see them and there he was this particular morning, his jellylike bulk firmly sat in the passenger seat. This was Flower's third lesson and the residents of Primrose House were all out in the garden as she stepped into the car.

'Ooh look,' said Rene, one of the other care assistants. 'Flower's going driving.' Everyone turned to look at Flower, who felt her face flush with embarrassment. She had her foot on the accelerator.

'Well, move, you silly moo!' boomed Ernie Bolland.

Flower accelerated and, forgetting the small issue of steering, headed straight over the roundabout in the middle of the drive, which contained a number of primroses, surprisingly enough. The residents of Primrose House were hugely impressed as she ploughed across, bumped off the other side and disappeared out of the drive without slowing down. A huge cheer went up as Flower roared off round the corner, with Ernie Bolland looking amazed, an expression he would wear once again that week when the young boy he picked up in the public toilets showed some interest in his life.

Flower found that her mind emptied every time she went for a driving lesson, which was not the best time for it to do that. She shaved an old woman's shopping basket on a zebra crossing, and even Ernie Bolland's penetrating baritone couldn't completely break through into the world of her thoughts. She was fretting about her next gig and the possible reappearance of the heckler and what his note actually meant. It sounded as though he wanted to have sex with her but maybe that was just the slant she was putting on it. Whichever way it went, she'd have to keep Charlie away from it all as she didn't want yet more trouble.

Meanwhile, Martha had been 'Mary-ed' as she called it, in other words trapped on her sofa while her miserable sister regaled her with all the elements of her miserable life. Normally, at the end, when Martha tried to say something, Mary tended to get up and go home. This time, for a change, they were actually having something approaching a conversation about their parents; as usual Martha had taken her mother's side and Mary, her father's. Mary couldn't bear anyone to show any kind of weakness, the legacy of many years as the oldest child being battered into submission by the Rev Brian, whilst being hauled up mountains, swimming in leg-mottlingly cold English seas and standing outside in all weathers preaching the word, which was really an excuse for her dad to get out of the house and away from the pathetic beseeching eyes of her mother who wanted a proper happy family.

'When's that thing due?' asked Mary unkindly, looking at Martha's Lump as though it was a lump of snot in her embroidered hanky. 'And have you told Dad who the father is yet?'

'What – so he can give me another fucking lecture?'

Mary visibly cringed at the F word as many people do who long to be able to use it. Mary thought her husband was a fucking wanker, her neighbours were fucking cretins and the kids were fuckwits. Hurrah for a Christian upbringing.

'It's due in about three weeks,' said Martha. 'Coming over for the big event?'

'I don't think so,' said Mary. 'Anyway, I've come to talk about Mother and Father, not the bloody ball of skin and bone you'll be ejecting out of your naughty.' (Mary hadn't really moved on from a childhood approach to sex.)

Martha had never heard Mary put it so charmingly and decided that as well as having all the best tunes, the devil had all the best descriptive phrases as well.

'So what about Mum and Dad?' said Martha, who was torn between hoping her parents would split up so her mum could come and help her with the baby, even if it meant having to clean up her act ... and wishing she'd keep well away.

'Well, since her foolish little foray here, I think things have slightly improved,' said Mary, 'but we need to keep an eye on them because Dad is just as likely to chuck her out as her go again, you know. He's nearly had enough.'

'Oh the poor bastard,' said Martha. 'It must be really hard for him having someone cook his meals, keep the house clean and shag him whenever he wants.'

Mary nearly vomited at this suggestion. 'That is b— disgusting,' she said, not even having reached the stage of the 'bloody' word yet.

'Oh come on,' said Martha, 'surely you must know the man is an animal? He twirls her on the end of it at least three times a week.'

Mary let out a strangulated scream. 'Shut up!' she shouted at Martha who was enjoying herself, but also being truthful.

'Oh grow up,' she said impatiently. 'Do you think they did it twice for us and a couple of times trying for Lazarus? He's over-sexed, is Brian. He's a fucking randy vicar, you silly cow, except he doesn't do it with anyone else except poor Mum.'

'I will not listen to this!' screeched Mary, and headed for the door. As she reached it, she turned and put her hand in her bag, pulling out a tin of ham. 'For you and the baby!' she shouted, lobbing it. Having thrown the javelin at school she didn't realise her own strength and the tin sailed past Martha's ear, out of the balcony window and landed on the car roof of some drug dealers measuring out some crack below.

A stream of expletives floated out of the car and it was a good job Mary didn't hear the myriad options available to her of meeting her death as they determined to pull limb from limb the person who had damaged their pride and their car.

Oh what a shame, thought Martha. The baby would have loved a ham sarnie just after it squeezed out of my *naughty*.

It was a pity it didn't sail in through the window of Sarah and Billy's flat because just at that moment Sarah was longing for a heavy object with which to defend herself. Billy was advancing menacingly towards her, having criticised everything all day and now looking like he might thump her again.

'Bloody useless, thick, pathetic, vain, ridiculous . . .' One adjective after another spewed so easily out of his mouth when it had been lubricated with alcohol.

And now for the physical part of *The Krypton Factor* challenge, thought Sarah grimly. And all this because Martha had phoned and asked her out for a drink on a Thursday night.

Chapter 12

Flower, Martha and Sarah arranged to meet on Friday night because Sarah had phoned sounding very breezy, in the way that over-optimistic hostages do, and told them she couldn't make the Thursday – but of course Flower and Martha detected beneath this unnatural cheefulness that a bit of domestic was going on and assumed rightly that Billy had been at it again. Martha, in the throes of a hormone surge, kicked the wall and cried, and Flower building up to a PMT session kicked Charlie and *he* cried.

Sarah was desperate to try and halt the descent into relationship hell for which Billy was lining her up. A nasty situation had been developing, averted only by a ring on the doorbell from a concerned neighbour asking if they were all right – something that shocked Billy, who made an excuse about the telly being too loud and letting his composure slip by finishing the encounter with, 'And mind your own business, you nosy cow!'

The nosy cow in question was Maxine who lived in the flat next door and had a husband called Sean, a kind sensitive bloke who didn't like the look of Billy and had avoided conversations with him in the communal hallway. Billy didn't care because he thought Sean looked under the thumb.

But before Friday and the great revelations by Martha Spinster of this Parish, Flower had another gig to get through, this time at a club on the outskirts of South London, one of these rather manicured well-off areas that is filled with a very high quotient of middle-class yobs, who obviously wouldn't be seen dead in a comedy club, but appeared to have sent their older brothers and sisters along. Flower was Charlie-less again as he had a bad headache sustained during Flower's two-day PMT window.

Flower was beginning to feel under siege with all the problems in her life: the driving lessons weren't going well, work was hard work, Charlie was being too suspicious, Billy was a nightmare and she dreaded her next encounter with the heckler, having had plenty of time to imagine a Hollywood woman-slasher blockbuster in which she was finally tracked to a disused comedy club and disembowelled.

This time Flower was working with Chas Lawrence, a very pleasant man in his forties whose friends had told him he was brilliant at telling jokes; emboldened by alcohol one night he had got up at a comedy club in Hastings and done five minutes of jokes which had gone down a storm. He'd then tried his luck in London and since then his career had taken off, but he had been ignored by telly people because being funny isn't enough.

Also on with Flower and Chas were Billson Tillson, a young man with a history of mental illness who tended to recount his thoughts to the audience and that seemed to be enough, and Lulu West, a solicitor, whose act consisted of describing famous murders and doing songs about them with a ukelele. Had her bosoms been two cup sizes larger, she would already have had her own series on telly.

Billson always started his act by staring mournfully at the audience for about a minute, which was a hell of a long time.

Tonight, he began by saying, 'My medication's not working so well this week,' and because he looked like a badly dressed owl, this worked well and the audience laughed and some clapped. Bilson continued, encouraged, 'When me and my twin sister Electra were eight my mother killed my father because he wouldn't mow the lawn and after she'd cut him up, we had to eat seventy fish fingers each for tea that night to make room for him in the freezer.'

Fewer people laughed this time.

'Next day I didn't have anything to take into school for cookery class so I took a bit of my dad's leg.'

The audience sensed something on cannibalism coming up and wondered if they had the stomach for it.

'Trouble was, my dad's leg got so badly burned in the oven, I wasn't allowed to eat it.'

Shuffling and coughing began and some people suspected that this odd character wasn't making it up. A mental-health worker at the back, more out of concern for what might develop than sadism began to shout, 'Off! Off!'

Bilson didn't need telling twice and he left the stage somewhat miffed that the terribly convoluted punchline he had prepared about being given a dead leg at school would never be aired at this particular venue.

Chas then came on and told a lot of old jokes that he had collected since he was a child and the audience breathed a sigh of relief that they didn't have to do anything except sit back and relax. Personally Flower thought there were too many sexist jokes in Chas's set but kept her mouth shut because this was the way things seemed to be these days. Also, when he got to the one about the lion-tamer putting his knob in the lion's mouth and hitting it on the head with a hammer with no reaction from the lion, she had to admit it was a funny joke and started to laugh, as the lion-tamer asked the circus crowd if anyone wanted to try it and an old lady answered, 'Yes, I'll have a go but you won't hit me too hard on the head with the hammer, will you?'

Chas stormed it and after ten minutes the audience were whooping and cheering. This made Flower nervous because she knew the content of her set would not be the material of choice for this particular audience.

However, that's what it's all about, she said to herself, appealing to the widest possible audience – so with as much of the trench spirit as she could muster, she walked onto the stage.

'Bit of a shithole round here, isn't it?' she started, which got a very respectable laugh, possibly a six on the Richter Scale. Flower loosened up a bit. 'Still,' she said, 'I live in Nunhead and the gardens round us aren't nearly as well kept as yours. Look!' She pulled a bunch of flowers from behind her back and smelled them luxuriantly . . . and the audience laughed and applauded.

Flower foolishly allowed herself the thought that for once it had started well.

'I hope you got those from my garden,' shouted a voice, ''cause I piss on them to water them, you know.'

The audience laughed very loudly, giving Flower eleven and a half seconds to come up with a funny reply.

'Fuck off Titchmarsh,' she ventured.

A big laugh.

'Hadn't you better have a sit-down, beautiful?' continued the voice. 'The scent of them flowers will knock you out, taken in through that conk.'

A bigger laugh, Flower's confidence sliding down into her boots and sweat springing up all over.

'Go fuck yourself,' came out of her mouth and she knew she was already defeated.

'I might have to if you're all that's on offer,' came the reply.

Flower struggled on for a bit longer but gave up and left as soon as she could. Dec, the club manager, was sympathetic but Flower could tell he wanted people who could handle the audiences and for some reason the self-confidence of most women comics is set at a different level from that of men; crumpling into a girlie heap comes so much easier to the female of the species. At least there was no note from the heckler this time. It was not long though before, in Flower's head, the heckler would be spelled with a capital H.

As Flower left the building she heard the mildly irritating tones of Lulu West's ukelele drifting out of the window and caught a snatch of, *'The Yorkshire Ripper stalked the streets of Leeds nightly, / Why couldn't he have helped us out and cut up Richard Whiteley?'*

Big laughs.

On her bike on the way home, Flower's mobile rang. It was Charlie.

'How did it go?'

'Shit,' said Flower. 'I guess Bromley's not my heartland.'

'Never mind,' said Charlie. 'Hurry home and we'll do it.'

Flower began to pedal faster, fearing Charlie might do it on his own if she didn't get there soon. Flower's phone made a beeping noise that signalled the arrival of a text message and like 90 per cent of the population when driving, she assumed that she could access a message and read it quite safely whilst continuing to pedal home through the cheerless South London night. Of course, Flower pressed a wrong button, tried to peer more closely at her phone and careered off the road and up onto the kerb which flipped her off and she landed on her bum on the pavement. More embarrassed than hurt, and cursing Charlie who had obviously decided to encourage her home for their tryst textually, she found the message.

Two nil it said, followed by a capital H, and it was enough to let the Grim Reaper clutch her heart and give it a good squeeze as she realised it was from the heckler. How did he have her phone number? This was getting spooky and she didn't like it. Perhaps she'd better tell Charlie. Well, at least she could tell the girls and see what they said although their advice, from the heavily pregnant, hormonally flooded Martha to the emotional knife-edge that was Sarah, might not be worth having at the moment.

'All right, love?' shouted a voice. 'That's not a chair, you know!'

She looked over to see a leering greasy sort of face poking out of an estate car. Fucking hell, she thought. I'm still being heckled. 'More's the pity, or I could ram a leg up your arse,' she replied and shuddered at her own creative limits.

The driver looked mortally wounded, as a lot of street hecklers do if you actually come back at them . . . well, either that or they stab you and it was Flower's lucky night.

Back at home, Charlie's erection had faded, been reactivated by a quick five minutes of his Mary Poppins video and then died again when Flower phoned him to say she'd come off her bike. They had an early sleep-filled night.

On Friday night the King's Head received Martha, Flower and Sarah into its dankness like little sperms into a big womb. The air was foetid and smoke hung in the air but they all loved it like a mangy old dog that refused to die.

Flower and Sarah were shivery with anticipation as they were about to find out who the father of the Lump was, a most unexpected development and one which they had assumed wouldn't happen until the Lump was about five and someone made a drunken slip of the tongue at a party.

Martha had steeled herself with a few drinks, knowing she shouldn't but this was a four-fag emergency and at least she hadn't given in and smoked, but as the Bloody Marys slipped down, she mused that at least she was introducing some Vitamin C along with the foetal alcohol syndrome. She regretted having to tell Sarah and Flower the truth, as she had rather enjoyed being a woman of mystery for eight months while they and her relatives pondered the gritty question of who could have impregnated her, and it had to be said that the Rev Brian had mooted the idea with Pat that someone had perhaps forced himself onto their daughter.

The etiquette for revealing to your two best friends the identity of the father of your soon-to-be-born child is not described anywhere in a manual so none of them really knew what to do.

Should I just come straight out with it? thought Martha. Put an appropriate record on the jukebox? Do a drumroll on the table? Mime it and make them guess?

'Come on then,' said Sarah, 'don't keep us waiting. It's Ted, isn't it?'

'Ooh, how could you?' said Martha. 'Me knocked up by that self-propelled dog turd! You are joking, I hope?'

'But he's got a nice sense of humour,' said Flower, 'and he's not that ugly.'

'Oh thanks,' said Martha, 'so that's my ideal partner rating, is it? *Not that ugly.* I can just see myself on a dating show with a couple of other mangled old bloodhounds competing for the attention of Mr Not That Ugly!'

'Don't be sensitive,' said Flower. 'I'm only pissing about. Spit it out. Is it Alan the Planet?'

'Not unless he's mailed me some Next Day Delivery sperm in a DIY postal experiment,' said Martha. 'I haven't seen him for ages.'

'Well, it must have been that bloke we met in that club in East London – what was his name?'

'Mohammed,' said Martha. 'Oh Gawd, I hope not. Besides, I didn't even sleep with him.'

'You said you did,' said Flower.

'Well, that's 'cause I don't like to appear too boring,' said Martha.

'Well, who is it then?' said Flower and Sarah who were now getting slightly irritated.

'It's . . . oh, I've just got to go to the loo,' said Martha. She saw their faces. 'No, I'm not arsing about. I thought you knew I had to go at least fourteen times an hour because the Lump has made my bladder shrink to the size of a weasel's bollock.'

Martha sat grinning on the toilet, taking an extra long time and wishing she'd gone into the spy shop in the West End and bought one of those pens you can activate to tape the conversation when you leave a room. She had concluded very sensibly that she would only hear stuff that would upset her and she was right.

'Well, it could be Junior,' Flower was saying. Junior was fourteen and lived next door to Martha with his family, but he was already the size of a small tree and had started having sex at the age of nine.

'Nah, not even Martha would stoop that low,' said Sarah.

'Want to bet?' said Flower, having witnessed Martha at a party in Southend once, so drunk that she was trying to seduce someone who was unconscious under a table.

Martha eventually reappeared from the ladies' toilet and stopped at the bar on the way to get some crisps, thus prolonging the agony even more.

'So who is it?' said Flower with more than a hint of petulance in her voice.

'It's Ted,' said Martha.

'But you said it wasn't!'

'Well, it didn't seem right that you got it first guess . . . sorry. Thought I'd better make it a bit more mysterious,' said Martha.

'Do you know if it's a boy or a girl?' asked Flower.

'I just know it'll be fat and mad as fuck,' said Martha, 'and Not That Ugly, with a penchant for pickled onions.'

Sarah, who had been having visions of them all looking much more attractive than they normally did, standing by a font, began to be less and less keen on applying for the post of godmother.

'So how did it all happen with Ted?' said Flower, having only met him once and thought he looked like he had committed many dark unpleasant deeds in alleyways with frightening women.

'I know this sounds awful,' said Martha, 'but it was in an alleyway behind the club one night when I was working late and we'd both had a few drinks.'

Sarah, who was obsessional about the attractiveness and cleanliness of her sexual partners, felt slightly nauseated whereas Flower found herself strangely excited.

'Go on,' she said.

'That's it really,' Martha shrugged. 'I got pregnant.'

'Have you told him?'

'No.'

'Why not?'

'Don't want to upset the baby,' said Martha.

'Surely he must have some idea? Does he not remember banging you in the alleyway?' said Sarah. 'Anyway, why didn't you have a termination?'

'Always sounds so nice, "termination", doesn't it? Takes all the emotion out of the proceedings whereas "abortion" . . . now that sounds like what it is – a bloody mess in every way,' said Flower.

'I want to have a baby,' said Martha.

'To wind your dad up?' asked Flower.

'No, it's not that simple. Obviously that's a welcome by-product, but I'm old and it would have been too late soon,' said Martha.

'And irresponsible.' Flower found herself sounding like a proper grown-up.

'Oh, bumholes to responsible,' replied Martha, echoing

the mating call of those single mothers who just want a baby to love and don't realise the torturous ties that last for life if you get a bad 'un.

'Well, here's to you,' said Flower, raising her glass. 'Good luck.'

'Yeh, good luck, you silly cow,' Sarah grinned.

The room darkened suddenly, because there, in the doorway like the sheriff in a spaghetti western, stood Billy.

Chapter 13

Flower gulped and Martha tried to sneer but was aware that the side of her face was twitching slightly with nerves. Billy looked angry but in fact when he arrived over at the table his face crinkled into a smile.

'All right girls?' he said in a way which was meant to be ironic and teasing but came out rather awkwardly and made him sound like a pimp.

'Hello,' they chorused.

'What are you doing here?' said Sarah uncomfortably with a fixed grin on her face.

'Oh, I finished early with the lads,' said Billy. 'Thought I'd find you three scalliwags in here.'

How did he manage to make 'scalliwags' sound like 'stupid tarts'? thought Martha and realised she was really angry with him. 'Why don't you give the poor girl a break and fuck off and leave us alone,' she said.

A look of terror crossed Sarah's face and she ground her

foot into Martha's under the table. Martha began to laugh hysterically. 'Ha! Ha! Only joking!' she said. Flower joined in with as natural a laugh as she could manage, which wasn't very.

Flower's mobile started to ring. Perhaps the only occasion it had managed such perfect timing. 'Excuse me,' she said.

It was Charlie at the other end to tell her someone from the Nightcap had phoned to ask where she was.

'Oh piss,' said Flower, 'I've got to go. I forgot I had a gig tonight.' She gathered everything in a flurry of roll-up tobacco smoke and jasmine perfume and headed out of the door in a huge panic, throwing, 'See you over the weekend!' behind her as she sailed out.

'I can see when I'm not wanted as well, girls' talk and all that,' said Billy. 'See you later. And don't be too late, Sarah, will you?' He disappeared into the gloom.

'What did you do that for?' said Sarah.

'What?' said Martha, whose short-term memory would have been seen by a geriatrician as definite proof of the onset of Alzheimer's. Then: 'Oh, sometimes I just get sick of pretending everything's all right with you two,' she snapped. 'He's a bully.'

'He's got his own problems,' said Sarah.

'Oh yeh? Tell me about them,' said Martha.

'I'd better go,' said Sarah.

'Oh come on,' said Martha, 'there's another half hour's drinking time left and we can't fall out over a bloke.'

'We're not,' lied Sarah, 'but I've just got to go.'

Martha, who often thought in visual clichés, saw in her mind a big wedge being hammered in and its thin end disappearing under a door.

'All right,' she said brightly. 'We'll talk over the weekend?' It was half confident statement, half question.

Sarah headed slowly home hoping Billy wasn't going to be in a mood. She got home and Billy wasn't even there.

Martha was left with her sparkling water, which she swigged back, making a hideous face, and off she went.

Flower got to the Nightcap in quite a short time as she had flown through all the traffic-lights on her bike causing many simmering motorists to shout abuse after her disappearing form. She wanted to stop and explain she didn't normally do it, but needed to talk herself into a horrible sarcastic comedy mood, so she turned back and tried to give them a dirty look, something some women just aren't very good at, especially if they are nice and middle class. Flower would no sooner dream of screaming abuse after anyone than killing them with a gun.

On with Flower that night at the Nightcap were Dick Knob and Will Hatchard. Dick Knob was on last and Flower before him. Will Hatchard was doing well when she arrived. He was a Liverpudlian whose naturally drooping moustachio-ed face suited comedy very well and his heckle put-downs were generally agreed to be so good that almost everyone else was doing them.

'Have you ever wanted to kill anyone?' Flower asked Dick as they sat in the dingy dressing-room through the dirty window of which they could just see feet and ankles going about their business in late-night Soho.

'Only a twelve year old who wouldn't suck me off,' said Dick, who often spoke as if he was onstage.

'No, seriously,' said Flower.

'Why? Do you want to kill someone?' said the unusually perceptive Dick.

'I felt like it earlier,' said Flower. 'Sometimes I really wish I had a gun . . . just to frighten them, you know.'

'Who's them?' said Dick.

'Oh, arseholes, that sort,' said Flower.

'I'll get you a gun if that's what you want, sweetheart,' said Dick, trying Humphrey Bogart and getting an old American stroke victim instead.

'You're kidding,' said Flower, open-mouthed.

'Not at all,' said Dick. 'You want to come with me down Canning Town tomorrow, I'll talk to some mates.'

Flower felt slightly unreal as though it wasn't really her talking. 'No, it's all right,' she said. 'It'd be mad.'

'Oh come on,' said Dick, 'it'll be a laugh. Then you can blow Charlie's head off.'

'It's not Charlie who pisses me off,' said Flower.

This pissed Dick off because he had fancied Flower for ages even though she was so different from the sort of woman he normally went for, brassy and not fussy.

'Whatever,' said Dick.

'I don't know,' said Flower, feeling icy.

'Well, give us a call on the mobile tomorrow if you fancy it,' said Dick.

Chapter 14

'Oh, somebody shoot her, please!'

A wave of laughter soared across the darkened room, hitting a demoralised Flower with the realisation that she wasn't a very sharp comic tonight, her self-esteem was starting to burrow through to Australia, and The Heckler was back. Yes, she had given him capital letters finally and it was obligatory for him now to torture her mentally before, in the final showdown, she rid the world of him, as a heckler not a person, she hastily added to herself. Being funny isn't something most people do consistently. Everyone has off days and the greatest fear of the comic is that the comedy muse will leave them sweating with fear in their unmade bed and fly into the mind of their greatest rival, raising his comedy skills to even greater heights.

Flower drooped and the audience actually began to feel sorry for her, but she hadn't learned to use that sympathy either and after a couple more stabs at put-downs which sounded like she was addressing a slightly irritable late-comer at a knitting circle, Flower gave up again and headed off the stage.

'I'll get the cunt for you,' said the ever-chivalrous Dick Knob as they passed in the tiny corridor.

'Thanks,' said Flower miserably.

'Right, where's that heckler?' said Dick Knob as he stepped onstage. 'It's a long time since I penetrated the arsehole of an arsehole.'

The crowd woofed with delight. They could feel he was in control and Flower crept to the back to watch the master at work despite the fact that his multiple paedophile references turned her into a prude she didn't recognise.

At the side of the stage from the bar appeared a hapless latecomer, a woman. Flower gritted her teeth knowing that Dick Knob would give it to her with both barrels. The woman was obviously plump even in the poor light and Dick prepared to destroy.

'No, love,' he said. 'Anorexics Anonymous is down the road.'

Blokey tittering.

'I'm not anorexic,' replied the woman with just the right level of irony in her voice. The crowd giggled. She continued, 'And I'm not anorexic because I eat a load of shit, whereas it appears to be the reverse process with you.'

Women laughing. Blokes half admiringly grunting. Dick Knob looked astounded.

'When's it due?' he asked, falling back on an old comedy standard for fat women.

'In about five minutes,' said the woman. 'Give us a hand, will you, it's your little bastard after all.' The crowd loved this and laughed and clapped.

Flower suddenly realised the woman was Martha and a slight frisson of envy ran through her at the ease with which her friend appeared to be responding to Dick Knob.

Dick Knob got filthier and filthier and then retired with as much grace as someone who is regularly cornered by paedophile-hunting vigilantes, could manage.

'Well done!' said Flower, grabbing Martha.

'Oh pooh!' said Martha. 'Just a lucky overflow of hormones at the right time.'

'What are you doing here?' said Flower.

'Didn't fancy going home after that depressing encounter with Billy. Needed a laugh. Looked in the *Standard*, saw you were on here et cetera, et cetera.'

'Did you see that bloke who was heckling me?' said Flower.

'No, why?'

'I haven't mentioned it before but he's been to a few gigs and heckled me.'

'Oh, how deliciously pervy,' said Martha, who had all the sophistication of an eleven-year-old girl when it came to sexual threat.

'It's not delicious,' said Flower, 'it's scary. He's left me notes and sent me a text message.'

'Wait to see what he looks like before you condemn,' said Martha. 'He might be gorgeous.'

'Oh, be serious, Martha!' Flower burst out. 'What can I

do? I'm so vulnerable up onstage and people always know where you are on as a comic, 'cause it's in the paper.'

'Sorry,' said Martha, 'but there's always loads of male comics around so surely they'd protect you.'

'I wouldn't bank on it,' said Flower. 'If Psycho Heckler comes at me with a breadknife, I can guarantee there will be a complete set of Kings of Comedy disappearing out of the door rather than run the risk of cutting short their brilliant careers.'

'Better get yourself a gun then,' said Martha.

'Do you know what—' said Flower and was cut short by the noise of Dick Knob being heckled off as he had gone too far again and started a routine about raping a chicken and the effect that had on the taste of it at Sunday dinner.

Flower and Martha left the club and decided to go to a late-night café and have some coffee and bagels.

The place was pretty full as it was a Friday and a few drunks wobbled in and out of the tables dispensing their alcohol-fuelled advice to anyone who didn't look like they could beat the shit out of them.

'Can I join you, love?' said one of the aforementioned, spraying Flower and Martha with the aroma of vomit and Special Brew.

'I'd rather you didn't,' said Flower, forgetting she was a comedian. 'We're having a private conversation here.'

'Piss off twat.' Martha tried the less empathetic approach.

'Oh, don't be like that, fatty-boom-boom,' he said, falling onto the corner of their table and hitting his nose which stared to squirt copiously, causing Martha to have the rather unpleasant thought that this blood fountain was riddled with God knows how many blood-borne diseases. He rose, clutching the gushing appendage.

'I said, "Go away!"' Martha screamed at him and half-heaved, half-punched the man in the shoulder, causing him to catapult into the next table and hit the ground.

'Oh let's go,' said Flower. 'It's horrible in here tonight.'

They left some money on the table and headed out into the night, not realising that Mr Nosebleed had not risen from his second visit to the floor but appeared to be knocked out cold.

'Call an ambulance,' said a punter who still had some of the milk of human kindness pulsing through her veins.

'Chuck him out in the street,' said someone else and the owner did the former though he wanted to do the latter.

The ambulance crew arrived and were not impressed. To each other they said things like, 'Just another fucking drunk, waste of bloody time,' whereas they appeared to be the epitome of professionalism as they loaded him onto the trolley and pushed him into the ambulance.

As they cruised through the streets of London towards a Casualty Department reminiscent of Hieronymus Bosch's *Garden of Earthly Delights*, they were so busy chatting about the weekends they were planning they didn't even notice that the final breath had left the man's body.

Martha and Flower walked on oblivious to the fact that they were murderers, discussing the incident of Billy's arrival in the pub.

'He looked like he was checking up on her to me,' said Martha.

'It could just be pure ordinary friendliness and niceness that he'd come to meet her and take her home,' said Flower.

'Why are you always so positive about people and their motives?' snapped Martha.

'I don't know,' said Flower, ''cause let's face it, every other person's a fucking arsehole these days.'

This shocked Martha who was only used to this kind of language from Flower at specific times of the month when she treated her as if she had had her drink spiked with testosterone.

As if to prove Flower correct, a gang of girls about eighteen years old appeared from an alleyway at the side of them and started to take the piss.

'It's fucking Laurel and Hardy,' said one and the others cackled like a hen-night posse. Flower and Martha quickened their pace and the girls, hungry for more excitement than teasing two women in their thirties, moved on.

'Do you think anyone ever shouts compliments when they heckle people in the street?' wondered Flower.

''Course they do,' said Martha. 'Stuff like, "Nice tits!" or, "Give you one!"'

'No, I don't really mean that,' said Flower. 'I'm talking more about something like, "Oh, you look like a nice friendly person who treats the rest of the human race as your equal".'

'Oh, come on, Flower,' said Martha.

'But why are all heckles negative and horrible?'

'You said heckles, that's not really what you get on the street.'

'Yes, it is. Pooh.'

Martha held her nose and her stomach heaved as they hurried past a big bank of bins which were being rifled through by a homeless person.

'Got any change, love?' he asked.

Flower began to shuffle through her pockets and found a pound.

'Cheers, darling,' said the man happily as though this wasn't a bitterly cold night, he wasn't dressed in filthy clothes and he didn't sleep nightly on a bed of dog shit.

'You're welcome,' smiled Flower, looking sickeningly beatific and, if she was honest with herself, feeling it too. The mood changed.

'Well fuck you, you patronising cow,' he shouted, throwing the coin onto the pavement with such rage that Flower and Martha were quite frightened.

'Come on,' said Flower and bent over to pick it up, at which point the man rather unceremoniously vomited on her back.

'Jesus Christ,' wailed Flower.

The man threw his head back, laughed like a demented clown and headed off into the night.

Martha was having trouble holding the contents of her own stomach in check as she dabbed ineffectually at her friend's back with half a crumpled tissue. Flower was filled with a by-now familiar wave of urban hatred.

'I could kill that old bastard,' she said.

'Ah, but could you?' said Martha, philosophical for a moment.

'If I had a gun,' said Flower, 'I'd soon put him out of his misery.'

'But he was quite happy until you did a Mother Teresa on him,' said Martha.

'No, I didn't,' said Flower.

'Did,' said Martha.

'Well, I'm just sick of being a perfectly ordinary, reasonably pleasant person and getting shit all the time,' said Flower. 'On the street, in the clubs, even at work ... by these people who quite honestly don't deserve to take up the space they do on the planet.'

'I know what you mean, but who are we to decide?' said Martha. 'I'd like to shoot that Billy through the block and tackle, but I don't want to go to prison and ultimately I don't want to ruin Sarah's life.'

'You might make her life,' said Flower, 'and let's be honest, our judgement is probably less flawed than your average Middle Eastern dictator.'

'Well,' said Martha, 'if you had a chance to disappear Billy off the face of the earth, would you do it?'

'You bet I would, man,' said Flower, who couldn't help lapsing into hippy vernacular from time to time, 'and I might be able to.'

She told Martha about Dick Knob's offer and Martha found herself encouraging her to at least go and get a gun, the power of it appealed so much to her, and as they walked along the dirty streets, she visualised several urban scenes in which she would threaten people and make them behave the way *she* wanted – finishing with a lovely scenario involving the Reverend Brian.

The night bus approached and the two women climbed on, going to the top deck so Martha could sniff the cigarette smoke of the alcohol-fuelled disobedients on top. This was a foolish mistake, because that night, like most nights, the night bus had become the transport of the Grim Reaper on his day off and was filled with a selection of the most unnerving and unpleasant individuals you could imagine, from barely conscious dribblers to groups of teenage boys with their young offender hats on. Flower and Martha huddled down into their seats, but the incident earlier made Flower somewhat of a nasal target.

'What is that stink?' enquired a teenager and elicited for some reason hysterical laughter from his mates.

'It's them two,' he said, pointing a finger at Flower and Martha. This was a cue for everyone else on the bus to breathe a sigh of relief and look out of the window while Martha and Flower got murdered or whatever.

Chapter 15

Being surrounded by a group of teenagers who have imbibed a selection of more imaginative substances than alcohol and drugs was not an ideal finish to the night.

These days, thought Martha, the contents of a chemistry lab were available to any kid from his friendly street-corner dealer for the price of a packet of fags, so God knew what biochemical imbalances were propelling their anti-social behaviour tonight.

One aspect of travelling in a big city at night is the reassuring knowledge that, should a situation get out of hand, no one will lift a finger to help. Numerous excuses flit through people's heads, all of them centring on the fact that risking injury for another human being you haven't even met just isn't worth it.

Knowing this made Flower feel very vulnerable indeed, and because of Martha's pregnant state she knew she would be called upon to defend her. She also knew that neither of them was attractive enough to warrant a front-page report in the paper if they were injured or killed, because it was required that you looked vaguely like a model if you got murdered. It was hard luck but, as a nation, nobody mourns the passing of the less attractive citizen unless they are important in some way. Flower decided to take responsibility and try the pacifist approach.

'Look, it's me who smells,' she explained apologetically like a Sunday-school teacher. 'A man was sick on me, right?'

One would have thought this was the funniest thing the gang had ever heard, as they indulged in hugely exaggerated laughing, rolling in the aisle, poking each other and generally swaggering around intimidating others with their laughter. The leader of the gang, however, sat in the middle of them, his pasty, impassive face belying an IQ of 140 and a wish to study medicine. Held back from achieving his goal by his unpleasant personality and parents who thought being a doctor was 'poofy', he made up his mind. 'Well, I don't like the smell. Let's get her off the fucking bus.'

The laughing stopped as it dawned on the fringe members of the gang, who were no more than overgrown ten year olds, what they were being asked to do. They knew disobeying this pizza base on legs would result in some sort of violence towards them and they would rather risk injuring someone by throwing them down some bus stairs than incurring his wrath. A few of them began to edge like cringing dogs towards Flower. Flower panicked and said things like, 'It's all right, I'll just go,' but she realised that they intended to have some sport with her whatever she said or did.

Martha was also aware that things were looking dodgy and tried to out-bravado the weaker teenagers.

'Come on, you little shits,' she said, trying to look relaxed. 'Pick on someone your own size i.e. someone smaller than me,' realising too late that the 'i.e.' was a bad idea and had only confused them.

The fringe members looked hesitantly at their leader, whose glare was unflinching, and realised they would have to do his bidding.

Martha's hand tightened round a Swiss army knife she kept in her handbag, fumbling for the blade and unfortunately coaxing out the bit that removed stones from horses' hooves. I'm sure that'll come in handy with one of these donkeys, she thought grimly to herself. She felt the Lump jump and twist inside her. Someone's up for a fight, she noted.

As the gang advanced, Flower started doing a sort of low whimpering that couldn't be heard by anyone except Martha.

'Don't worry,' said Martha. 'We'll be OK. Something'll turn up.'

Everyone else on the bus was listening to every word and holding their breath, and a few communicated desperately with their eyes to their partners. A middle-aged couple on holiday from America knew full well the consequences of intervening, having tried it in New York and been beaten for their troubles; a younger couple from South London who had just got engaged simultaneously decided they didn't want to be stabbed on a bus before their wedding for the sake of a hippy covered in sick. Four drunk students knew enough of London Transport to keep their lips buttoned, and a slightly older but smaller gang of teenagers knew they were outnumbered and stared resolutely ahead.

That left, sitting quietly at the front of the bus waiting patiently for his moment and equipped to deal with this situation physically and mentally, a certain Mr Michael Randall who spent many a Friday night sitting expectantly on the night bus waiting for things to erupt. Up to this point they never had and it was ironic, he thought to himself, that he was being called up as a gallant knight for these two unfortunate-looking girls who had recently joined his self-defence class. He had not acknowledged himself to them, in fact he never did to anyone when he was on one of his jaunts, just in case he had to hit them or humiliate himself in front of them.

It would be reassuring to report that Michael Randall rose magnificently from his seat and stood at the top of the bus, eyes blazing and weapons poised, but he was too weaselly for that. He just sort of slimed to his feet and with the anger of ten men launched himself screaming towards the fracas, something he had read was essential to terrify the enemy, from the rebel yell of the Confederates in the American Civil War to the blood-freezing roar of the raggle-taggle Scots at Culloden.

The teenagers were truly shocked that what appeared to be a skinny, human version of Golem had decided to take them on and felt confident that Ant, the one with the biggest punch, could take him out. Before Ant could manage this though, Michael Randall had all but blinded him with two fingers poked without mercy into his eyes. Ant fell to the ground screaming and holding his face.

Drama queen, thought Martha.

Spurred on by this vicious assault on their manhood by a stoat in a car coat, Ant's mates Jez and Luca took their chances. Jez took a swing at Michael Randall, missed and received a size eight in the bollocks, perfectly placed with a terrible force. He too hit the deck screaming. Luca pulled out a knife and held it gleaming for a split second before Michael Randall took it from him in one deft move and brought it down into his thigh. This made Martha wince at the memory of trying to open a toffee tin on the bus as a schoolgirl with her compasses and stabbing herself in the leg.

The gang thought that safety in numbers was the only answer now and Dom, Lob and Taz, who sounded like three forwards for Charlton Atheltic, broadsided Michael Randall in an attempt to get him on the floor and kick the crap out of him. But Michael Randall had lived this scenario too many times in his head to get it wrong at this point and, bringing out a rounders bat ('more easily concealed, thicker and more convenient to handle'), he played their heads like a xylophone until they retreated down the steps at the end of the bus wondering why they felt like cuddling their mums, who had given them nothing but grief since they were little kids.

This left the gang leader Moz alone and seething as his lieutenants fell around him and he sat trying to sneer as Michael approached, confident even despite the carnage, that he could handle whatever this little man chose to throw at him.

But Michael Randall had something special for Moz. Within seconds he had whipped out what looked like a helmet, around which he had attached a band of metal which could be tightened. Before he knew what had happened, Moz sat with a kitchen colander on his head as Michel deftly tightened it and threw the Allen key out of the window. It was snug enough to hurt a lot but not to do any damage, and as he strolled back down the bus and winked at Martha and Flower, the whole bus erupted into laughter as a pained-looking Moz made his way down the stairs and out onto the street.

Moz got to know the meaning of heckling on the long walk home that night as, 'Hang on, I'll bring me spuds out,' and 'Careful your brain doesn't leak out,' assaulted his ears along with some more pithy efforts.

As night rolled on, Michael Randall lay in bed grinning silently next to his wife and Martha and Flower changed their minds about not going back to his class.

Chapter 16

Martha and Flower were rather sobered by their night-bus experience and decided to go to Martha's for a drink and to get some perspective back into their jaded lives.

Flower knew that Charlie would be waiting at home to see how her gig had gone. He had been only slightly suspicious when she discovered a last-minute booking on a Friday girls' night and he had offered to go with her, but she was so near to the place and he was so far, he was persuaded to stay at home.

Charlie sounded relieved when he heard Martha had turned up at the show and Flower had kept him apprised of their progress across London on the mobile, leaving out the less savoury details.

Of course when they got back to Martha's, Flower couldn't wait to wash the contents of the vagrant's stomach off her back and got into Martha's shower as if it was hippy heaven while Martha did her customary hunt for booze which always turned up something, on this occasion half a bottle of Greek brandy which looked quite palatable but tasted like liquidised tyres. The two didn't notice the ersatz taste however as they mulled over the night's events and the conversation turned to Billy again.

'Just say,' said Martha, 'that we shot him.' She realised she was becoming keener on the idea. 'I mean, nobody would know it was us. For a start, nobody except us knows about the violence.'

'Sarah would know it was us,' said Flower.

'But surely she'd realise we were doing her a favour in the long run.'

'Oh I doubt it,' said Flower. 'Besides, we couldn't keep it a secret for ever – what we had done would somehow spill out in the pub. We'd be pissed one night and tell Doreen and she'd bloody tell everyone.'

'What, Barmaid Ceefax? No never,' said Martha.

'Anyway,' said Flower, pouring herself another brandy, 'why kill Billy? He's not that bad.'

'I know,' said Martha, 'but wait till Sarah commits to him and then she's got years of shit up ahead, which we could save her from now.'

'But we haven't tried anything on our list yet, except me talking to him,' said Flower.

'I'm just impatient to take the bastard out,' said Martha and they both laughed.

'Where's your list?' said Flower. 'What else have we got?'

Surprisingly, given all the slightly unpleasant debris that was still lying in Martha's flat even after an attempt at

cleaning, she managed to produce an intact list almost immediately. Martha surveyed it. 'We've got the sublime and the
ridiculous here,' she said, 'from talking to him to trying to
split them up, to trying to turn Sarah into a lesbian, to a
contract killing, to tampering with the brakes on his car.'

'Oh yeah – and you'd know how to do the brakes on his
car, would you?' said Flower.

'I would, actually,' said Martha, 'seeing as when I lived
in the village I knocked around with a mechanic for quite
a while.'

'Did you ever find out anything useful?' said Flower.

'Such as?'

'Oh, you know, how to change a wheel, that sort of thing.'

'Oh Christ no, nothing that dull,' said Martha.

'So let's do his brakes,' Flower heard herself say and
then laughed at how odd it sounded. Martha began to laugh
too and they were nearly onto the guffawing stage when
the phone rang. Considering it was one in the morning,
both girls felt their hearts leap and each separately wondered
whether Billy could have heard them and was phoning to
threaten them.

It was Charlie.

'It's only Charlie,' said Flower with her hand over the
receiver because she knew he would be offended by the
'only', and in their relief, they began to laugh.

'What's going on?' said Charlie irritatedly, assuming he
was being discussed and laughed at.

'Nothing,' said Flower, always an unsatisfactory reply.

'When are you coming home?' said Charlie.

Flower felt like saying, 'When you change the fucking record,' but in fact said, 'Not long now.'

'Look, I'll come and get you,' said Charlie. 'Be there in twenty-five.' As usual Flower had no time to agree to this.

Martha, serious for a moment, said, 'Look – if Billy doesn't settle down with Sarah and increase his battering in direct proportion to how long they are together, he'll just do it to someone else.'

'I know,' said Flower, 'but it's not our job. One in four women suffer domestic violence, but we can't kill a quarter of the blokes in the country.'

'It *is* our job,' said Martha.

'Why?' said Flower.

'Because we're pissed as farts,' Martha replied, starting to roar with laughter again and wetting herself slightly in the process, because of the pressure of Lump. She didn't tell Flower. Oh God, thought Martha, I am pissed and I'm about to have a baby. I must be more sensible. And this made her laugh even more. She bent double and headed for the toilet, trying to stop any more urine leaking out. On the way back, she noticed that Flower had taken up Martha's list and was adding some things. Rudely, she snatched it from her. 'Therapy?' she read dismissively. 'Waste of bloody money and effort.'

'I'm not getting into the therapy argument again with you,' said Flower.

'And what's this,' said Martha. 'Anger fucking management?'

'You need fucking swearing management,' said Flower.

'Oh, come on though,' said Martha. 'A load of violent wankers sitting round in a circle saying, "And then I hit her with a hammer", what bloody good is that going to do?'

'Look, I didn't say anything before, but Charlie went to one to see what it was like,' said Flower.

Martha began to laugh again.

'Oi!' said Flower. 'What's so funny?'

'Did he get battered?' Martha chuckled.

'How did you know?' said Flower.

'It was just so inevitable,' said Martha and carried on laughing as the door-knocker sounded.

'It's all right, it's only Charlie,' they said together.

But it wasn't Charlie, it was Pat, Martha's mum, having risked a second expedition into the heart of darkness.

'Mum?' Martha was pissed and pissed off and hadn't realised yet that so was Pat.

'I've been shopping in town and then to a pub,' said Pat.

In their drunken state this struck Martha and Flower as extremely funny and even at the age of thirty-eight and thirty-five they tried to suppress childish explosions of laughter.

'Been to a pub? But you've never been to a pub with Dad, let alone on your own, and what are you doing here at this time of night?' Martha realised some role reversal had taken place.

'I missed the train,' said Pat.

'Have you phoned Dad?'

'I've texted him,' said Pat. 'Some boy in the pub showed me.'

'You what?' Martha's mother seemed to have been replaced by a socially disinhibited teenager. 'Has Dad got a mobile?'

'Oh yes,' said Pat, 'he's got a really wicked Nokia.'

Martha felt queasy.

Martha wondered if Pat had had a stroke and decided to investigate further in the morning. 'Keep an eye,' she whispered to Flower as she went to check that her bedroom wasn't too revolting to put her mother in.

'But I'll have a drink with you two,' protested her mother as Martha tried to steer her by the elbow into her room as though she was a ninety-year-old occupant of an old people's home.

However, Pat relented and fell asleep almost immediately. Martha marvelled at how she'd made it safely across the estate again and wondered whether maybe there was a God.

As she walked back into the sitting room Flower said, 'Fucking hell, Marth. Has your mum left the planet temporarily?'

'I don't know,' said Martha. 'I'll find out tomorrow.'

Another knock at the door heralded Charlie, who had seen Pat wandering around outside the kebab place and dismissed her as a vagrant.

'It's fucking freaky out there tonight,' he said. 'That dope we got yesterday is strong, Flower, but I'm sure I just saw a bloke with a colander on his head and there's some weird old lady wandering about outside.'

'Yeh, that's my mum,' said Martha.

'Oh ha, ha, you're so funny,' said Charlie.

'I mean it,' said Martha. 'She's in my bed asleep.'

'Bollocks,' said Charlie.

'Tell him,' said Martha to Flower.

'No, honestly,' said Flower, 'it's true.'

'Oh, pull the other one you two drunken old tarts,' said Charlie laughing.

'Right,' said Martha, pointing. 'There's my room, go and look.'

'What is it, bucket of water on the door?' said Charlie. 'Blow up doll in the bed?'

'No, it's my bloody mother and don't wake her,' Martha told him.

Charlie wandered into the room and could just make out a shape under the bedclothes which he assumed was made up of pillows. He sat down on the edge of the bed and gave the shape a good prod.

'Hello Martha's mum, you old slapper,' he said.

A hand appeared from under the duvet and grabbed his groin area and he nearly went through the ceiling. The look on his face as he arrived back in the room with Martha and Flower told them he'd found Pat and that she'd found him. Martha also had a colander on her head.

'Come on, Flower,' said Charlie, 'time to go home.'

For once Flower didn't argue.

The following morning everyone had a hangover except Sarah who had gone to bed early and woke up feeling refreshed and healthy. She decided as Billy lay snoring, not something one expects handsome men to indulge in, that she would wander down to Martha's, have a coffee and see how the Lump was coming along, and try to pump her for some more details of the Ted encounter.

Martha looked bloody awful, a mop of greasy hair perched on top of a sallow face with two bloodshot eyes the only splash of colour. 'What time is it?' she said in a voice reminiscent of a frog.

'About ten, mate,' said Sarah. 'Put the kettle on, I'm dying for a coffee.'

Martha's hideous appearance was further emphasised by the fact that Sarah looked like a Swiss milkmaid in the complexion department. Martha went to put the kettle on and shouted various bits of conversation through to where Sarah was sitting, not really noticing that she wasn't answering but occasionally 'umming' or grunting. Martha made her coffee in a cup whose contents looked a couple of days old and did Sarah the honour of rinsing hers under a warm tap.

'Flower had a terrible heckler last night,' she said as she carried the coffees into the room and realised that Sarah had a very angry expression reminiscent of the Rev Brian on her face.

'What the fuck is this?' she demanded, waving a pad at Martha.

'It's a pad, dear,' said Martha.

'And what is this list on it?' said Sarah.

Martha realised in a millionth of a second that it was her and Flower's list for sorting out Billy. Did it have his name on it? Or had she torn it off? Was he identifiable from the different suggestions? She took a gamble.

'Oh, I'm writing a book at work,' she said.

'Bullshit,' said Sarah. 'It's about Bill, isn't it?'

'What makes you say that?'

'I can just tell,' said Sarah.

Great, thought Martha. It hasn't got his name on then. 'Look,' she said aloud. 'I don't really want to ... that is, I'm a bit embarrassed – well, you'll find out sooner or later. My mum's here and my dad's been knocking her about.'

'No!' Sarah was astounded. She thought the Rev Brian only had a bark.

'Don't say anything if she comes in,' said Martha, 'but Flower and I were pissed last night and we made a list of how we could help my mum.'

As if summoned to explain herself, Pat appeared at the door with Martha's dressing-gown over her clothes looking drained of blood.

'I'm sorry, dear. I think I might have been drunk last night,' Pat said. 'It won't happen again.'

Chapter 17

While Sarah was round at Martha's, Billy was at home watching a Saturday-morning football programme on television. A piece of his mind, however, and not the bit he always gave Sarah, was on something else. It wasn't sex, although men apparently think about it every seven seconds. Who researched that particular statistic? Billy wondered. Who was their control group and wouldn't men just say they were thinking about sex, rather than owning up to musings on scaffolding, say, or macramé?

Billy had decided recently that he really, really liked Sarah, could tolerate her weird friends and could quite happily settle for this life he had with her. He had all but given up the adolescent hope of the leggy model/porn star/actress with exploding bosoms beckoning to him in a bar one night and thought at the age of thirty-two he should probably be sensible and squirt his semen into a permanent seedbed. However, like most men, a tiny bit of him clung onto the vain hope that even though he was happy in a relationship which made him want, for the first time, to sort out his violent temper, especially when drinking, he could still make room in his sexual calendar for a dirty woman. Why do my thoughts always sound like a bad porn film? he asked himself.

Billy, unlike some violent men, was aware of just how bad his bad behaviour was, knew it needed to be curtailed and wondered if there was any help for people like him. His violence couldn't be put to good use as a championship boxer or inner-city comprehensive deputy headmaster so he had better deal with it. Billy knew that when his temper started to mushroom, he became a thug; anyone, even someone he had decided he loved, could fan the flames and make him so full of rage that he questioned whether this deep-seated anger would ever go away. Maybe some poncy *Guardian*-reading arse from North London could guide him towards being a better person, but he doubted it. Billy couldn't help it that his critical voice was directed outwards, towards others, whereas most women's are directed inwards. He would always find weaknesses in others; it was just a question of how he dealt with them.

As he lay on the settee thinking, Sarah opened the door and came in, calling out a greeting and dropping her bag on the hall table with a crash, which ever so slightly irritated Billy, who was still daydreaming. He thought about shouting something but checked himself. Sarah then clattered into the bathroom and he heard her running the shower and wondered whether she would leave the shower curtain outside the frame and get water on the floor, not to mention leaving the soap in a glutinous mess. He also wondered, briefly, why she was having a shower and within seconds had concocted a scenario in his head in which Sarah was being fucked up against a wall by a workmate of his called Craig, until he actually began to believe this scenario. He found himself dialling Craig's mobile number to see whether he was at home in Hertfordshire and, after a brief chat in which he invented a spurious reason for calling, wondered how Craig could have got home from this liaison so quickly.

Sarah, unaware of this ominous mind-ratcheting, was singing some dreadful song that was in the charts. This was one of the many things Billy didn't understand about Sarah and other women; she didn't have a favourite band, knew nothing about the people who performed the music she did like, had no inkling of back catalogues, who played saxophone on B sides and who managed bands through the difficult times. *And* she never put CDs away.

Sarah, in the meantime, was in the shower preparing for her usual beauty routine. Some girls do, some don't. The ones who don't can't be arsed and are irritated by the ones who do because it underlines their neglect of what has become, over the years, a fundamental girlie obligation. Martha, for example, thought cleansing, toning and moisturising was a waste of time and believed that advice from various cosmetic companies to do so was a ploy to scare women into a phobia about wrinkles, thereby forcing them into a continuous frenzy of beauty product acquisition. She told people she didn't buy beauty products on principle but, in fact, on a Saturday night would slap on the slap with the best of them. Flower didn't use anything and didn't need to, and her lack of beauty product use was based on the fact that she had been told by someone once that some beauty creams were made from the aborted foetuses of French nuns and try as she might to get this image out of her head, every attempt at moisturising evoked the unpleasant feeling that she was rubbing a baby into her cheek.

Sarah, however, was meticulous and spent hours at the beauty counters of the biggest department stores, weighing up the pros and cons of various products and listening intently to the generalised bullshit of the immaculately plastered women with their flawless foundations, huge panda eyes and encyclopaedic celebrity knowledge.

After rubbing in a sizeable amount of coconut oil when she left the shower, Sarah started from her feet and worked her way up using three different sprays to keep her fresh for feet, armpits and a spray that is euphemistically termed an 'intimate' deodorant because it masks the pungent smell of woman with an industrial-strength floweriness that can kill puppies at ten yards.

Sarah then tackled the problem of removing hair from the bits of her body it shouldn't be on, in her case legs, armpits and face. She was scrupulous about her face as she couldn't help associating moustaches with comic-book lesbians. This was perhaps because your average teenage street heckler did too and she lived in fear of being on her own or worse, with Billy, when the, 'Oi, like the 'tache!' heckle came, the consequences of which would be a hugely bruised ego or hugely bruised teenager. Sarah had tried hair removal creams but they smelled like they were burning a hole through her jaw and left a lingering taste in her mouth which made her think of crop spraying. She waxed her face then tackled what seemed like big sprawling bushes of hair on her legs but were in fact rather sparse clumps of light growth. Her armpits were also dealt with, and try as she might, she just couldn't get the image of a plucked chicken's arse out of her head when she raised her arm to inspect the work. Nails were pared and moisturised and cuticles driven back. Eyebrows were savaged. Hands were slathered in cream and ears were probed with cotton buds.

It was at this point that Billy began his routine.

'What the fuck's taking you so long?'

Sarah heard the bad temper in his voice and felt like childishly running through a list of her bathroom tasks until he either walked off and left her alone or exploded. Instead she managed a cheery if somewhat strained, 'Out in a minute!' Unfortunately this wound Billy up even more.

'Why can't you just be like the fat sow?' He shouted, the 'fat sow' being what he considered his ironically fond name for Martha but which irritated Sarah.

'What do you mean?' she shouted back.

'You know – never bothers with the routine shit, shaving, all that bollocks, got a badger under each arm.'

'Don't be horrible!'

'Or the hippy with her pissy little natural fibres and

patchouli this and that, smells like a navvy underneath it all.'

Billy was warming up into his weekly stand-up routine about what was wrong with Sarah's friends.

'Oh, leave it for once, will you,' snapped Sarah, balancing on one leg as she checked the soles of her feet for unnatural growths, stains or fungal outbursts. She couldn't hear Billy draw a big breath but she could imagine it.

'Yeah, and Flower never washes . . .' he began.

Oh not this again, thought Sarah. 'Just shut the fuck up,' she said quietly.

Billy must have had an ear-trumpet to the door because he seemed to hear. 'Pardon?' he said.

'Nothing,' said Sarah, well aware that wasn't an adequate answer.

For some reason that Billy couldn't fathom, this made him really angry. 'What do you mean nothing!' he screamed and Sarah jumped at the ferocity of it all.

She appeared from behind the bathroom door with a shiny, 'tache-free face, pink, shaved legs and those weird things you use to separate out your toes when you are painting them. Because she looked so silly, Billy at this point should have just laughed and forgotten his rising temper, but this was textbook Billy; his temper was on the way up and he couldn't stop it until all his bile had leaked out.

'Look at the state of you,' he said very unkindly and Sarah, cowed by him most times, but emboldened by her visit to Martha's den and the weird behaviour of Martha's mum, slammed the door on him. This was quite enough to justify Billy really going mental and he began kicking the bathroom door. Sarah got quite scared and locked it. This escalated things and Billy began to kick harder, shouting, 'Don't lock me out of my own bathroom!' which taken as an individual statement, sounded pathetic.

Sarah began to laugh which made Billy feel foolish and humiliated and then there was no going back and he laid into the door with an extravagance he reserved only for his most violent moments. Sarah could not believe that the man she lived with was thrashing his way through solid wood to get at her. She wondered what he would do when he'd kicked the door open and so did he.

They didn't have to wait long because the bathroom door, rotting slightly as they do in rented places, flew off its hinges, hitting Sarah on the head. Sarah, along with many others, had often wondered if you really saw stars when you got a blow on the head.

You didn't.

She did, however, feel sick and had acquired the quickest headache she'd ever known.

'What did you do that for?' she asked, already knowing that the answer was, 'Because I am an out-of-control tosser.' Without thinking, she picked up a soap dish and chucked it. It sailed past Billy's ear and smashed against a mirror in the hall. Oh dear, seven years' bad luck, she thought. That's a bugger.

Billy stepped onto the incandescent rung of the temper ladder because of the hall mirror incident and swung a punch at Sarah who couldn't believe he had done it and in her scramble to get away, tripped and fell, banging her head on the sink as she went down.

At that point, as there always is in a farce, there was a knock on the door. Both Billy and Sarah felt their stomachs lurch. Billy didn't want to be discovered in flagrante as it were and Sarah didn't want him to look bad even at this stage of the escalation. They thought about keeping quiet and not answering but Billy felt it too risky.

'Stay there,' he said to Sarah and opened the front door.

It was Charlie, who had never seen Billy's eyes looking quite so wild before. He would have been happy to turn round and go, but he was on a mission from Flower and it had to be done.

'Mate, hiya,' said Charlie, trying to sound like he wasn't about to be doubly incontinent with fear.

'What do you want?' replied a surly-eyed Billy.

'Well,' said Charlie, 'don't take this the wrong way, but do you want to come to a group for sorting out violent behaviour with me – you know, for a bit of a laugh like?'

A gigantic fist connected with the side of Charlie's face and his legs crumpled under him.

Chapter 18

Charlie limped home nursing a very sore jaw and wondering why he had been involved in violence yet again. It seemed unfair that he, who had spent his life trying to stop various wars, keep foxes alive, pay the workers a decent wage and curb the power of the police, always ended up getting smacked in the gob.

Flower had got used to Charlie coming home with a bruise somewhere on him so she didn't really take much notice when he skulked into the room holding his face and muttering darkly. Eventually irritated because she couldn't hear a relaxation tape she was listening to and therefore feeling very unrelaxed, she said, 'What is the matter, Charlie?'

'He hit me,' said Charlie in a voice that demonstrated he was getting used to it.

'Who?' asked Flower, still not really listening.

'Billy Bloody Arseface Taylor, that's who,' said Charlie.

Finally Flower sat up and took notice. 'Billy hit you?'

'Yep,' said Charlie. 'Something weird was going on at that house of pain. I heard shouting and stuff being chucked, then I did my little speech and the bastard chinned me.'

'Did you see Sarah?'

'No, I can't say I did.'

'Well, did you hear her?'

'No,' Charlie admitted.

'So you don't know if she's dead or alive?'

'Oh, don't be such a drama queen,' said Charlie. 'Of course she isn't dead.'

Flower reached for the phone and dialled Sarah's number. Billy answered.

'Hello, can I speak to Sarah?' said Flower.

'No,' said Billy. 'She's not here.'

'Well, where is she?' Flower could hear the anxiety in her own voice.

'Gone shopping,' said Billy. 'I'll tell her you called.' He hung up.

'He's killed her,' said Flower. 'I'm going to call the police.'

'And what good are those fascist wankers going to do?' said Charlie.

Irritated, Flower said, 'This is not the time or the place for a rant about the police.'

'Nor is it time for a pre-menstrual fantasy about suburban murder either,' said Charlie, who recognised the symptoms.

'I do not have PMS!' screamed Flower.

'We call it good old PMT in England, I think you'll find,'

said Charlie, from whom anti-Americanism tempered with unwarranted chauvinism occasionally escaped.

'Call her mobile,' he suggested, so Flower did and Sarah answered sounding rather muted but perfectly alive.

'Are you all right?' asked Flower.

'Is Charlie all right?' countered Sarah. 'I'm really sorry.'

'Not your fault,' said Flower. 'Do you want to come round?'

'No, I'm out shopping. I'll buy a new skirt, I think, and that'll help.' Sarah had some insight into her shopping trips but only on a very superficial level. Flower always said if someone called it retail therapy once more to her face she would hit them, but Sarah wouldn't even know what retail therapy was.

'Did he hit you?'

'Only with a door and not on purpose.'

Flower's hormones dictated that more melodrama entered their conversation. 'He's going to kill you.'

'Yes, please,' said Sarah.

'What?' said Flower. 'You want to be killed?'

'No, I'm having mustard on my hot dog . . . eating always makes me feel better,' said Sarah.

'When you've had a door on your head?'

'I can't hear you, you're fading,' said Sarah.

In Flower's book of mobile etiquette this was always an excuse to get away. 'Stay on the line,' she said desperately, sounding like a police negotiator talking to a hostage taker and then she tried, 'Stop fucking pretending you're out of range,' but Sarah had gone. Flower set about texting her, very slowly, as she had learned neither text language nor speed on the keys and ended up doing laborious longhand. *Call me, let's sort things out.*

This text went mistakenly to Martha who texted back twenty minutes later *On my way*, too late for Flower to head her off and have a relaxing afternoon obsessively cleaning the flat or being cruel to animals, both of which were the special features of her PMT. Charlie and the cat cowered and Flower cleaned until there was a ring on the makeshift doorbell and Martha rolled in waving a scrappy bit of paper in front of her and announcing, 'We've got to crank things up a gear. I'm assuming you have something to report. Make me herbal tea and I'll kill you.' Then she flopped in a big pregnant heap on the mattress.

Flower explained Charlie's visit to Billy and Sarah, and Martha admired his courage mixed with extreme foolishness as she felt she could have predicted that poor Charlie might get floored by puffing Billy. She thought Charlie very sweet but a bit useless and decided that given the opportunity she wouldn't have any sort of sexual encounter with him.

Billy was different. In a strange echo of her mother's attraction to the brooding bad temper of Brian, there was something about Billy's sulkiness that fascinated Martha. She would melt down a drain if Sarah ever found this out though, as it was an unacknowledged cornerstone of their friendship that they would never sleep with each other's partners. Martha realised she was blushing and that Flower was staring at her.

'Pah, hormones!' she said in an exaggerated fashion and tried to cover her face. Flower, used to hormonal explosions of her own as well as Martha's, didn't connect Martha's redness in any way with an assessment of the suitability of her and Sarah's partners for her bed.

Then the two friends sat down together and re-examined the list which contained the following elements:

Flower talk to him.

'Not much use,' said Flower. 'In fact, a bloody waste of time. I reckon it just made him feel more angry.'

'When did you do that?' said Charlie who, as usual, was eavesdropping.

'Oh, I just bumped into him in the newsagents,' said Flower.

'I thought you . . .' Martha said. Flower pinched the inside of Martha's arm really hard '. . . bumped into him in Sainsbury's.'

'For fuck's sake, girls,' said Charlie, 'does it really matter?'

Flower and Martha exchanged a look.

M talk to him.

'All right,' said Martha. 'I'll have a go.'

'Are you sure?' said Flower. 'You know he's getting worse.'

'Oh, I'll be all right,' said Martha. 'Surely he wouldn't whack a big pregger lady?'

'Yeah, you're right,' said Flower. 'Next?'

Martha showed Flower the list where it said:

Charlie talk to him.

Martha put a line through this.

Anger management?

Martha put a big question mark next to *anger management*.

'Right,' she said. 'Those are our initial options. I'll talk to Billy and then we'll reassess it again, because if he's as uncooperative with me as he was with you, then maybe we need to go a little more drastic. A little tinkering with their relationship maybe.'

'Oh, I'm not sure,' said Flower.

'Not wimping out, are you?' said Martha.

'Hardly,' said Flower. 'I was going to suggest we by-passed the relationship bit and just had him beaten up.' Charlie made his best axe-murderer face behind Flower's back.

'Silly me,' said Martha, 'I was forgetting the old PMT. Look, I'll talk to Billy-Boy and then we'll take it from there, all right?'

Flower nodded.

The rest of the list said:

Their Relationship
1. Split them up.

1a. Sleep with him.
1b. Find her new bloke.
1c. Find her a woman.

Threaten Him
Get him beaten up/kill him.

Flower and Martha left this for another day.

Chapter 19

Martha thought long and hard about talking to Billy. She considered the neutral ground of a pub and then decided it would be difficult to be truly private. She thought of the local café – not a problem being truly private there, because nobody in this working-class area ate health food. Once they realised they couldn't get a cardiac arrest from the veggie fare on offer they had stopped coming in.

Martha's Lump was due in the next couple of weeks and because this was her first pregnancy she had convinced herself that it would plop out on the due date, despite the fact that over three-quarters of babies steadfastly refuse to come out on the day the doctor has predicted. Lump was now more of a human than he/she had ever been and she could feel his/her little hands pushing her skin and occasionally she caught a heel as Lump turned round trying to get comfortable. The only image in Martha's mind was John Hurt's character in *Alien* whose demon baby disgorged itself at the dinner table, a vision that wouldn't go away.

It was at this point in the process that Martha started to worry about how she would cope with looking after Lump, especially if it was an alien in some way.

Greasy Ted had offered to keep her job open for her, still not realising that it was his sperm that was responsible for Martha's state of approaching maternity and secretly feeling rather regretful and envious that she was having some other bloke's baby. It had never occurred to Ted to examine dates and compare them with his and Martha's encounter round the back of the club; he had assumed that some more long-term no-good bastard she had been with had dumped her at the news of pregnancy. Try as he might, though, he couldn't get any information out of her. As Ted ran a lap-dancing club in Soho and looked like a portly trainee for the Rule 42 area of a prison, one might imagine that he would be seedy and unpleasant, one step away from a rapist, but in fact Ted was the sweetest, gentlest, funniest bloke who, but for his hideous appearance, would have been a real catch.

Martha was worried that the combination of herself and Ted would produce some minor version of the Elephant Man and it had entered her head that she would have to have the child adopted if she couldn't bear to look at it, or if it was quite sweet, but had a huge head.

Martha had done her best through her pregnancy to behave like a demure prima gravida but had found the healthy diet and no drinking and no fags rule extremely difficult to obey. She had not drunk much but had found herself gasping for a drink some nights when she needed to steady her nerves. When she thought about her 'chat' with Billy, she definitely needed to steady her nerves.

She eventually decided to get Billy round on the pretext of helping her with her computer. Martha had managed to set up email with the assistance of a socially awkward nerdy type on the other end of the phone who kept tutting when she used less than technical language, but now she wanted to expand things and save some of her work onto disc so she didn't lose it. She had acquired a secondhand CD burner, but had not the slightest idea what to do with it and had been meaning to phone Billy, who worked with computers, to ask for his help. Ted also knew his way round a computer, but Martha was worried that if she invited him back to her place, because he was so funny and she liked him so much, she might cave in and tell him it was his child inside her womb.

So Martha called Billy at work and asked him to come, and because she genuinely did need help and had mentioned it to Sarah, who in turn had told Billy, nobody was suspicious. After Flower's rather cackhanded approach to Billy, this rendezvous was set up with all the subtlety of an established computer dating agency. Billy had been only too happy to agree to help Martha because, since the incident with the bathroom door, things had been icy at home. So he set off from work that evening feeling very glad, as he picked up an evening paper and a sandwich, that he wasn't going home for a bit and that he had Sarah's blessing because he was helping out one of her friends.

Martha, on the other hand, was in a frenzied state of anticipation. The bit of her that fancied Billy and that she had barely acknowledged, to save her the embarrassment of having to admit it to Sarah, had dictated that he could not be entertained in a flat that smelled of many unpleasant substances, from washing waiting to be done, to last night's dinner. As Martha slogged furiously, feeling that this must be what it was like laying waste to rainforest as she chopped through the flat with a hoover and dustpan and brush, polish, duster and a sweet-smelling spray to squirt at anything that ponged, she had a strange sense of fear mixed with a tiny bit of deliciousness that Billy was going to be in her flat *alone with her* for at least a couple of hours.

Martha had not totally ignored the fact that she was going to give Billy a stiff talking to, but like many women, she truly believed that if Billy was with her, he wouldn't hit her. She pulled herself up when she realised that she was feeling too fond of Billy and kept telling herself that he was a violent person who hit her friend and therefore was not deserving of little thrills of anticipation.

Foolishly, given her pregnant state, Martha, then began to consume a six-pack of strong lager that she had found at the back of her wardrobe, obviously placed there at some time or other by a selfish party-goer who did not want to waste the alcohol content on a lesser man or woman. Martha thought she would have half a can to steady her nerves as she began to get the speech together in her head that she would give to Billy. As she hoovered, she slurped, and suddenly three cans had gone and she felt a bit drunk and a bit guilty. It was rather late in the day to get Lump pissed before she/he left the all-encompassing safety of her womb, but she was sure Lump could handle his/her booze. Martha could think of nothing nicer than floating pissed in a warm sea.

By early evening, she still had lots of clearing up to do, but unfortunately her enthusiasm for the job had dribbled away with the fourth can, so she gathered up armfuls of rubbish and threw it all under her duvet: a cat tray, some pudding, a heap of dirty knickers, a cheap bottle of wine with the top not quite on, some leftover pizza and a home colonic irrigation kit. Just as the duvet floated over this bizarre collection of goods, there was a knock at the door. Martha got up to answer it, stumbled and realised she was quite pissed. I should be ashamed of myself, she thought, but I'm pissed so I won't bother.

'Hiya,' she said to no one in particular, well practised in disguising her pissedness, following many a Sunday dinner at home after a session in the pub. She felt warm and altruistic towards the world as she opened the door, although this leaked away when she saw how unsmiling Billy's face was. He had been in the local pub and was the worse for two barley wines, an uncommon drink these days, but which could be labelled the tipple of the unreconstructed psychopath, so often has it featured in scenarios in which some blokes go off to kick the shit out of some rival football fans, burgle an empty property or bring some woman to the point of tears.

'Come in,' urged Martha, trying hard to remember

whether Billy would know she knew about the bathroom door incident. Of course he fucking well does, she said to herself, then realised she was slurring her unspoken words and swearing in her thoughts, which was a very bad sign.

Billy came in showing a remarkable degree of restraint at the sight of the recently tidied earthquake that was Martha's flat. For Martha, each can of extra-strong lager had given her flat that gloss of neatness and a cachet which it simply didn't possess.

'Sit down,' she said, pointing to the kitchen table.

'Shall we just get started?' said Billy, looking at his watch. 'I've got quite a lot to do this evening. Where's your computer?'

Martha led him through to the room where the computer sat; the room was currently being occupied by Pat, who had decided to stay a few days but, because Martha had thought she would definitely screw things up if she was around, she had persuaded her mother to go to the West End and see a show. 'Seeing a show' was something that Pat's generation thought was a huge treat and she did not need much persuading, saying she would be back at eleven. Martha looked at her watch. It was 7.21 p.m. so she had almost four hours to get round to the topic of Billy's violence, have him lose his temper and retrieve the situation with her remarkable people skills before Pat got in. After half a lifetime Martha still didn't realise that she *had* no people skills.

Martha turned on her computer and Billy set about plugging bits in and clicking the mouse on a confusing array of icons at a remarkable speed. Martha felt too confused to ask him what he was doing. She had always had terrible trouble with electrics. Only last week, for example, a charming old West Indian guy like the universal grandfather of the world had come round and fixed her video for what seemed a laughably small fee and Martha had felt so grateful towards him she nearly cried.

'Can I try my handiwork?' he had asked and Martha had gestured at the pile of videos and said, 'Pick any one.'

As the picture spread onto the screen she realised that there in front of their eyes were two naked men one of whom was anally penetrating the other with gusto. 'It's an Italian art film,' she managed to get out as she observed the horrified look on the poor guy's face and thought to herself, Why did I even bother to say that?

The grandfather repair man left, sadly turning down her tip.

Billy seemed to be coming to the end of whatever complicated thing he was doing to her computer. He'd saved various files for her and the technical language swam past her like hieroglyphics made verbal as she nodded, pretending to understand. How to keep him there and talk about Sarah was now the problem.

'Can I get you a drink?' she said and was surprised when he looked enthusiastic about that idea. She found some vodka and scrubbed at a glass in the sink. Billy swigged it back in one, smiled and the evening seemed to begin.

Martha felt relaxed. Lump had drifted off to sleep inside her and chatting in a friendly fashion, she and Billy strolled into the lounge. Billy walked out onto the balcony and, in an extreme and by now predictable hormonal mood swing, an idea occurred to Martha in her drunkenness that she could throw him off the balcony and make it look like an accident. End result: a favour would have been done all round.

She began to estimate how much force she would need to run at him, and tip him over into the blackness of the South London night. She started to convince herself that this would work, and even with the handicap of Lump, set off at a trot towards the balcony to see whether she could go through with it. As she got nearer and the ridiculous idea became more of a reality, her heart started to pound. 'I am a murderer,' she said to herself under her breath and prepared to launch herself at Billy.

'Hi, Martha.'

It was Junior from next door, the biggest, most mature teenager in the universe, who was watering something that Martha had always assumed was cannabis, but was in fact lemon verbena.

'Junior, hello,' Martha said breathlessly.

'And who's this?'

She introduced them. There was some boring banter and then she and Billy went inside.

'Look, I want to talk to you about Sarah,' said Martha.

Then, with absolutely no warning, Billy kissed her, a proper hungry kiss with a pushy tongue involved.

I can't believe this is happening, they both thought simultaneously.

Then the kiss turned into physical contact which was hard, fast, urgent and, thought Martha delightedly, really really filthy. Clothes were ripped and unborn babies were woken as the pair somehow got to the bedroom.

'Be careful,' said Martha.

'What's the best way to fuck you, baby?' said Billy.

He ruined that by adding the 'baby', but I can allow a few minor blips past my style radar, thought Martha.

In the darkness of the bedroom, they threw back the duvet and jumped onto the pile of rubbish. Some crunching and splatting occurred, accompanied by some sounds of disgust and then normal service was resumed.

When Pat returned humming 'Climb Every Mountain' she was faced, looking from the lounge through into the bedroom, with a framed arse rhythmically penetrating her daughter. She turned and went to bed tutting, not even stopping for her customary glass of water.

Chapter 20

The first of Martha's senses to be assaulted the following morning was her nose, when she realised that cat litter had somehow worked its way into the equation of debris on which they had slept. Yes it was foolish, perhaps, having a cat that she hardly ever saw and living on the twelfth floor of a council block. She spent far too long worrying about Plop too, fantasising about her being captured by local schoolchildren and arriving home minus vital organs or limbs. But all Plop ever did was live up to her name by defecating copiously in her litter tray and occasionally elsewhere in the flat, a situation which had become blown out of all proportion since Martha's pregnancy with the risk of that unpronounceable disease that can be picked up from cat excrement.

Martha ran over what she could remember of the night before with Billy and found herself blushing at some of the things they had said to each other. Was it still 'they'? she wondered, eyes tightly closed as if to ward off the inevitable repercussions of last night. Or was it, as usual, just herself, the regretful lover having sneaked out under cover of the sort of unconsciousness only extreme amounts of alcohol can guarantee. She hardly dared look and reluctantly opened one eye.

Christ, he's still there, she thought.

She tried to open the other eye and discovered it was gummed shut with Mother Nature's post-binge glue. A wave of guilt flowed over Martha at the knowledge of what she had done to one of her best friends, and she berated herself further because this hadn't stopped her feeling that she'd quite like to do it again now.

Billy had half a pizza stuck to his face which just made him look even more delicious. Martha noticed it was a Margarita, her favourite. Lump kicked inside her and hormones surged as she rolled towards Billy and he responded.

Pat came out of the bathroom to see an early-morning repeat of what she had witnessed the night before, and assumed it was one of these sex marathons people under fifty could still manage. Little did Pat realise the degree of exhaustion with which her daughter was conducting this tryst, but at the same time the passion was intense and enabled Martha to put every effort in rather than snoring, which is what she really wanted to do. Besides, she reasoned, this might be her last opportunity for a very long time.

Billy, who, somewhere in the middle of the night, had assumed he would be repulsed when sober, found himself handled more expertly and delightfully than he could ever have imagined, and his plans to brusquely exit Stage Left pursued, he imagined, by a desperate Martha, melted away. Like all good things it was over pretty quickly, and as they lay staring at the ceiling the enormity of the cover-up required began to roll over them.

Martha went to the kitchen to make tea on the sticky surface that passed for a worktop and listened to the answerphone. There were three messages on it.

'Hi Martha, it's me. Is Bill there still? It's two-thirty and he's not home. Perhaps he said he was going on somewhere. Call me, can you? Bye.'

'Martha, call me, will you. It's Sarah.'

'Martha, it's Flower. Will you at least call Sarah and tell her what you know.'

Martha, who had always fancied being a Catholic as they seemed so much less banally psychologically disturbed than their C of E counterparts, for the first time understood what true guilt was as a wave of it engulfed her, almost causing her to sit down on the floor.

Billy had also heard the messages and came shamefacedly out into the hall with all his clothes on.

'I'd better go,' he said.

Pat, listening at the door, thought, Yes, you better had, my lad.

'Are you sure you won't stay and have some tea?' said Martha, aware that even this light-hearted question sounded rather desperate and hoping that Billy couldn't see the image that burned into her brain which portrayed Martha,

Billy and the Lump, now a beautiful baby, as a little family group in Battersea Park in the children's zoo, smiling and strolling. She wondered to herself why an alternative image of him drunkenly beating her hadn't surfaced ahead of the family group.

'No, better go,' he said.

Shall I ask him whether there'll be a repeat performance? thought Martha, briefly forgetting he was one of her best friend's boyfriends.

I hope she doesn't ask me if we're going to see each other again, thought Billy.

Just as Martha was about to humiliate herself by asking that very question, Pat quickly emerged from her room and holding out her hand said, 'How charming to meet you, and you are?'

'. . . Just going,' Billy managed to say and slid with an enormous sense of relief outside the front door.

'Seemed like a nice young man,' said Pat, as the door shut.

The phone rang. Unfortunately, Martha hadn't decided on her strategy yet so she coughed very loudly as her tearful friend left another message asking her to call.

Pat, whose hearing was very acute, had made out the gist of the message and looked sternly at her daughter.

'Oh dear, have you made love to a friend's fiancé?' she said.

Martha couldn't help herself, she laughed out loud at her mother's choice of words.

'Mum,' she said, 'I am in my late thirties and what I do

is none of your business. I don't want to upset you, but you just have to accept that I am an adult and wrong as they may seem, I make my own choices.'

This would have been a perfectly acceptable plea for independence had not a huge tear rolled down Martha's face, as she finished her little speech. Pat's stomach lurched as it always did when one of her little girls was upset and the two stood there with Martha crying as hard as she ever had and Pat trying to fold herself round her daughter's mountainous bump but not succeeding very well.

Sarah and Flower were in a café quite close to Martha's when they saw Billy walk past.

Sarah had phoned Flower in a panic when Billy didn't come home because it was the first time it had ever happened and Flower had gone over to keep her company until Charlie's phone calls got very frequent and she left about 2 a.m.

Sarah hadn't slept all night and Billy, who had started the night as someone who was beginning to irritate her slightly and with whom she might finish, not least because of the increasing violence, became by the morning a saintly and generous man whom she loved madly and who very occasionally was violent, probably because she goaded him into it.

Flower was not happy when she heard Sarah eulogising Billy as if he were St Francis of Assisi. It had crossed Flower's mind that Billy and Martha had spent the night together, but she didn't dare suggest it to Sarah, who was thinking it too, but wondered if it would be betraying her friend to even consider it. Flower had borne the brunt of Martha's hormonal outbursts during this pregnancy and therefore believed that any behaviour was possible.

'Billy!' screamed Sarah and ran out of the café.

Billy's heart missed a beat and his brain began to work overtime.

Sarah ran towards him as though he was a soldier come back from the war, but halfway across she remembered he had been out all night and skidded to a halt several inches from him.

'Where the fuck have you been?' was the unlyrical enquiry that escaped her lips.

Billy had decided to play it indignant and the plot his brain had delivered to him began to spray out.

'Look, Sarah, I'm sorry – I was round at Martha's and she felt really rough, thought the baby might be coming so we ended up going to Casualty and they took her in to see the doctor and I fell asleep in the waiting room and then Martha thought I'd gone home because she looked in the wrong place and they woke me up about seven this morning and I went and had some breakfast and now I've just been round to Martha's to see if it's all right. Christ, she's your friend – *you* should have been looking after her.'

'Sorry,' was Sarah's automatic response. Then she thought, Why am *I* saying sorry? He's the one who didn't contact me, and so she said this.

'I did. I bloody called you on your mobile,' bluffed Billy. 'Did you have it on all night?'

'Er . . .' Sarah began to falter. 'Why didn't you leave a message?'

'Well, I would have, but Martha was having a really bad spasm and I . . . well, I just got distracted. Most of the time I had it switched off in the hospital.'

'Then why didn't you call me later?'

''Cause I fucking fell asleep, for Christ's sake,' said Billy, managing to talk himself up to the moral high ground.

Flower, who was lurking in a gawky fashion in the background, didn't believe a word of it.

'Flower!' Suddenly Billy's voice burned her brain.

'Yes?' she answered.

'You believe me, don't you?'

'Yes,' said Flower and hated herself.

Sarah turned to her with an expression of semi-disbelief and appeal.

'I think he's telling the truth,' said Flower wanly.

'So, let's all go back to Martha's and see how she is,' said Sarah, looking for a flicker of guilt, panic or whatever.

'If you like,' Billy said casually, feeling relieved she couldn't see an EEG which would demonstrate the level of electrical activity in his brain: he could have run a power station on it. The three of them turned in a formation and headed down the road towards Martha's estate.

Martha nearly fainted when she opened the door to see the three of them. In the split second that followed, she assumed that Sarah hadn't pronounced her guilty of the worst betrayal of friendship because she hadn't hit her yet. But she had absolutely no idea what Billy had told the girls and therefore she waited for his lead. He, on the other hand, didn't want to make it too obvious by saying something like, 'Hi, how are you feeling after our trip to Casualty after you felt bad and I couldn't phone Sarah because of the emergency nature of the visit and then her mobile was turned off but anyway we thought that we'd pop round and see how you are.'

Instead he said, 'Feeling OK now?'

Sarah was watching them like a madwoman for signs of betrayal.

'Yes, much,' said Martha.

'Poor you,' said Flower, 'having to go there.'

Where does she mean? wondered Martha and took a lucky guess given her condition but just to be safe didn't mention the word.

'Yes, it was awful – noisy, dirty.'

'That's the NHS for you,' said Flower, confirming it for her.

Sarah was still glowering, trying to decide whether Martha looked like she'd been banged senseless all night or not.

Then Pat appeared out of the spare room. 'Hello everyone,' she said brightly.

Please, prayed Martha, don't let her give the game away. She turned towards her mother and made a panic-stricken face which Pat correctly interpreted as a clue that some sort of subterfuge was going on. Rather than put her foot in it she withdrew, making an excuse about having to wash her girdle.

Martha now had the floor and decided to trowel on the

drama. 'I'm so grateful to Billy for taking me to Casualty and bearing with me,' she said. 'I felt bloody awful, like my insides were gradually being squeezed through my intestines to be shat out.'

'Yes, thank you, Martha,' said Flower, who was weedy about this sort of thing.

'Why didn't you call us?' said Sarah.

''Cause I was worried it had all gone wrong and I was going to lose the Lump and I just didn't know how I would react,' said Martha, and then felt incredibly guilty that she had used her unborn baby as an alibi for her unfaithfulness.

'Oh Martha, I'm really sorry,' said Sarah and Martha felt even worse because she realised that the corner had been turned and Sarah now believed that she and Billy had not done anything. She felt her eyes welling up with tears and realised that Billy was looking at her with contempt.

She just wished that everyone would piss off and leave her to get her head in gear and her story straight.

At that point Junior from next door popped his head round the balcony and said, 'Fucking hell, Martha, were you banging a bloody football team last night or what?'

A portentous silence followed.

Chapter 21

Pat, without so much as a backward thought, stepped into the breach.

'It wasn't Martha, Junior,' she said. 'After all, she is nine months' pregnant. No, it was me. Embarrassed as I am to admit it, the Rev Brian was visiting and we got carried away.'

Junior felt physically sick at the thought of these two people of advancing years copulating noisily, not to mention wrinkly bits of skin flapping with wild abandon, forgetting that he possessed similar younger but equally wrinkly bits too and looked a bit silly himself when they were undulating furiously.

Flower also found herself disgusted at the thought of Pat and the Rev, and then shovelled in some political correctness from somewhere to get her conscience back on an even keel. After all, she reasoned to herself, why shouldn't old people couple in any way they want? If they could cope with it, surely their younger relatives could turn a blind eye to the fact that they were being horribly carnal for their age.

Junior was seeing Martha's mum through new eyes. 'Oh, right you are then, Mrs Harris,' he said and slunk back to his balcony area to text all his friends and tell them what stomach-churning sexual practices were going on right under his nose.

Everybody shifted uncomfortably once Pat had made her revelations about her midnight shenanigans with the Rev Brian. Flower noticed that Billy had a little smirk on his face. Martha's expression was one Flower had never seen before nor was it intelligible as representing any recognisable emotion. Her nearest stab at it would have been an animal previously in great pain having been freed from a trap.

'Well, now we know Martha's all right perhaps we'd better go,' suggested Billy tentatively and everyone started to move towards the door. He and Sarah wished Martha and her mother an awkward goodbye and headed through the rubbish littering the walkway to play Lift Lottery, the game that is so popular on London's council estates.

Flower, who didn't want to catch them up, thereby giving them a chance to talk about the schism in their relationship thrown up by last night's absence, hung back. 'Can I just use your loo?' she said and headed off towards it wondering why she had asked and whether there is ever an occasion when access is denied by anybody. Surely it would be more sensible just to inform Martha she was off to use her toilet, but English manners forbade this as a faux pas more serious than urinating openly in a pot plant and Flower preferred to forget that particular birthday.

In the toilet Flower pondered the convincingness of Pat's statement and decided that it wasn't true and that she was covering up for Martha. But why would Martha do something as stupid as fucking Billy, especially when she knew what had been going on between him and Sarah? Before she had a chance to stop herself, Flower realised she was not just having a pee; something bigger, fashioned by obsessive consumption of bran was heading out, another huge catastrophe of etiquette and frowned upon by all but the most libertarian of toilet-owners. 'One should always shit in one's own toilet,' she mused to herself, pleased with her homespun homily but not really sure what it actually meant apart from what it literally meant.

Left alone for a couple of minutes, Martha said to Pat, 'Thanks a million for getting me out of trouble there, Mum.'

'I don't approve, Martha,' said Pat, 'but you're in enough trouble as it is,' throwing a glance at the Lump. 'Also,' she went on, 'I've decided to go back to your dad.'

'Mum, you can't,' said Martha. It was a pain having her there, but apart from her bedroom, which was out of bounds, the place was looking almost normal.

'It's my duty as a wife to be by your father's side, to love him, cherish him and do my best in the kitchen, at social events and between the sheets,' said Pat.

'Yes, thank you, Mother – that will do.' Martha was trying to banish a vision of the Rev Brian rhythmically rocking aboard the good ship *Pat*. 'Look, Mum, Lump's due in a couple of weeks, and Dad's a pig.'

'Don't call him that. He is my husband.'

'Oh, rub it in, why don't you?' said Martha, although she wasn't convinced that having the Rev Brian as a husband was better than having no husband at all.

'Who is the father, dear? Please tell me and then Brian could have a word with him,' said Pat.

'What, crowbar in a quick shotgun wedding at St Faith's?' Martha snorted.

'Don't be silly, dear.' Pat had the ability to fly Martha back through time and make her feel about six years old.

'Sorry,' said Martha. 'Look, do you want me to come on the bus with you to the station?' She was 99 per cent convinced that her mother would reject the offer.

'Yes, that would be lovely,' said Pat, much to Martha's horror, and went into her bedroom to pack her bag.

Flower came shamefacedly out of the loo. 'Sorry,' she said. 'Just sort of happened.'

'Don't worry,' said Martha. 'You eat so much greenery your shit smells like horse manure.'

'Fancy a lunchtime drink?' said Flower, who thought if she just twisted Martha's arm a bit she could find out the truth. She knew her friend of old. Martha's inability to keep a secret was famous and she would obviously be dying to tell someone.

'Sure,' said Martha, 'but I've got to go to the station with Mum first, then we could go somewhere up town. What about Charlie?'

'Oh, he's taken the day off work to go on some demo somewhere,' said Flower absentmindedly, little realising that at that very point in time the size eleven of a policeman was booting a pavement-bound Charlie extremely hard up the arse.

Flower, Pat and Martha set off, finding Lift Roulette in their favour for a change. As it spewed them out at the ground floor, a little gaggle of twelve-year-old girls who looked forty-five set up the sort of cackling that one only expects from bona fide witches, as they looked the bedraggled trio up and down.

'Do they do eye of newt at Sainsbury's?' enquired Martha as they passed, causing a blank look to pass over their faces, which was immediately replaced by their habitual maniacal giggling.

Pat, although she didn't like to admit it, was terrified and was glad she had her daughter and Flower there, although had she really thought about it she might still be terrified, because a heavily pregnant woman and a tall willowy pacifist are about as much use in a fight as Kylie and Danii Minogue. Pat decided she must toughen up.

They got a bus fairly quickly and huddled together for emotional warmth as a series of disturbed people did their party pieces for their fellow travellers. This happened often enough for Martha to have christened it London Transport Psycho Cabaret. Always fascinating and a surefire touring success, she reckoned, but quite scary to watch as occasionally the acts picked on members of the audience, as the middle-aged drunk with a selection of last week's dinners down his suit did now.

'Here, you fucking old slag,' he directed at Pat who, emboldened by being sandwiched between Flower and Martha, replied, 'Yes, what can I do for you, you miserable, pissed old wanker smelling of sick?'

Martha began to laugh and Flower did too.

'Fuck you!' shouted the drunk, shocked by the lack of terror he had engendered in this sixty-year-old woman.

'It's highly unlikely that you are going to fuck me,' said Pat, 'so why don't you just fuck *off*?'

Everyone on the bus began to laugh, and the drunk, betrayed by his public and heckled down by a member of the audience, shambled off at the next stop.

'Mum, that was brilliant,' said Martha.

'I don't know what came over me,' said Pat.

'The Reverend Brian, according to what you told Junior this morning,' said Martha. Luckily Pat didn't understand this and continued to bask in the glory of the open spot comedy guest who has stormed the show against the odds. However, this made Flower sit up and take notice and wonder whether Martha had let something slip that she could perhaps work on.

They reached Liverpool Street station without any further mishaps and saw Pat onto the train. Her newfound confidence had made her sort of crisp round the edges and Martha knew that her father was in for a roasting when Pat got home. She smiled to herself as the square of window containing Pat's face shifted out of view up the platform.

'Where shall we go for a drink then?' she asked Flower.

'Let's head up to the Barbican, shall we?' said Flower, who secretly loved all the street performers and winced as Martha said, 'No stopping for those wanky jugglers though.'

They found a wine bar with huge glass windows that looked out onto passing shoppers.

'Two orange juices,' said Flower to a barman who could have been dead a week, he moved so little and looked so pale.

'You're joking, aren't you?' said Martha. 'Get me a Bloody Mary.'

'Do you think you ought to?' said Flower.

'Flippin' heck, when did you turn into Grandma pissing Mussolini?' said Martha. 'If you're not careful, I'll ask him to make it a double and put a sweet sherry in it.'

'Haven't you heard of foetal alcohol syndrome?' said Flower.

'Look,' said Martha, 'you have to be glugging meths from conception for that to happen, and apart from last night I've barely touched alcohol during this pregnancy.'

'Last night?' said Flower. 'I thought you were in Casualty.'

'I was,' said Martha, rather pathetically.

Flower felt confident at this point that Martha would topple.

She did. Out it all came, squirting everywhere with no punctuation, emphasis, or emotion, but a lot of capital letters because Martha couldn't decide whether to weep, celebrate or beg for more. Martha didn't spare Flower any details.

She, Sarah and Flower had never been coy about filling each other in. She only felt sorry that this session could not be shared with Sarah too.

'Oh Martha, I can't believe it. What happens when Sarah finds out?'

'She won't,' said Martha.

'Yes she will,' said Flower. 'You told me almost immediately. You'll crack within days.'

Martha knew she was right.

'And Billy's a violent man,' said Flower accusingly.

'Not with me he wasn't,' said Martha.

Flower realised she had been reduced to an 'Oh Martha,' machine as each new comment of Martha's brought out another sigh of despair.

'Anyway,' said Martha, 'I might kill him. I nearly did before I slept with him, you know.'

'Oh Martha,' Flower said automatically, then added, 'That is bullshit.'

'Honestly, Flower, it's not,' said Martha. 'These hormones flooding round your system make you want to do so many weird things. If I hadn't been so desperate for a fuck I'd never have jumped Billy.'

'Wouldn't Junior have done,' asked Flower, adding, 'if you were desperate?'

'What – and be had up before the beak for underage sex?' said Martha. 'No, ta.' Then she stopped talking for a while and just stared.

'Are you OK?' said Flower.

Martha wasn't. She felt warm all round her thigh area

and realised that her waters were breaking. It seemed, for a second, like a big warm sea swirling round her and she stood up helplessly as she tried to work out how much of what felt like a tributary had flowed down the main gangway of the wine bar.

There was quite a lot.

Flower saw it and thought Martha had wet herself, and much to her shame was logging it away in the area of her brain that memorised things her friends did which could be worked into a comedy routine.

The half-dead barman, bearing something enormous on a plate that Martha had ordered, stepped unsuspectingly onto the skidpan created by her amniotic fluids and slid almost gracefully towards the bar before he fell, bruising his coccyx very badly in the process.

'Quick, call an ambulance!' shouted Flower and the sleepy bar sprang into life.

Within minutes an ambulance sped up and two para-medics scooped up the beleaguered barman, leaving Flower and Martha to run along behind protesting that they needed an ambulance too.

Chapter 22

The staff at the local Accident and Emergency weren't particularly impressed by Martha and seemed far more keen to move the half-dead barman into a cubicle for treatment. To Martha it was the most momentous time of her life, whereas to the A and E staff, another cursory welcome into the world of a squealing mass of redness was about as dull as it got.

'But my water has burst,' shouted Martha at the disappearing arse of a very officious, obviously sexually frustrated and childless staff nurse.

She turned and said, '*Its* waters have broken actually, and I suggest you just go home and wait for the contractions.'

Martha, who had based her knowledge of pregnancy and birth on Hollywood films and adverts rather than actual textbooks, which she kept meaning to get round to reading, but just hadn't, turned dejectedly to Flower and suggested they went home.

Flower nodded and got her special emergency tenner out from her mobile phone case to pay for a cab as she felt the situation demanded it. Her phone had been turned off in the hospital and when she turned it back on, it rang immediately telling her she had six new messages, all from Charlie, of course, the next more urgent and louder than the one before and seeming to convey that some injury had occurred during the demo and that he was off to get some treatment.

So while the cab driver gave Martha a rundown on the births of his six children, Flower called Charlie.

'Shit,' he said in reply to her enquiry about how he was, followed by his description of the trajectory of the policeman's boot.

'So just how far up your arse did it go?' enquired Flower, oblivious to the fact that the cab driver, a confirmed homophobic, was getting completely the wrong idea.

Martha gave her a look after which point she became barely audible at the other end of the phone and Charlie assumed she was in a bad reception area and hung up.

Contractions started even before the cab had reached its destination and Martha wondered whether they should turn right round again and head for the hospital but Flower vaguely remembered that you should wait for a few hours, until as she put it rather unscientifically, 'They're really fucking killing you,' before you ventured off to hospital.

'Should you go and minister to poor Charlie?' said Martha, silently praying, an odd thing for the wayward daughter of a vicar to do, that Flower would stay with her.

Flower was so used by now to Charlie's encounters with the constabulary and his resulting injuries that she promised she would stay for the day and keep an eye and then accompany Martha into hospital.

So what do you do on a day when your Lump is about to become a real baby?

Martha felt she should do something dramatic and memorable. Flower suggested in that case she might want to have a stab at cleaning her bedroom, and strangely enough, as is often noted with the late stage of pregnancy, a nesting instinct overtook Martha and she swooped into her bedroom and began a major clear-up of evidence from her liaison the night before, coupled with the removal of grime of months. After several hours and increasing pain, she had created quite a nice little haven for her and Lump to exist in for the first few weeks of Lump's life.

By early evening the frequency of contractions had increased enough for Martha to ring the hospital, having glanced at her book of what to do if you're having a baby, and tell them she thought labour was imminent.

The hospital agreed and Martha asked when the ambulance would arrive. There was a hollow laugh on the end of the phone echoed by Martha when she realised she would have to get there under her own steam. A scrabble of immense proportions round the flat produced only one pound seventy pence and of course Flower had spent her emergency tenner on the cab home from the previous encounter at A and E.

Martha was bereft and in pain. 'Oh fuck, what are we going to do, Flower?' she said.

'We could get a cab one pound and seventy pence worth of the way and then hitch,' said Flower, knowing as soon as the words had come out of her mouth how stupid they sounded.

Martha chose to completely ignore her statement. 'Who do we know with a car?' she said.

'Billy?' ventured Flower.

'Oh I can't,' said Martha. 'If Sarah turns up, I won't be able to keep quiet.'

This sentence was interrupted by a loud screaming response to the pain shooting through her pelvic region, leading to Junior on the other side of the wall speculating that Pat was at it again.

'Well, what about Ted?' suggested Flower.

'Oh, you are coming up with a lot of good suggestions,' said Martha, through clenched teeth. 'Let's get my dad along and really have a good time or maybe anyone else I've fucked that I totally regret who has a car and might be able to take us to the hospital in that sort of hideous tortured silence only the memory of a mistaken sexual encounter can produce.'

'Well, there was that one that gave you warts,' said Flower.

'Ah yes, Henry,' said Martha. 'Yes, he's got a very nice motor – go on, call him.'

Flower looked aghast and should have been because Martha had reached the stage where the whole experience had resulted in her truly losing her marbles and she would have been prepared to do anything.

'I don't know Henry's number,' said Flower lamely, at which point Martha began to sob.

'I am not going on the fucking bus,' she said with a snot accompaniment.

Junior, hearing the commotion, appeared round the balcony. 'What's occurring?' he said.

'The fucking baby's fucking coming and I fucking haven't got any fucking money for a fucking cab or I fucking can't think of a fucking way to fucking get there and I've fucking had enough and I don't want to give fucking birth in this fucking rathole,' said Martha succinctly.

'Man,' said Junior, 'I didn't think you were supposed to swear that much until the thing was actually, like, coming out.' Then an image of that very thing happening made him feel so queasy he had to sit down.

'Just do something, Junior!' screamed Flower, getting carried away with the momentum of it all and putting too much pressure on an emotionally under-developed four-teen year old.

'Right,' he said. 'Back in a minute.'

Then Junior went out and nicked a BMW, something he was very accomplished at, and drove it back to the flats, beeping incessantly until Flower looked over the balcony to see him gesticulating wildly twelve floors below and signalling to them to come down.

'Where's your bag?' said Flower.

'There,' said Martha, pointing at her very grubby handbag.

'No, silly,' said Flower. 'Your bag that you have packed

ready for the hospital with all the stuff for the baby and your nightie and that.'

'Oh, give us a fucking break,' said Martha. 'Who do you think I am? Bleedin' Mrs Beeton? Of course I haven't got a bag packed. There's more interesting things to do in life you know than sit in my room deciding which nightie's going to look most attractive with placenta splatted all over it.'

'Jesus, Martha,' said Flower and ran madly around like a recently decapitated chicken throwing a selection of totally inappropriate things into a supermarket carrier bag.

Junior beeped very loudly. He could see a police car patrolling through the estate and thought it was not a good idea to get arrested now.

'Right, let's move,' said Flower.

Martha lay on the floor and wailed, 'I don't want Lump to come out! What the hell am I going to do? I've got no money, no permanent job, oh my God I can't cope.'

'You'll be fine,' said Flower in the manner of a brusque psychiatric nurse, because she found herself ever so slightly irritable now and was surprised that, as a hippy social worker, she couldn't disguise it properly.

Martha sensed the change in her tone and decided to get a grip. She stood, grabbed the carrier bag, found her keys and ushered Flower out of the flat.

Into her mobile phone, Flower was saying, 'Yes, actually having it – well, not literally, Charlie, there's nothing poking out yet, but we've got to get to the hospital. In Junior's car. No, Charlie, I categorically do not fancy Junior, never have, never will. I'll call you later when I have some news.'

Junior virtually catapulted Martha headfirst into the back of the car and Flower had to run alongside and jump in, he took off so quickly.

There was no sign of the police now but the traffic was terrible and their progress slow. Junior was caught between being a fourteen-year-old black kid who had just stolen a BMW and the risks that engendered if they were spotted, and wanting to get Martha to the hospital as quickly as possible because she was making such an awful noise and he knew he would throw up if he saw blood or vomit. Besides, he couldn't hear the radio.

'How are you going to pay the congestion charge?' enquired Flower.

'What?' screeched Junior, who was now unfettered by caution and doing fifty-five down a bus lane.

'Well, I think we've entered the area,' said Flower.

'I'll enter your fucking area,' said Martha, clutching the Lump. 'Bloody congestion charge when I'm about to split open.'

'Sorry,' said Flower. 'Only trying to help.'

Junior's mobile phone rang. It was his mum who was the only individual who prevented him being able to see himself as a local gangster. Flower could hear him being given a hard time.

'Mum, I gotta go,' he protested. 'I'm on business.'

'Don't you hang up on—'

He did.

Their arrival at the hospital was a chaotic affair, Junior

having driven the wrong way into the Casualty Department and blocked an ambulance containing a seriously ill man. Had Junior not decided to get into a verbal abuse session with the two ambulance men about the moral rightness of his case, they would all have got inside a lot quicker.

Eventually though, Martha gratefully felt herself being slung into a wheelchair and closed her eyes as she was wheeled down a series of corridors. A whiff of cigarette smoke struck her nose and she realised she was dying for a fag. She opened her eyes to see the big pasty face of Mr Cancer only a few inches away from hers.

'Give us a puff,' she said and grabbed his cigarette, adding, 'Go! Go! Go!' to Junior who raced her off down the corridor with Martha puffing like a fat train until they reached the labour ward.

Junior was left like a dumped bridegroom at the door of the labour ward as Flower explained that he was not the father, while a stern midwife thought to herself that she didn't believe a word of it and women of Martha's age would have sex with absolutely anyone to get a baby. Alternatively, she might be a lesbian who had resorted to a turkey baster with her girlfriend – the vulture in a dress, she thought to herself.

The next twelve hours were a total surprise to Martha, consisting as they did of many things that were entirely unexpected. There was pain, sure enough, and she was well aware that might be the case. However, solutions to the pain were not as satisfactory as she had been led to believe by her sister and some friends. Having attempted gas and air and finding it about as effective as a paracetamol for a mastectomy, she moved on to pethidine (rubbish) and an epidural which worked brilliantly on one side and not on the other.

Flower turned into a blurry face that occasionally loomed up in front of her looking concerned and she followed instructions as if she was sleepwalking. She breathed when told to breathe, panted when told to pant and pushed when told to push and at 3.30 in the morning a great big bugger of a baby boy covered in blood and goo exited from her vagina and began to scream the place down. Stern midwife's features softened, Flower cried and Martha let out a noise which was a mixture of extreme joy, hunger, sadness, exhaustion and amusement and then she slept.

Some hours later a noise woke her and she looked up to see a line of people including Flower and Charlie, the Rev Brian and Pat, Sarah plus black eye and Billy, and Greasy Ted, the bugger's dad.

Chapter 23

Martha wasn't sure who to start on first. They made her think of skittles in a bowling alley waiting for her to knock them down, in which case, inevitably, she started with her father.

'What are you doing here?' she said accusingly.

'Well, I was in London for a conf—' he began, when Pat cut him off and said, 'Come on, Martha, did you really think we wouldn't come to celebrate the birth of our daughter's first child?'

Martha felt that now would be a good time to express some of the feelings she'd been suppressing for years, under the guise of the Just Given Birth Hormone coursing through her body and making her uncontrollably honest. She could visualise Pat explaining this to her father as he fumed in the car on the way home. This was one encounter she *wasn't* going to lose out on, and perhaps the fact that her best friends were there to witness it wasn't such a bad thing. She motioned to people to sit on the few weedy chairs that were around and marvelled at the fact that somehow she had ended up in a private room. She wasn't sure why; it could have been her threats to the midwife that went on after the baby was born – threats which are supposed to stop once labour is ended but in Martha's case became louder in volume and more unpleasant.

'So what are you going to call it?' sneered her father and it was the sneering that was responsible for Martha's reply.

'Jesus,' she said.

Rev Brian looked aghast and Pat looked equally shocked by proxy. There was some giggling too. Greasy Ted threw his head back and roared with laughter and Sarah just continued to look pissed off and stare at the floor.

'That is sacrilege!' bellowed Rev Brian. 'I'll give you twenty-four hours to think about it, and after that time if you persist with this pathetic idea I will never speak to you or see you again.'

He exited with as much melodrama as he could muster, with Pat in tow talking all the time in a low voice and trying to calm him down, not realising that over the years it never failed to wind him up even more.

Two down and a mere five to go, thought Martha and decided to apply her truth-telling hormonality to the others in the room. 'Ted, why are *you* here?' she said. Ted appeared from behind a big bunch of flowers. From such beauty, ugliness comes shining through, thought Martha and wondered if that was a famous quote or just her own effort.

'Well, as your employer,' said Ted, 'I happened to phone

Sarah and ask her how you were getting on and she'd just heard from Flower about the baby so I thought I'd better pop down and see how you were and give you congratulations.' He sounded stilted, less funny and less relaxed in this setting.

'Just as well you did,' said Martha, 'because it's your baby.'

There was a look of such tragic proportions on Ted's face that she thought he might hit her. Instead he said, 'You fucking cow, Martha,' threw the flowers on the floor and walked out of the room. Martha noted that she felt really upset, but how could she tell if it was genuine?

'You idiot,' said Flower. 'What did you do that for?'

Martha felt slightly ashamed so she went on the offensive. 'Oh, mind your own business, you flaky hippy and leave me in peace – and take *him* with you.' She pointed to Charlie.

Flower was knackered and grumpy, and didn't need a second invitation. She grabbed Charlie by the hand and almost lifted him off the ground they left so fast. Martha felt like a spectator at her own funeral.

Just then, Martha's mobile phone rang. She picked it up, looked at the caller display, pressed the answer button and just said, 'Fuck off.' Then she turned back to the remnants of the baby-welcoming party, Sarah with her black eye and Billy shuffling uncomfortably from foot to foot.

Martha sighed, then opened her mouth and said to Sarah, 'Another black eye, I see. No need to wonder where *that* came from. Well, if him hitting you won't make you leave him, perhaps this will . . .' She didn't finish the sentence because a stinging slap caught her on the side of the face.

It was Billy.

'You're hysterical,' he said. 'We'll come back when you're feeling better. Come on, Sarah.' He led her from the room.

'That went well,' said stern midwife, coming out of the ensuite toilet.

'Just get me my morphine,' shouted Martha, who believed if a Class A drug was written up for you legally, you might as well take full advantage of it.

Martha pondered the enormity of what she had done while Jesus slept. She only had to hold out twenty-four hours and her father would never speak to her again. Oh, what bliss. She didn't know what to do about Ted, about whom she felt rather regretful, and as for her outburst to Flower – that was completely ridiculous: she had no axe to grind there at all. And Flower had been a tower of strength. Poor Sarah, her intervention couldn't have been more text-book stupid.

I must sort everything out when I leave here, thought Martha, suddenly grateful for a few moments' peace. Little did she realise that with a baby in tow, finding the time to sort things out was about as likely as her father reappearing at the door and saying, 'Fuck it, love, why not have another one and call it God?'

There was a knock on the door. Oh Christ, who is it now? thought Martha. 'Yes?' she shouted grumpily.

Junior opened the door and slunk into the room. He had a hunted look about him and the reason for this was revealed soon enough when he was followed in by his mum and two policemen. Jesus, in a worryingly anti-authority response to their arrival, woke up and started to cry very loudly.

'Will you explain to them, Martha,' said Junior. 'They don't believe my story about the BMW.'

'I'm sorry,' said Martha, looking blankly at him, 'I don't know who you are.'

A smile spread over the face of the younger copper.

'Only kidding,' said Martha and turned to Junior's mum. 'Look, I'm really sorry, Mrs Shakespeare,' she said. 'I know I shouldn't be encouraging him into bad habits . . . it was an emergency.'

'So I see,' said Junior's mum, picking up Jesus and asking, 'What's he called?'

'Haven't decided yet,' said Martha, wondering for the first of many times whether she could go through with the Jesus thing, especially given there were so many fundamentalist churches in her area. Jesus quietened down as soon as Mrs Shakespeare picked him up and Martha felt rather jealous.

'Oh, he's absolutely gorgeous,' she said. 'His daddy must be really pleased.'

'Hmmm,' said Martha.

The older policeman coughed in an attention-seeking sort of way.

'Yes, finish your business,' said Martha, 'and then please get out of my room.'

'Can I ask you a couple of questions, madam?' he said.

'Look,' said Martha, 'I'll tell you exactly what happened.

I was about to have a baby and I didn't want to go to hospital on the bus. Call me a snob if you want, I had no money for a cab and so Junior very helpfully got a car for us to get there quickly and safely. I'm sorry he stole it.'

Junior nodded solemnly.

'Well, I suppose that puts a marginally different complexion on things,' said the senior policeman, looking like he had enjoyed saying 'marginally'. His colleague nodded.

'We'll be in touch, son,' said the older one.

They left leaving an awkward Junior and his mum by the bed looking around as if they had never seen a hospital room before. Junior's mum suddenly stirred.

'We'd better go too,' she said. She turned to Martha. 'Look, girl,' she said, 'is the father around?'

'I'm not really sure,' said Martha. 'I should have a better idea by the end of the week.'

'Well,' said Mrs Shakespeare, 'if you need any advice on coping with the little lad, let me know, or I'll babysit or whatever.'

'Thank you,' said Martha. 'I'd be grateful of that some-time, I'm sure.'

Suddenly she was alone.

'But I'm not alone, though,' she said out loud.

'No, you're not alone,' said stern midwife, coming into the room with some tablets for her.

'You're right, Jesus is with me,' said Martha, evoking a rather strange look from stern midwife. If she did plump for 'Jesus', Martha could tell there were going to be many moments like this when people would think she was a

Christian of the over-committed variety. As for poor Jesus himself, how would he cope in the playground? Would he be bullied, laughed at, maybe worshipped – who could tell?

Martha could still extricate herself from the 'Jesus' commitment. Only a small roomful of people had heard her pronouncement and she would lose no face by saying she'd decided to change the name of her baby to Wilson or Brad or one of those fashionable surname-type names that every poor little bastard in South London had been saddled with. Why not Harris? Harris Harris, there was a name to contend with.

She was pondering this question when Jesus/Harris began to cry and stern midwife suggested she feed him as Martha was too knocked off to come up with that obvious solution to his distress. Up until this point her attempts at breast-feeding had been singularly unsuccessful but it now felt like things were reaching a crisis point and Jesus's cries rang louder and louder round the room, giving rise to awful dark fantasies in Martha's mind that she wouldn't be able to feed him and the poor little guy would just fade away to nothing.

'I killed Jesus,' she said to herself.

Stern midwife, who was in the process of trying to attach the baby's mouth to Martha's nipple in that matter-of-fact way nurses have, which is reminiscent of an irritated plumber trying to force a bit of washing machine to fit another bit, wondered whether she should call the duty psychiatrist to come and examine Martha, who could be suffering from post-natal psychosis. She thought perhaps to be on the safe side she would.

Martha was beginning to realise she had already claimed the name in her own mind for her little boy and whatever the emotional cost, ridicule or threat he might have to suffer in the future, she would stick with 'Jesus'. Besides, if it all got too much, they could move to South America where there were hundreds of Jesuses running around.

At this point, Flower put her head round the door. 'Do I still have to piss off?' she said.

'Oh I'm sorry,' said Martha, having a brief respite from the raging torrent of hormones that was turning her from the person she thought she knew into a labile, over-concerned, huge squirting machine of vicious maternity.

Flower looked relieved. 'I think I got off lightly in the Martha Attack Line-Up,' she said. 'How do you think your poor parents are?'

'I don't care,' said Martha. 'It's me and Jesus against the world,' adding, 'Yes, I know I sound like a fucking funda-mentalist Christian.'

Stern midwife was still there and both Martha and Flower were desperately trying to ignore her but Martha's pain and irritation levels were so high that she slapped stern midwife away from her breast as if she was a particularly big horsefly.

'Ow!' said stern midwife and then smiled in a scary, nursing fashion, saying, 'Aah, you young mothers are all the same.'

'Are you taking the piss?' said Martha.

The baby finally slept, seemingly satisfied and Martha

wondered if she would require surgery to put her nipples back on.

'Did you notice Sarah?' said Flower. 'I know in the middle of all this gory glory that we shouldn't be taking on anything, but the state of the poor girl . . . Let's sort this bastard Billy out once and for all.'

Chapter 24

Martha was surprised by Flower's fierceness and her resolve because she herself, having been prodded, poked and opened up to allow a rather larger-than-life new human to pass through, felt that the last thing she wanted to do was sort anything out.

'Look, Flower,' she said pathetically, 'I've got a new baby, I've alienated my parents, I've not even let my sister get as far as the ward before I got rid of her, Christ knows when Ted is ever going to reappear and talk to me, and now you want us to do something drastic to Billy.'

'Not us,' said Flower. 'I'm quite prepared to take responsibility for it if you support me and we can talk about it.'

'Well, what are you going to do?' said Martha.

'I'm going to get a gun,' said Flower.

Martha laughed uproariously. Flower didn't. 'Oh come on, mate, a water pistol maybe or a staple gun to nail his bollocks to the carpet, but a real gun?'

'A fake gun wouldn't work,' said Flower.

'Wouldn't work killing him, do you mean?' said Martha, horrified.

'No,' said Flower, equally horrified. 'No, wouldn't work when I threaten him with it and tell him to lay off Sarah once and for all.'

'He'll laugh in your face,' said Martha. 'He'll assume it's a fake and he'll piss himself.'

'I don't think he will,' said Flower, 'because I will know it's real so I'll scare the shit out of him.'

'And where are you going to get a gun? I know it's rough round our way, but they don't sell them in the MiniMart, you know.'

'Dick Knob's going to get it for me,' said Flower. 'In fact, I'll go with him and get it. Might work out into a good routine.'

'Oh what, the I Went Up The East End And Bought A Gun Illegally To Threaten Someone routine . . . might be a slight giveaway,' said Martha. 'And by the way, when are you seeing Mr Knob?'

'I'm working with him tonight in West London,' said Flower.

'Don't,' pleaded Martha, suddenly overcome by misgivings.

'It'll be all right,' said Flower. 'What you don't realise is it's better that I have it than if they sell it to some fourteen-year-old car thief.'

'Like Junior, you mean?' said Martha.

Flower looked at her watch. 'Jesus, I'd better go,' she

said, then she remembered the baby and added, 'Oh sorry.'

'Don't worry,' said Martha. 'I realise what I'm taking on if I give my son a name that incorporates so many scary concepts and even a swearword. Maybe I should just call him "Fuck". What do you think? "Fuck Harris". Does it suit him?'

'No,' said Flower, 'stick with Jesus, it's growing on me. Look, I've got to rush now or I won't have time to get home and rub some stuff into poor Charlie's back before I go to the gig.'

Flower passed Mr Cancer and the tubercular gang on her way out and disliked herself intensely for wishing she had a gun now to put this pasty bastard out of his misery too. Who would miss him? she wondered. Did he have someone who loved him somewhere? Was there a woman who was that disturbed? She decided there must be, considering women write to serial-killers and want to marry them. In fact, Martha's liaison with Billy was a very minor version of that. Flower decided she must keep an eye on Martha and hope that she didn't start corresponding with a convicted killer.

Mr Cancer had no idea of the amount of hate that was surging through Flower's veins as he called, 'Hello, beaky,' to her disappearing back.

She turned and not being able to help herself said Martha's line, 'Well, at least I haven't got cancer.' She didn't wait for the consequence and headed straight off down the road not realising that Mr Cancer just wanted to be loved like everyone else and a big fat tear rolled down his cheek.

Charlie was a bit miserable as well when she got home. He had been wondering to himself why he couldn't just have a girlfriend who had normal friends instead of Martha and Sarah both of whom, in Charlie's opinion, were too high maintenance.

Flower wondered if she should tell Charlie she was going to go ahead and ask Dick Knob to get her a gun. They had discussed the whole thing generally and for a couple of hippies found they were pretty right-wing in their attitudes towards the state of the streets of London, crime and how it should be dealt with. Charlie had noticed, though, that Flower was becoming increasingly combative and leaving him behind in the hang 'em and flog 'em department. He had thought of arming his girlfriend with some sort of weapon to protect herself with when she was out alone, but to be quite honest a gun had never occurred to him and had Flower told him, he would have been very patronisingly negative about it.

Flower was nervous. She had been booked for that night's show, rather than been given a five-minute guest spot. The venue was a university in West London which was having a ball to celebrate its 50th anniversary and had decided to throw a few comedians to the students at the end of the evening as gladiators weren't allowed any more. Therefore, the gig didn't start until eleven and Flower's stomach kept telling her that they would all be very pissed and probably quite abusive. On the bill with her were Dick Knob and

Muff Diva, an innocent hippy filling in a filth sandwich, she thought to herself. However, she liked Muff – real name Alison Hughes – and even though Dick Knob came out with nauseating stuff for some reason it didn't bother her.

Dick Knob picked Flower up at the corner of her road in a black car that looked American ('it's paid for itself in twat') and they drove up through the centre of town where a flat just behind Paddington regurgitated Muff Diva, looking decidedly queasy. 'Food poisoning or up the fucking duff,' being her assessment of the situation.

They headed for the A40 and after an hour or so stuck in traffic reached the hallowed portals of what looked more like a science-fiction film set than a university. Here they met a slightly pissed union representative called Dan who was going to compère the show.

The dressing-rooms were at the back of the stage and were positioned near the toilets so the full aural effect of the alcohol-sodden students could be assessed by all three. Dan said they would start in about half an hour and managed to procure them three warm bottles of lager, a packet of crisps and a plate of sandwiches that looked as if someone had already tried them.

Some sort of dancing and screaming was going on and Flower felt her sandwich hit the pit of her stomach and begin to make its way up again. 'Butterflies' was not a good way to describe the process within her entrails, more like the iron grip of fear which simultaneously had stimulated her bladder and loosened her bowels and threatened a total system shutdown.

At this point, before a really awful gig, Flower always tried to imagine the worst that could happen to try and calm herself down. A person jumping onto the stage and killing her never entered into it, however; it was always the fantasy of a killer heckle that made the audience cheer for minutes on end and led Flower to sadly slash her wrists in the pissy, makeshift dressing-room, that gripped her imagination.

Muff Diva was doing a few breathing exercises because she had been to drama college; had he done a warm-up, no doubt Dick Knob's preferred method would have been a wank. Flower just sat with her head in her hands wishing herself back home and to the age of five when she was happy.

Dan appeared in the dressing-room, said he would do about five minutes and left bravely for the stage having neglected to tell the intrepid trio that he hadn't compèred before and he didn't really know how to do it. What's more, he was now very pissed.

'Evening, fellow pissheads!' was his opening salvo and then he vomited on the stage and staggered off.

'Quick,' said a technician, poking his head round the door to Muff Diva. 'You're on!'

Muff Diva was in the toilet when all this happened, she went on stage like a lamb to the slaughter, slipped on the sick which she didn't see because the stage was dark because the spotlight operator was pissed as well and had put it on too late, and went sailing into the audience who assumed it was part of her act and just threw her up and down as if she was up the front of the big stage at Glastonbury. Her queasiness rising to the surface at this treatment, Muff vomited onto someone's head and a riot looked certain until Dick Knob, a seasoned campaigner at these sorts of events, got a hold on the proceedings by walking to the mike, dropping his trousers and revealing a small chicken strapped to his penis. He then did several minutes of execrable material on sexually abusing pets, turned to the side of the stage and said, 'Please welcome a little Flower!'

The mêlée of people seemed to explode as Flower walked on. The noise was huge, the lights blinding and the microphone seemed such a long way away. The stage had been cleared and as Flower reached the microphone, suddenly the mood changed, the audience quietened down and Flower realised that the friendly crowd were pleased to see her and waiting expectantly for her to begin. For the first time that day she relaxed.

'Fuck me, it's the bastard daughter of Barry Manilow and a fucking yeti,' shouted a voice into the silence, followed by perhaps the purest ripple of laughter building to a crescendo of hysteria that Flower had ever heard. Inside she cried. Outside she did too. There was no option but to leave the way she came on and from that night onward the gig came to be known by (the mainly gentlemen of) the comedy circuit as The Hippylezzer Fiasco and went to prove that girls couldn't handle the really rough gigs.

Flower was downcast in the dressing-room after the gig and Dick Knob was probably not the best person to comfort her as he put everybody's problems in a sexual context and, 'I bet loads of them wanted to get in your knickers, love,' was not really what Flower wanted to hear.

She waited until Muff Diva had disappeared to the toilet again to have another puke and said to Dick, 'I want to get that gun tonight.'

'Now come on, love,' said Dick.

Flower took a gamble. 'Forget it,' she said. 'You're always pissing about. I'll go somewhere else.'

'No, you're all right,' said Dick, who had actually spoken to a mate of a mate about it. 'Look, I'll make a call, we'll drop Muff off home and then I'll take you there, OK? Have you got any money on you?'

'How much will I need?' said Flower.

'Two hundred quid or thereabouts,' said Dick.

'I doubt I'll get paid,' said Flower. 'That fucking heckler, it was the same one I always get.'

'A stalker, you mean,' said Dick.

'Well, I'd never thought of it in that context so thanks for layering on an extra level of fear,' said Flower.

Dan the vomiter had been replaced by someone more studious-looking with glasses called Phil who came backstage with an envelope of money.

'Don't forget the promoter's ten per cent,' said Muff, as they divided it up.

'Bollocks to that,' said Dick and carried on counting.

Flower's mobile rang. 'How did it go?' said Charlie.

'Hang on a minute,' said Flower. She went outside and said: 'Look, they've postponed it until two in the morning.

Sorry, I'm going to be really late. I'll call you when I'm on my way home.'

Charlie for once didn't have the energy to complain. He must be feeling really crap, thought Flower, and she resolved to get home quickly.

They drove through West London, silent until they reached Muff's house. Muff had been quiet and thoughtful all the way home and had been thinking about having children and how she was going to achieve it without having to ask any of her gay friends to bang her or masturbate into a jar.

'Cheerio,' she said absentmindedly.

'She almost sounded like a heterosexual there,' said Flower perceptively.

'Well, I'd enter the dragon,' said Dick.

'You'd enter a Pot Noodle,' said Flower, a sense of humour creeping back into her comedy, the life having all but been squeezed out of it at the college ball.

Once free of Muff Diva, Dick turned the car towards East London and after about half an hour they were crawling along through Whitechapel looking for number 137. It turned up next to a funeral parlour.

Very handy, thought Flower and, standing in a dirty pool of yellow light, Dick, who had called ahead on his mobile, pressed a grubby over-fingered bell and footsteps echoed down the stairs towards them. Flower, who had had a few steadying beers, was starting to ask herself what on earth she was doing here, but luckily for her, her PMT phase was virtually upon her and she could justify the purchase of a gun very easily in that mood.

A good-looking scruff answered the door. 'Hi Quent,' he said to Dick.

Flower was astounded, 'Your name is never Quentin, is it?' she said.

'Well, of course it is, or he wouldn't have called me it,' said Dick, not his customary relaxed self for a few seconds.

'Quentin What?' said Flower. 'Double-Barrelled, is it?'

'No, and neither's the gun,' growled the good-looking scruff as he led them up the stairs, turning round to say to Dick, 'Don't she know then, Quent?'

'No, she don't,' said Dick furiously.

'Pratt,' said the scruff.

'Oh, he's not,' said Flower. 'He's all right.'

'No, that's his name,' said the scruff.

Had Flower not been close to incontinence, she would have laughed.

By now they had reached a sitting room of sorts where two other men were watching telly and looked disinterestedly at Flower, because they were off their heads, rather than her assessment that she wasn't attractive enough.

'Right,' said Scruff. 'Got your money?'

Flower produced her two hundred quid and expected her gun to be handed to her carefully wrapped in an oilskin. Instead Scruff took it out of his pocket, fished a bit more and produced three bullets.

'There you go,' he said.

'Is that all the bullets I get?' said Flower.

'How many cunts do you want to shoot, love?' said Scruff and the two men on the settee laughed.

'Can you show me how it works?' said Flower, convinced she sounded like a slightly demented Enid Blyton schoolgirl.

The bloke dextrously opened the gun, shoved the bullets into the chamber, clicked it shut and said, 'Look, that's the safety catch. If that's not on, you'll have your fucking foot off.'

And that was it. So simple, so banal and so untheatrical, thought Flower as they decended the stairs, but unfortunately there's more than three cunts I *do* want to shoot. But never mind, I'll make do for now.'

Chapter 25

Billy and Sarah had fared badly as a couple since the night before Jesus was born. The black eye visible to everyone in the post-natal ward had been courtesy of Sarah's six-year-old neighbour Keanu and his new baseball bat, but she didn't even bother to tell anyone any more.

Sarah was still suspicious and angry about what she presumed was Billy's infidelity with her best friend, but scared of rocking the boat, so she did what many women do in her situation: she directed the anger inwards and hey, presto! – became depressed.

Billy, on the other hand, was angry with himself, contrite for what he had done, but unable to come clean and tell Sarah the truth, because he feared, wrongly, that this would finally finish them off and he had decided that he couldn't manage without her. There were so many dark aspects to his seemingly normal facade that he wanted to come clean about, the legacy of having a rather nasty father with an unhealthy interest in porn and a mother who let it all slide past her without any kind of challenge. He wanted to tell Sarah all this and was surprised, as no other woman in his life had ever engendered that kind of trust and Billy just knew if he could get through this crisis, then their relationship could work happily and without violence.

Of course, it never occurred to Billy to seek psychological help because he came from a background in which the conscious mind, let alone the unconscious one, got about as much respect as a busload of social workers, when compared to the achievements, wealth and array of material acquisitions that signified success. Billy's parents would rather have been killed than found themselves saying to their son, 'We don't mind what you do, as long as you are happy, son.'

Hence, any sign of emotional weakness was equated with lack of strength and so Sarah's withdrawal into herself just got on Billy's nerves. He found this harder to cope with than her anger which had simmered under the surface for ages but had been denied many times with the sweetest of smiles.

Sarah, whose repertoire of emotional rescue plans consisted of shopping, health farms and more cigarettes than usual, had decided something drastic was called for if she was going to get back on an even keel and conduct herself sensibly enough to save the relationship between her and Billy. 'Christ, why do I want to save it?' she asked herself time and time again. 'Hasn't Martha done me a favour by sleeping with him?' (Sarah had decided that this was the truth of the matter and however much she tried to deny it to herself, couldn't see any other option than to believe her instincts.) Sarah's attitude towards Martha oscillated between a kind of grateful resignation, an acceptance of the altruistic nature of their liaison and such extreme anger and hatred that she wanted to physically damage her and her child.

Having thought long and hard about how to feel normal again, she decided the only way was a makeover after which the new confident, sparkling Sarah would emerge strong and ready for anything because she'd had a bit of a haircut and a new eyeshadow colour. She managed to get a cancellation at the hairdresser she normally went to, called in sick to work and sat staring blankly at her reflection as the stylist, Bal, tried to tempt her into something which sounded utterly ridiculous and nothing like the kind of haircut she could tolerate.

'Well, how about a bob then?' said Bal distractedly in between chews of a piece of gum long overdue for ejection.

'No, it's not me, man,' said Sarah. 'I want something spiky – something, you know, gammon.'

'You what?' said Bal whose command of the English language wasn't anything to write home about either, but did extend to knowing that bacon had never featured in the description of a style of hair.

'Hang on love,' he said and went off to ask Mia, the apprentice, who read books.

'Oh, she probably means "gamine",' she said, and seeing

Bal's blank expression added, 'you know, sort of Parisian street urchin look.'

None the wiser, Bal headed back and decided to razor Sarah's hair a bit more and bluff the rest of the way.

When he had finished Sarah looked as if she had recently been tarred and feathered, but being unaware of this concept, as it had never happened in Maidstone where she came from, she quite liked the result.

She then headed on to her favourite department store in the West End, which she knew could give her a new face, as she had called in advance to check. In a small booth with someone called Maria whose chat and nuclear perfume would have filled a cathedral, she struggled not to lose her temper, particularly when flashes of insight told her just how point-lessly pathetic what she was doing really was. Maria used a lot of melodramatic words to do with stripping away and starting again. She 'rejuvenated', 'repaired' and 'exploded', 'electrified', 'evoked' and 're-evaluated' until Sarah convinced herself that this was real and it would work.

Finally, after stepping out of the booth looking like an LSD casualty who has just been on a bender, she went up to the fashion department and bought herself a dress which would have looked good only on someone with anorexia nervosa and not on Sarah who was, although not fat, a sort of healthy chunky. She decided to wear the dress and headed home, being ignored for the most part by London's populace who will pretty much accept any sort of behaviour without raising an eyebrow – from wanking to murder to badger-baiting – and so had no idea that she looked very bizarre.

Shop windows and the mirror at home reinforced that message but somehow in her head Sarah had turned her look into a positive state of eccentric yet interesting beauty. She therefore almost forgot her transformation and so could not understand why Billy was standing in front of her, having come in from work, helpless with laughter.

'My God, it's Mata Hari on Es,' he said through the laughter and Sarah lashed out at him.

'Go fuck yourself, you bastard,' she shouted and gave him a slap so hard across his face it hurt her hand.

Billy's emotional make-up was such that he shot first and asked questions later and without even thinking, he lashed out and caught Sarah below the eye, flooring her. It was the eye that had escaped Keanu's baseball bat last week and so Sarah knew she would have a pair of Panda eyes to make excuses about.

Billy immediately returned to his everyday self. 'Oh my God, I'm so sorry,' he said. 'I did it automatically. Sarah, believe me – I didn't mean to.'

Sarah couldn't even speak. She got up, tore her new clothes off, kicked her shoes against the wall and flung herself into the bathroom where she locked the makeshift door and dunked her poor shaven head under the shower, while Billy stood nonplussed outside trying to think how he could retrieve this situation.

Then Sarah stuck her head round the door and screamed, to his complete amazement, 'Everything would be all right if I had a baby!'

*   *   *

Meanwhile Charlie and Flower were discussing Martha's situation and the Ted scenario.

'Ted is a knobhead basically,' said Flower. 'He runs a dingy club for wankers in Soho and Martha should never have had anything to do with him.'

'His heart's in the right place though,' said Charlie.

'Oh for fuck's sake, Charlie,' said Flower, 'the man is not much better than a pimp, and you're trying to big him up.'

'At least I'm not trying to speak a language that's far too young for me and makes me sound ridiculous,' said Charlie.

Flower didn't even hear what Charlie had said as she was wrestling with the huge question of whether she should tell him that she had bought 'a shooter' as Dick Knob rather pathetically kept calling it. She decided against it and thought that if Charlie came across it in a second make-up bag in her handbag she would say she was hiding it for Muff who was easily scary enough to be carrying one around.

'Are you listening?' said Charlie. 'You seem preoccupied by something, have done all day. Was it such a bad gig last night?'

'I'm just tired,' said Flower, 'and I want a baby.'

Charlie nearly fell off his chair, which wasn't difficult to do as it was one of those foam ones which tip over easily. In fact a young policeman who had visited them a couple of months ago to ask Charlie a few questions about his involvement with a group that caused a lot of trouble at demonstrations had found this out to his cost as he plunged sideways off the chair, ending up in a heap with his helmet on the side of his face and all he could see as he looked up was two giggling hippies.

They weren't giggling now though.

'What on earth has brought this on?' said Charlie, whose paternal feelings were well and truly buried inside him, obscured by things he planned to do in his life which didn't allow for the irritation of a baby – hitchhiking across Australia for example, and then living rough in the outback for a year. Unfortunately he hadn't discussed these plans with Flower so he knew it was going to be difficult to convince her that he hadn't just come up with them this minute.

'Jesus has brought this on,' said Flower, and for a moment Charlie thought that she was even more disturbed than he had imagined before he steered his mind back to Martha's offspring bawling its head off in the local hospital.

To be honest, he thought to himself, that puce little bastard doesn't engender any fond feelings in me. 'Look,' he said to Flower, 'it's not like I don't want to have kids with you, Flower, 'cause I really do, but not yet. I mean, your comedy career is just starting to take off.'

'That is bollocks and you know it,' said Flower, 'especially after last night's fiasco. Look, I'm in my mid-thirties, right, and if we don't start trying soon I won't have the chance.'

'We can't afford it,' said Charlie lamely.

'We could if you stopped smoking so much dope,' said Flower, 'and if we stayed in a bit more.'

Charlie's sinking heart dived a couple more feet towards

his boots. 'Let's go out and talk about it, shall we?' he said. 'I can't think in this place, I need some space.'

They headed out of London on the bus towards a scrubby bit of countryside they knew in Kent which was near enough to London to give the leaves on the trees dirty hems that were not visible to the naked eye, but made Flower and Charlie feel they were truly in a rural paradise, when in fact they were barely out of the suburbs. As usual they brought with them a big bottle of cider and their books. Charlie was reading something incomparably dull on the ecosystem of Scandinavia and Flower was revisiting Dickens's *Barnaby Rudge*, a book she had read as a child and came back to every five years or so for emotional comfort.

Having left behind the grimy, slightly urine-tinged smell of the bus, they sniffed the air optimistically and headed off down the country lane which led to a little glade in some woods by a stream which no one else seemed to have discovered. Charlie had grabbed something he called 'a picnic' from the kitchen but it turned out to be a tub of cous-cous past its sell-by date, two spongy apples and some chocolate biscuits. So they had biscuits and cider lying on a blanket, side by side, alternately reading and looking at the sky and inevitably the combination of these things led Charlie to want sex.

He took Flower by surprise, as he landed on top of her with very little warning and began to remove articles of clothing in a completely random way until Flower was left with one sock and shoe on and a grubby vesty thing which she used for security when she was a teenager and hadn't quite been able to part with.

Charlie, who was easily bitten in rural settings and got cold if he so much as removed one of his seven layers of angora, only stuck outside his clothes the absolute minimum necessary to complete the sexual act – and the fact that Flower laughed uncontrollably when she saw it coming towards her only increased his desire.

Flower lay back and allowed Charlie to do his thing and as she gazed up at the sky became aware of some movement just out of her line of vision and quite a lot of giggling.

'Charlie,' she whispered furiously.

'Oohaah,' was all Charlie could manage.

'Charlie!' hissed Flower. 'Someone's looking!'

Charlie quite liked this idea and the pumping got harder. Then two faces appeared from behind two trees to reveal a couple of, spotty teenage boys filled with fascination and concentration and obviously giving each other the boldness not available to them as individuals.

'Stick it to her, mate,' said one of the boys, whose nocturnal consumption of pornography on the internet had convinced him that this was an appropriate comment to make to a couple in their thirties found fucking in the woods.

Charlie had reached his climax and was now on the downward spiral of self-loathing that characterised many of his sexual encounters with Flower and with other women in the past, something he had not thought to explore in any way but just accepted. However, here was someone to rail against and even better, teenage boys, a breed he hated and so did Flower.

Charlie rose to his feet, zipping himself up and managed to afford Flower some decency by kicking their rug towards her. Flower decided to put the blanket over her head like a prisoner facing the paparazzi and come out when Charlie had sorted it.

Charlie reached the pair who, rather than legging it, as is the wont of most teenage boys, decided to stand firm because this hippy bloke looked a little bit easy to knock down. Teenage boys they were, but through some miracle of feeding they were the size of men but the threat they posed failed to strike Charlie as anything less than minimal.

'Clear off,' tried Charlie, holding in reserve worse language, should it turn nasty.

'Go fuck yourself, hippy man,' said one of the boys and suddenly the sky seemed to darken as Charlie realised he had misjudged things and might get a kicking yet again. He held up his hands in a gesture of surrender.

'Look, I don't want any trouble,' he said. 'Just leave us alone, will you.'

'I think you need to be punished,' said the other boy, 'for shagging such an old dog in the woods.' Both of them bent over double at the hilarity of this remark and Charlie, a veteran of many aggressive encounters with the police, who after all weren't so different from these teenage boys, seized his chance and punched a fist in the general direction of the nearest boy's chin.

It connected and with a scream of pain, he staggered backwards.

'Do you want some too?' said Charlie to the other one, who was a massive coward and only buoyed on these occasions by his mate.

He began to cry.

'Now fuck off the pair of you,' he said, hoping they couldn't spot the fact that he was trembling.

The two ran off. Charlie turned to Flower. 'What about that then?' he beamed, full of self-congratulation.

Flower was crying.

'Babe, what's the matter?' said Charlie. 'We stuffed the fuckers.'

Flower had, however, been imagining what could have happened and in her mind had visualised some terrible scene of torture and death, her and Charlie at the mercy of the two boys.

All the way home on the bus Flower kept putting her hand in her handbag and feeling the gun. Little did Charlie know, but she had been so close to getting it out. She had wondered if she could have got away with just waving it, or whether they would have thought it was a replica gun and forced her to use it. In which case, had she shot one she would definitely have had to shoot the other, and that would have left her with only one bullet – and she wanted more than one.

Chapter 26

Jesus is three days old today, thought Martha. I wonder why my dad hasn't been in touch?

Ted stood at the open door for a long time watching Martha with his baby. She didn't notice him. She was so taken up with trying to get the breastfeeding thing right; she felt she must master it, if only to piss off stern midwife who was convinced she couldn't do it. Ted felt so fond of Martha for a few seconds that had she not done this awful thing to him of failing to reveal his paternity, he felt it could be all right between them.

Suddenly Martha became aware of Ted's presence and before she remembered the atmosphere that had prevailed last time they saw each other, was pleased to see him and felt an enormous amount of warmth towards him.

Ted's facial expression turned thunderous and set the agenda for the next few minutes.

'I'm sorry, Ted,' said Martha. 'I know I've done the

wrong thing and hurt you, but I was worried if I told you, you'd try and make me do something I didn't want to do.'

'And so that has allowed you to keep this whole affair to yourself. I don't suppose you'd ever have told me, unless I caught you on the day he was born,' said Ted. 'Well, I've seen a lawyer and I'm going to try and get custody.'

'You're joking,' said Martha cheerily but her heart swooped down to her boots.

'I'm not,' said Ted.

'On what grounds?'

'On the grounds that you're likely to be a rotten mother,' said Ted. 'I have seen your flat, you know, and many people would say that it's not fit for human habitation.'

'You bastard! You don't know anything about my mothering skills, do you?'

'I know enough,' said Ted, 'and I know that it's always the women who win in these cases but I'm going to do all I can to fight you. In fact, I may contact your father – I'm sure he'd help me.'

'No way,' said Martha. 'I refuse to give you permission to see him.'

'What do you think this is, some Victorian novel or something?' said Ted. 'Do you really think you can stop me seeing your dad? Don't be so bloody ridiculous. In fact,' he continued, 'once I dig up some stuff about you at work, I can't fail to win. You could have a drug problem.'

'I don't do drugs,' said Martha.

'You don't have to,' said Ted. 'I can make it *seem* like you do – and I can tell them you used to steal from me.'

'They'll just send me and the baby to prison and then I will definitely not see you,' said Martha.

'I don't know how you could do this to me,' said Ted. 'I thought we got on.'

'I'm sorry,' said Martha miserably. 'Anyway, where are *you* going to live with the baby if you get custody – in that smelly bedsit above the club?'

'Oh no, I've got big plans,' said Ted.

'The baby can't come and live with you. He'll cry all the time.'

'Why?' said Ted.

'Because of your ugly face,' said Martha.

It was a gamble, but Martha had always been able to make Ted laugh and she prayed for the second time that month that it would work.

Ted could hardly believe that in the middle of such an emotional debate, Martha had dared to do a Ted Is Ugly joke. He stared expressionlessly at her for a few seconds and then his great cavernous pitted face began to show signs of creasing and within less than a second he had thrown his head back and begun to laugh as if he would never stop.

'I'm sorry,' said Martha, 'I really am,' and she began to cry, and just for good measure, Jesus joined in.

One of the nurses who was doing the medicines wheeled her trolley into the room to find all of its occupants heaving out huge great sobs as if their respective worlds had ended.

From that moment onwards, it seemed to Martha that the whole situation became more bearable once Ted had been included in the family. She had asked to stay in hospital for a couple of days because she couldn't face going back to the flat yet, knowing that she had alienated most of the people she loved. However, once she and Ted had managed their reconciliation, she asked the medical staff to let her go. There was no reason to keep her there as Jesus was perfectly healthy and Martha was as healthy as she ever would be, which was not very.

Martha and Ted tried to have a discussion about the future but found they were not very good at it, and so they agreed that Ted would go back to the flat with Martha, stay for a couple of days, and then they would come to some sort of a decision.

Ted had made no reference to the fact that his son was called Jesus and Martha didn't allude to it for fear of pissing him off. Between them they packed Martha's stuff and Ted went off home to get a few belongings and dutifully arrived back to pick Martha up. As they sailed through the portals of the hospital, Martha pointed out Mr Cancer to Ted, in order to introduce him into the world of strange people whose lives collided with hers from time to time.

Junior, who had been waiting for the call to nick another car for the journey home, was surprised to hear the hustle and bustle going on in the flat next door and the cry of the baby. He stuck his head round the balcony, to be greeted by Ted's big face inches from his. It quite frightened him.

'Who might you be then, mate?' said Ted in the style of an East End villain, which he was quite good at.

'I'm Junior,' managed Junior. 'See you later, man,' and

scuttled back to his side, pondering the arrival of this big ugly bloke, and what it could mean.

Martha wasn't coping terribly well with Jesus. The breast-feeding still wasn't properly established and so the baby seemed pissed off and hungry all the time. Martha was knackered and frustrated and just wanted to sit in front of the telly and stare blankly at it and then go to bed. But on day three of Jesus's life she realised it would be a very long time before that sort of freedom was available to her.

'Look,' said Ted, 'I can tell you're knackered – why don't I take The Big J with me down the bookies in his pram and you have a bit of a kip and take it easy.'

Martha felt herself screech, 'Because a three-day-old baby should not be going in the fucking bookies,' and wondered why she had suddenly acquired the voice of a seventy-year-old witch.

'All right then,' said Ted, 'I'll just stroll round the park for an hour.'

Ted was not acquainted with the vicissitudes of life round Martha's way, as a stroll in the park usually meant at the least being pelted with dog shit by the seven year olds or being stabbed by the thirteen year olds.

Martha explained this to him, in her high-pitched witchy voice and they came to the compromise that Ted would put Jesus in the baby seat in his car, drive somewhere nice, get him out and take him for a walk then put him back in and be home within three hours – the amount of time Martha had decided could elapse between one feed and another without him starving to death.

Ted also noticed that the number of baby things accrued by Martha was minimal: a crappy frayed Moses basket that Flower used to keep her CDs in, a few little sleepsuits from Junior's mum and some blankets. He wondered what Martha had been doing with herself for all that time before the birth and felt like he was starting to get to know her a bit better and was somewhat perturbed by every little extra bit he was finding out.

Martha didn't want Ted to go out with Jesus, but she was so exhausted, she found it hard to put up any real resistance. She was beginning to realise just how fooled she'd been by all the pictures of motherhood painted in the media. As she looked at herself in the mirror, noting the rings under her eyes, nipples she could light the gas with and the raging tempest that used to be her vagina which now felt like a racecourse for horses with pointy hooves, she almost fell asleep on her feet.

Jesus and Ted meanwhile were having a wail of a time on the Embankment. Ted had decided to give Jesus his first real thrill and take him on that big revolving wheel on the South Bank of the River Thames. In their pod on the London Eye were a few mothers with their school-age children; the mums all looked at Ted in a horrified way when they saw what a very young baby he had with him. Could he be a paedophile who had stolen it from somewhere? they wondered. Perhaps he was an extra in some play in the West End and the baby was a prop. As far as they could tell, the baby was quite attractive so Ted couldn't possibly be a blood relative.

Oblivious to all this speculation, poor Ted nodded at everyone in a good-natured fashion, making the women clutch protectively at their children, who found this very irritating since they had far more idea of what a paedophile was than their mothers did and could tell that Ted was a good bloke and no threat to them.

Back at home, Martha furiously burrowed her head under the pillow, willing herself to go to sleep in the few precious hours she had been given. Jesus was up all night squawking and complaining and therefore, as the book said – Martha had finally taken a look at it – it was important to get some sleep while you could. What Martha didn't realise was that this was the dreaded *third day* – only vaguely alluded to in the books for fear of its huge impact, and underplayed by everyone except the new mother experiencing it, or the partner or friend on the receiving end.

Martha finally gave up on sleep and did something her father had always told her *not* to do – she turned the telly on in the middle of the day. There was an item about children's clothes and within seconds Martha had collapsed into a raging torrent of weeping and sadness which she found impossible to comprehend as this just wasn't her. She switched to another channel, which was showing a documentary about a couple getting married, and this only made her worse. This is absolutely bloody ridiculous, she thought, sobbing her heart out. Finally she changed to another channel on which a very dull-looking bloke was explaining something about trigonometry, but there was a pathos in his movements and the way he was dressed that lifted Martha's distress to ever greater heights. She lay on the chair, snot flying everywhere, each fiery vein in her eyes red and bulbous, and her chest heaving out great racking sobs of despair, completely perplexed as to why this was happening.

Had Ted any idea that this was going on, he would sensibly have run as fast as he could in the other direction until the fourth day dawned. But poor old Ted had only glanced at a new mothers' magazine article in the newsagents and this didn't really give a complete picture. So he returned like an innocent smiling child into the hall of the Mountain King, unaware that a savaging of monstrous proportions was about to hit him.

No sooner had he got the pram into the hall containing a peacefully sleeping Jesus than Martha screeched at the top of her voice whilst aiming the nearest thing to hand at him – a heavy shoe. The content of her outburst went as follows:

'Ted, you fucking arsehole, you're not fit to be a father you piece of slime, get out, go and hang yourself, you hulking great piece of shit, I hate you I hate you I hate you!'

Ted, who had left Martha on the lowest level of screeching, was speechless that after three hours' relaxing time she had managed to crank herself up to this height. Something in the back of his head told him to keep calm and that this wouldn't last, whereas another little voice kept prodding him, saying, 'She's like this all the time, mate. You don't really know her.' He sank into a chair.

Bad move. Martha launched herself at him like a nuclear-powered sack of potatoes.

'How dare you! How dare you!' she screamed as if sitting down could be equated with torturing an animal and eating its vital organs.

'What have I done?' asked poor helpless Ted.

This was the cue for Martha to launch into another tirade about Ted's resemblance to an axe murderer, and in the end he was forced to join Martha's screeching society to get his point across.

'*What the fuck have I done?*' he shouted in a voice that could be heard several flats below.

Martha could only keep tapping her watch furiously with her finger but with such force Ted feared she might break it. 'Ten minutes!' she screamed. 'Ten minutes! I thought you'd been murdered and the baby had been kidnapped!'

It dawned on Ted that this was all about him being late and he wondered what Martha would do if he really did something wrong. He decided to try and play the conciliator.

'Look, sweetheart,' he said, and Martha just collapsed into tears on the chair again.

'No one's ever called me that,' she wailed. 'Do you mean it?'

Ted knew if he said, 'No,' he would be killed and he kind of did mean it anyway. Amazingly, Jesus slept through this verbal hurricane, leading Martha to believe that he must be in a coma.

'Fucking hell, Ted, let's take him down the hospital,' she said.

Thankfully at that moment, the community midwife knocked on the door.

Chapter 27

The community midwife was called Tangerine and should have been related to Flower, so similar were their backgrounds. Born in the sixties to a couple who had conceived her at the Isle of Wight festival, they had chosen 'Tangerine' because it was their favourite fruit, colour and half a band name at the time. 'Tan', as she called herself, just had to put up with it; in fact, she'd developed a bit of a comedy routine because people always asked her what Tan was short for, and she delivered it with the weariness of the long-serving circuit comic who has never made it on to telly. Tangerine, as the psychology books would predict, given her background, had a conservative approach to childcare and a horror of babies being thrown into rucksack-type affairs and carried off round the world when they were obviously desperate for a routine. She did her round amongst the council flats of South London, moving from one single mother to another, to families of children with several different fathers and on to homes where drugs, alcohol and violence were high on the list of domestic pastimes, with the pained expression of a constipated Madonna, as though all these people were doing it deliberately to get at her personally.

So when Ted answered the door, unattractive as he was, poor sod, Tan could at least see from the way he was dressed that something approaching respectability clung to him and breathed a sigh of relief. Then she entered the flat and saw that chaos was king and poor Martha, hardly even aware that one bosom was poking out, sat hunched in the corner of the settee, ravenously devouring a bowl of bran to try and get yet another sluggish part of her body moving.

'Tea?' said Ted and Tan stipulated an ordinary bog standard cup of the cheap non-scented variety which made Martha warm to her immediately. Tan had spent too many years pouring the vile leaf tea of one inappropriate shrub or another down her throat to take pot luck any more.

When Ted returned with the tea and more types of biscuits than Tan had ever seen in one tin, she relaxed even more, and looking at the sort-of-well-suited couple, said, 'Well, how's it going?'

Martha and Ted said, 'Shit,' and 'Great,' at exactly the same time and so began Tan's job of the great unravelling of the emotional epicentre of the earthquake that is a new baby. She started on Martha, as she had always felt that if she could get the mother on her side the rest would fall into place and she had to do it quickly as she only had eight days left of her allotted ten to establish The Tan

Dynasty before some badass health visitor hoved into view with her liberal views and her over-relaxed structure.

'Just tell me how it's been,' she said to Martha in a brisk but kindly way, enough anyway to set Martha weeping again.

'It's been hard,' said Martha, gathering up Jesus from his cot and snuggling him to the bosom that wasn't sticking out. 'I love him to death but I just feel like I don't know what to do with him. He's starving hungry most of the time and it kills me to feed him, but in the hospital they said I shouldn't give him any formula milk and I should stick at it, but it's like being tortured. Ted and me were up all night, weren't we?'

'Oh yes,' said Ted, managing in those two simple words to convey the overwhelming pain of the experience.

'And sometimes,' Martha went on, 'I know I shouldn't, but I feel like I'm a big blob of nothingness only here for Jesus to feed off.'

'Who?' said Tan, thinking, Surely I misheard that?

'Oh just a silly family joke,' said Ted and Martha concurred.

'Well,' said Tan, 'I'm sure you won't feel any better if I tell you that most new mothers feel like this, like they are floating unanchored in an unfamiliar sea, and need to be tied down – and the way to do that is to try and impose a bit of order on your day, even if it's only regular mealtimes or putting Je— your baby down for his sleep at the same time.'

Martha produced a packet of crisps from somewhere and began to munch them.

'And stop eating crap if you're breastfeeding,' said Tan who, although she didn't march with the Breastfeeding Brownshirts, thought if Martha was going to try it, she might as well do it properly.

'Don't worry too much about housework either,' said Tan, even though she had already realised that housework had never been a priority in this flat. Tan took Jesus from Martha and had a look at the various important bits.

'Happy with changing, bathing and all that?' she said to Martha.

'Oh, can I have a bath yet?' said Martha.

'I meant the baby,' said Tan.

Ted pissed himself laughing at this and Tan thought what a nice bloke he was, even if his face let him down really badly in the first-impressions department.

'More tea, Midwife?' said Ted and Tan nodded, feeling very comfortable in this rather messy highrise with these two friendly incompetents and their poor unsuspecting baby.

There was a loud frantic knock on the door. Ted answered it. It was Flower and she looked in a state. Ted was only just getting to know Martha's friends and naturally there had been very little time or inclination on Martha's part to give him the rundown on them as they had either been exhausted, marvelling at Jesus's face and appendages or laughing hysterically when Ted tried to change Jesus and got a mouthful of urine as he failed to realise that a tiny baby penis is a bit of a water pistol, unless controlled.

'Are you all right, Flower?' said Martha who, even through

the fog of new motherhood, had detected that her friend was emotionally charged.

'Yes, but Sarah's not,' said Flower. 'I came round, I didn't want to talk on the phone about it. I knew you'd be in.'

She was aware that the dynamic in the house had changed since the arrival of Ted and wondered if she was free to blurt out anything she wanted to in his presence or whether they had to play Boyfriend's-Here-Keep-It-Clean, a game Martha had initially been hopeless at and had had to be taught by Flower, after shrieking across the room at a party to Flower and Charlie, who'd just got together: 'Hey, Flower, do you remember when you were hitchhiking in France and you fucked those two brothers from that pig farm?'

'Tan, Flower, Flower, Tan,' said Ted, trying to do the introductions before Flower launched into her tirade about what Martha guessed might be Sarah's latest drama.

'Hi Tan,' said Flower. 'It's Tangerine, I guess, is it?'

'Well yes,' said Tan. 'How on earth did you know?'

'Well, being a "Flower" has enabled me to sniff out a hippy name at twenty paces,' said Flower. 'And which pop festival were you conceived at?'

Tan laughed. 'Isle Of Wight. You?'

'Nothing so romantic,' said Flower. 'A squat in Kennington.'

'Anyway,' said Tan, 'I won't interfere any more, you've obviously got things to talk about. Nice to meet you and if you ever set up a support group, let me know.'

'I'll walk you down,' said Ted, who was just being nice,

but Martha felt the slightest of twinge of what – jealousy? Surely not! How on earth could she be a potential possessor of this great lummox of a man to the exclusion of other beasts of the field that might want to have a go on him? She put it down to hormones and turned to Flower.

'Tell me,' said Martha, somewhat sarcastically, 'Sarah and Billy – not getting on, are they? He's never been very nice, has he?'

'Don't take the piss,' said Flower. 'This is serious.'

She thought that Martha seemed strangely distracted, and although she was not the world's best listener, at least Flower had always been able to get Martha to focus on a good story if it had all the hallmarks of a soap opera – which the Sarah and Billy saga certainly did. What Flower did not realise, and what Martha would have strenuously denied because she was as yet unable to see it herself, was that Martha was very subtly taking on the mantle of motherhood, because it is impossible not to unless you are either emotionally damaged in some way, or you didn't really want a baby in the first place.

For the rest of her life Martha would carry with her this slight lack of concentration on what anyone else was doing; a constant small percentage of her attention permanently focused on her child or children. And Flower would just have to put up with it until she had children herself and did the same thing. Until that time she would just be irritated by it.

Martha picked up Jesus and started to feed him as best

she could, being extra clumsy because she was performing in front of someone.

'Oh, how did the gig go the other night?' she asked, and although Flower really felt very strongly that she should get onto the latest in the Billy and Sarah drama she couldn't resist talking about her stand-up.

'The heckler guy was there again and I'm beginning to get a bit bloody scared, if I'm honest,' she said.

'Saw old Tangerine into her car,' shouted Ted, coming through the front door, then seeing that Flower and Martha were in discussion and that Jesus must be asleep or feeding as his only three modi operandi at the moment were crying, eating and sleeping, he went into the kitchen to wash up and listen to some sport on the radio.

'How's it going with . . . ?' said Flower, inclining her head towards the kitchen.

'All right, I think,' said Martha. 'I can't do it for six weeks though, and I feel I should as we've only done it once in our whole relationship and I'm even having trouble remembering that. Anyway, I'll tell you more when we're on our own.'

'All right,' said Flower. 'Anyway, this gig the other night – God, the compère was shit and pissed, you'll never guess what he did when—'

Flower's mobile rang and seeing it was Sarah, she answered it. The conversation was brief and annoyingly opaque for Martha, who could tell that things were worse and that something had happened, peppered as Flower's responses were with a selection of 'Oh fucks' and 'my Gods'.

Flower finished by saying, 'All right, I'll see you there. Yeh, Sar, I'm sure that'll be fine. Don't worry.'

'Well?' said Martha.

'She's only gone and walked out on him,' said Flower. 'I can't believe it. There's absolutely nothing for us to sort out now.' This was said with some regret. 'It's what we always wanted to happen, thank God – what about that, eh?'

'She'll be back with him in two days,' said Martha matter-of-factly.

'Oh, don't be such a bloody pessimist,' said Flower. 'We can spirit her off, do that thing they do with people who have joined weird religions, sort of deprogramme her.'

'I do have the slight problem of a three-day-old baby here, you know,' said Martha.

'Oh sorry,' said Flower, 'but he does seem to sleep for quite a bit and Ted can have him for the odd hour, can't he? Hey, and guess what too?' She looked at Martha and said in a high stage whisper, 'I've got a gun.'

Martha sat up and Jesus fell off her breast and started to cry. Martha tried to reattach him.

'You are joking,' she said.

'No, I'm not,' said Flower. 'I'm going to point it at him and scare him.'

'Point what at who?' said Ted, coming into the room.

'Oh, I was telling her about Jesus's weeing feats,' said Martha, shocked that her spongy brain had managed to come up with something and even more shocked by what Flower had just told her.

'Anyway,' Flower said, 'I'd better be going – you know, to get Sarah.'

'But you haven't told me what's happened,' said Martha.

'I haven't got time,' said Flower. 'I'll call you later. See you, Ted,' she added. 'Bye, Jesus,' and she was gone.

'Nice to see your friend, was it?' said Ted who, if he'd had any inkling about the content of their conversation, would have worn a very different expression on his face. 'Come here, my son,' he said, picking Jesus up from Martha's lap and holding him aloft, looking up at him with a smile as wide as his suit. 'How are you, my lovely, lovely little one?' he said, and started to laugh with what he thought to himself must be pure joy.

Jesus responded by vomiting and pretty much hitting the target of Ted's open joyous mouth. Martha, ever the supportive mother and partner, began to laugh, but the effort of trying not to resulted in a volcano of hilarity which Ted, even though he was on the point of throwing up himself, felt he could not avoid joining in.

When it had all calmed down and they sat in front of the telly with pizza and chips, not having taken Tan's advice to junk the junkfood very seriously, Ted turned to Martha and said, 'Do we really have to call the poor little fucker Jesus?'

Martha, who had just been waiting for a get-out clause that wouldn't imply weakness on her part, was overjoyed.

'Oh all right,' she said, trying to contain her delight, 'but unfortunately my dad will be really pleased and he'll be round here pestering us, you know, and trying to poke his nose in.'

'I don't give a toss,' said Ted, 'as long as we aren't respon-sible for the little blighter getting his head kicked in in the playground, like I did.'

'Why, was Ted a particularly weird name in your school?' said Martha.

'It wasn't me name,' said Ted, 'it was me fucking phizog.'

'Your fucking what?' said Martha.

'Phizog,' said Ted. 'You know . . . face.'

'What language is that and from what era does it come, old man?' said Martha.

'You cheeky cow,' said Ted, 'I'm only eleven years older than you.'

'So how do you think we're getting on?' said Martha, out of the blue. 'Out of ten?'

'Ooh, I'd say about a seven,' said Ted. 'How about you?'

'About a two,' said Martha, and Ted jerked his head up to see that she was smiling.

'I don't half fancy a—' he stopped.

'A what?' said Martha.

'You know,' said Ted.

'But it's not safe, I don't think,' said Martha, very strongly seized by a similar desire. 'Oh fuck it, let's have a go. Just go easy round . . .' and finding herself strangely coy. 'Oh, you know.'

So there on the carpet, in front of the telly with the recently de-named Jesus bawling his head off indignantly, Martha and Ted had a go at some form of sex which involved hands and mouths far more than it did a certain orifice. It was hot, frantic, sticky, funny and immensely enjoyable and set Martha off weeping again, as Ted lay exhausted on the carpet wondering whether she was going to cry like this on a regular basis for the rest of her life.

Chapter 28

Flower met Sarah in the pub and it seemed so strange that Martha wasn't there.

The first of many meetings without her, Flower thought, although in the summer she supposed they could all meet up in the garden. Fresh air and breezes weren't really Martha's thing, but from now on they would have to be unless she achieved the title of The One Mother In London Quite Happy For Her Child To Do Passive Smoking.

Sarah had very heavy eye make-up on and looked like a panda but Flower didn't realise that she actually looked like a panda underneath as well. Much to Charlie's reluctance, she had offered to let Sarah sleep at their flat until she found something more permanent, but after what Martha had said, she wondered whether the split would be fleeting and fragile.

Sarah was a little bit dubious about sleeping at Flower's, which showed she had not quite been taken over by the madness of the heartbroken woman, or she would have slept in a wheelie bin. She thought the flat was probably unhygienic and full of cockroaches, so made a mental note not to sleep on the floor if at all possible.

'So what happened?' Flower's voice interrupted her musing.

'Well,' said Sarah, 'I went for the big one, for a complete makeover, came home hoping it might make a difference to our lives and the bastard laughed at me.'

Flower, not familiar with the concept, had to ask what a makeover involved, considering Sarah had a really bad haircut and her skin was the worst Flower had ever seen it.

'So you decided to leave him because he didn't like it?' she said incredulously.

'Oh shit no,' said Sarah. 'No, it all went off after that.'

'How?' said Flower, who felt so pleased she had never had a relationship like this and now never would.

'I shouted at him and hit him, he hit me back, I locked myself in the bathroom, he broke the door down, I hit him with a chair, he hit me with the towel rail, I kicked him in the bollocks, he threw me into the wall, I scratched him with my nails and he kicked me,' said Sarah, starting matter-of-factly and finishing tearfully.

'Oh Sarah, I'm so sorry,' said Flower. 'You poor thing, did you call the police?'

'Oh Christ no,' said Sarah. 'They don't give a toss and anyway I'd probably change my mind about it all before the first form was filled in.'

'It's your flat,' said Flower. 'Why don't you get him to move out?'

'Great idea,' said Sarah. 'I'm sure if I wagged my finger at him he'd go really easily.' She started to cry again.

'Look, let me get you a drink and we'll make a plan,' said Flower.

At the bar, she phoned Charlie and said, 'I'll be back soon with Sarah, is that still all right?'

'S'pose so,' said Charlie, who was thinking rather ungraciously of the limits it would put on his sexlife if Sarah was quivering with tears on the sofa. He very generously, he thought, neglected to mention this.

Flower wrinkled her nose, as the man next to her at the bar smelled unpleasantly cheesy. She looked at him: he seemed vaguely familiar and she suddenly realised that the cheesy chappie buying a large sherry was the Reverend Brian Harris. He obviously didn't recognise her, and maybe she should have left it that way, but something made her say hello to him.

He turned, a sneer ready on his face. 'Yes, and who might you be?' he said.

'I'm Flower, Martha's friend,' she said. 'We met in the maternity ward at the General.'

'Oh yes,' he said distastefully, as though he had met a decomposed, talking rodent. 'And how is the girl?'

'Sorry, which girl?' said Flower, having briefly lost the plot.

'My daughter, of course,' he said. 'You young people have no concentration.'

At that point Flower's mobile rang. Normally she would

have left it, but some instinct told her to answer. It was Steve Marchant, who ran the biggest chain of comedy clubs in the country.

'Hi, Flower,' he said, 'Steve Marchant here. I'm afraid Muff's had to pull out of our late show at the Comedy Store on Sunday night – just wondered if you'd be available. Three hundred for twenty minutes, OK?'

Flower could not contain her delight and began to jump up and down shouting, 'Fuck, you're joking!' at the top of her voice.

Steve laughed and said, 'See you soon, then.'

The Reverend Brian looked as if he had been hit with an axe. 'Language please,' he said. 'And now I really must be getting home.'

'Aren't you going to see Martha?' said Flower.

'Not if she persists in using that sacrilegious name, no,' said the Rev.

'She's thought better of that,' Flower told him, having no idea whether she actually had or not. 'Please go and see her, she really loves you, you know,' and wondered why she had an image at that moment of Martha punching her in her head.

'Was that Martha's dad?' said Sarah, as Flower sat back down.

'Yeh,' said Flower. 'Fancy him or what?' And then decided, given the solemnity of the proceedings, that was inappropriate and added, 'Sorry.'

'Come on,' said Sarah. 'Let's go before Billy comes in here looking for me.'

*   *   *

Billy was at home crying with his head in his hands wondering why it had all turned out so badly and why he was such a bastard to women. He knew he was pathologically unable to show vulnerability and was coming to the realisation that if he did not change, he would never be able to make a relationship last. A little voice in his head said to him that he could not change without help and it was the first time that it had occurred to him to think about that. But with any problem that he needed to sort out, there was always a period of stubbornness and reluctance before he took any action and therefore Billy told himself that he would leave it a few days, let the fog in his head clear and then patch things up with Sarah and sort himself out. He knew Sarah loved him and although he knew, also, that he had weakened their bond, he felt fairly confident he could strengthen it again.

The problem with going to stay with a friend when you are emotionally turned upside down is that you should ideally be in your own environment in order to be able to make sensible decisions about your future. Sarah, having been in Flower and Charlie's flat for approximately seven minutes, had already made the decision to go back to Billy if he asked. She realised, looking in her make-up bag, that she had forgotten to bring her eyelash-curlers, a piece of equipment so essential to her equilibrium that she decided to go back to the flat and get them.

'You are joking, aren't you,' said Flower.

'No, I really need them,' said Sarah. 'Really really really, Flower.'

'Well, if you *really* need them, Charlie will go,' said Flower.

Charlie gave Flower his, 'In the kitchen, now!' look beloved of couples who have guests but need to slag each other off.

'Just going to the loo,' said Flower, leaving the room and two minutes later Charlie got up. 'Just putting the kettle on,' he said. 'Raspberry leaf tea?'

Sarah, who unlike Martha knew everything there was to know about pregnancy and its effects, said, 'No thanks, Charlie, I'm not trying to elasticate my vagina to give birth. I'll have a coffee, please.' She knew this was just an excuse for Charlie and Flower to reconvene in the kitchen and sobbed silently to herself, thinking of the times she and Billy would do the very same.

In the kitchen Charlie said, 'No fucking way am I turning up on that tosser's doorstep and asking for pissing eyelash-benders.'

'Curlers,' said Flower. 'Oh please, Charlie.'

'No,' said Charlie. 'You'll have to go.' He waited for Flower's next protest but it didn't come.

'All right,' she said. 'I'll go,' thinking she could give Billy a fright and warn him off Sarah.

Of course, the nearer she got to Billy and Sarah's flat the more ridiculous it all seemed to her, and she couldn't quite believe that she and Dick Knob had actually gone to that place and got that gun quite so easily. Charlie's stories of Albanian gangsters looking for contracts to kill people for as little as three hundred quid must be true then. She phoned Martha for moral support, not a great idea given Flower was riding her bike and Martha was difficult to hear.

Flower said, 'Hi Martha, I'm going to collect something from Sarah's for her and I'm going to threaten Billy with this gun I've got.'

'Ted, hold his head, not his bleeding leg, he'll drown – sorry, what was that?' said Martha.

'I'm going to wave the gun at Billy,' shouted Flower.

'Don't be silly,' said Martha. 'No, not you, Ted. That's fine.'

'Can you come and help?' Flower bawled.

'No, of course not,' said Martha, 'but phone me as soon as you've seen him. You wanker, I told you not to do that!'

'Pardon?' said Flower, then she hit the kerb and fell off.

Flower wasn't injured, yet when she thought of the enormity of what she was about to do, she found herself wishing she had been badly hurt and taken to hospital so she didn't have to go through with it. Somehow she ended up at the entrance to Denbigh Mansions and with a trembling hand rang the bell. Her mobile rang at the same moment, which made her jump, and when Billy's voice sounded through the intercom all he heard was a high-pitched, strangled noise.

It was Charlie on the mobile. 'Are you all right?' he said, realising he had been cowardly sending Flower.

'Go away!' she hissed. 'I haven't been in yet,' and into the intercom, 'Hello Billy, it's Flower. Can I talk to you?'

Billy told himself to keep calm and accede to whatever

demands Flower might make or Sarah might make through her. He buzzed the door open and Flower climbed slowly up the stairs where Billy stood at the top looking absolutely huge.

'Don't tell me,' he said. 'She wants her eyelash-curlers.'

Flower was astounded that Billy had a feminine side and kept telling herself that he had been very nice to Martha.

'Hang on,' said Billy, 'I know where they are,' and he disappeared into the bedroom, reappearing within seconds with a smile on his face, saying, 'Here we are. Send her my love, won't you?' as though Sarah was just going on a long weekend with the girls rather than having been thrown round her own flat by him, causing her to run away.

Flower stood still for a very long time, trying desperately to decide on a course of action.

'Anything else?' said Billy, who had decided at all costs not to ask Flower to beg Sarah to come back to him, and had vowed not to threaten any of Sarah's friends. He was so charming that Flower, to her complete shame, found herself fleetingly wondering if Sarah was exaggerating it.

Billy coughed. 'Is Martha well?' he enquired, as if pushed to make polite conversation.

'Fine,' said Flower and thought, I can hardly wave a fucking gun around and tell him to watch it now.

'Right then,' she said. 'I'd better be going. Shall I give Sarah a message?'

'You can say I know we both let it get a bit heated,' said Billy, 'and I for one am very sorry.'

'OK,' said Flower hesitantly. 'See you then.'

Suddenly she was on her bike and on the way home, the video of the incident in her head having been completely erased by the reality. She called Charlie. 'Yeh fine,' she said into her mobile. 'See you in ten minutes.'

Then she called Martha. 'Couldn't fucking do it.'

'Thank Christ,' said Martha. 'Hoped you'd come to your senses.'

'Oh thanks,' said Flower. 'Cheers. Oh, by the way,' she added, 'saw your dad in the pub and did a terrible thing. Told him you weren't calling Jesus, Jesus. I think he might come round.'

'He's already here,' said Martha.

'Oh, right you are. I'll be off. What are you going to call him then?' she added, almost as an afterthought.

'Got to go,' said Martha annoyingly. 'Talk to you later.'

'I've got a gig at the—' started Flower then realised she was talking to air.

Martha's dad was indeed sitting there looking marginally less grumpy than usual. He had called Pat from a phone box to tell her the good news and Pat had been so relieved, having felt awful about just trotting after him at the hospital.

'So, what are you going to call him?' said the Rev.

They had all reached this point because the Rev had arrived in the middle of a screaming row about the name. Flower had really landed them in it, having to come up with a name on the spot. Ted wanted to call the baby Melvin after his father but Martha told him that no way was any child of hers going to have a sex-offender's name. She herself wanted to call him Jude – at which Ted remarked that his son wasn't going to have a girl's name. A furious, noisy statemate had been reached, coinciding with the Reverend's arrival. The Rev Brian stood grinning on the doorstep, thinking to himself what a relief it was to finally hear someone giving Martha as good as they got.

'So what *are* you going to call him?' repeated the Rev, as Ted and Martha stared with pure hatred at one another.

'Melvin,' said Martha.

'Jude,' said Ted, and they fell towards each other and laughing, kissed slurpily.

'Thank you. That was all I wanted to know,' said Rev Brian, getting up and heading towards the door.

Chapter 29

Sarah couldn't see herself holding out much longer at Flower and Charlie's flat. There was an alien feel to their lifestyle that made her realise what she was missing about home: the familiarity, the comfort, the ordinariness which, balanced against the odd black eye now and again, surely won out. She knew she was underplaying the whole situation in her mind, and that things must have been bad to drive her from her home, but even so the memories faded and were replaced by longing.

Charlie and Flower did their best, bought breakfast cereal that they wouldn't feed to their worst enemy, a tabloid newspaper that made Flower feel physically nauseous to have in the house, and Charlie even kept his mouth shut about Sarah's incredibly daft ideas on politics. However, the pair of them were beginning to feel the strain and after a miserable few days in which Sarah had gone zombie-like to work in the mornings and returned looking even less animated at night if that were possible, they decided to cheer her up by taking her on a demonstration on the Saturday, followed by a gig in the evening, and then to Flower's big important gig at the Comedy Store on the Sunday.

Sarah did her best to look enthusiastic, but couldn't help drooping. She so desperately wanted to go and hide in her room but her only respite in the small flat was to go and sit on the toilet; she had gone out to walk aimlessly round the local park, but several approaches by professionally disturbed people and comments on her appearance had put her off. As time passed, she did begin to feel a glimmer of excitement about the demonstration. This was something she had never done in her life, because every time something with a tenuous political connection came on TV, her mind ceased to function. She had, however, seen fighting in the streets between Charlie lookalikes and the police so she wondered if it might give her the chance to sublimate some of her anger and have a bloody good scream because dragging herself round the shops after work every night didn't seem to be doing the trick.

Flower felt sorry for Sarah and increasingly aggressive towards Billy and the rather empty sad person he had created. Worst of all, she felt angry because she knew how fiercely Sarah wanted him back.

Flower was nervous about the big gig coming up on the Sunday, but was pleased she had a small gig to practise at in Kent before it happened. Coincidentally it was in Maidstone, Sarah's home town and they were going to meet her mum, Connie, at the pub where the show was on. According to Sarah, Maidstone was the equivalent of the Deep South of America and Flower would have more than enough of a challenge from the local toothless pig-stickers, who liked nothing better than frying London comics.

At last, it was the end of the week and Sarah sat with Flower and Charlie in the tiny sitting room and prayed they would turn on the rather battered telly and let her slump in front of it. No such luck. In an attempt to entertain her and keep her mind off her pain, they had invited a male friend of theirs called Sim to come round. Sim was a story-teller and had been travelling abroad for six months. He had called Flower and Charlie to tell them he had picked up lots of new stories and promised to come over for an evening of chat and food.

In the toilet for some brief respite from what Charlie told her was called 'world music' Sarah started to ask herself what the fuck a grown-up bloke was doing telling stories. She wanted to call Billy on his mobile and have a laugh about it, because that was one of the things they did well together. She wished he would phone her, but had no idea that Billy was playing the long game and steadfastly resisting any kind of contact to reel her back in.

Someone knocked on the door of the toilet and Sarah jumped. 'Ych?' she shouted.

'Sim's here,' said Flower. 'Are you coming out?'

'In a minute,' said Sarah, steeling herself for the weird-ness that Charlie and Flower had lined up for her.

Flower had phoned Martha and asked her if she, Ted

and the baby wanted to come round and meet Sim.

'I'd rather make a hole in my stomach, pull my entrails out with laundry tongs and fry them while they're still attached,' was Martha's answer, with poor Ted holding the baby and saying in a conciliatory fashion in the background, 'There's no need to be quite so direct.'

When Flower grumpily reported Martha's answer because she didn't have a huge sense of humour about their friends, Sarah had to bite her lip to stop herself laughing and wished herself round at Martha's flat living in cheery squalor, but she knew that would have palled by now too. So she sighed a big sigh, put something approaching a smile on her face and entered the land of storytelling.

It was much as expected. In Sarah's later description to Billy: 'He talked a load of bollocks about pixies and that for fucking hours,' whereas Flower had enthused to someone at work about Sim's 'amazing grasp of the world Zeitgeist and his cherishing of the human race'. Sarah medicated herself with wine throughout the evening and therefore sailed close to damming poor Sim's flow on a number of occasions with stifled giggles and the occasional, 'for fuck's sake!' Because she was sleeping in the main room, she couldn't go to bed until they did and Charlie rolled joint after interminable joint. Sarah had tried it once many years ago and it had made her giggly and slightly hungry but she thought she might as well have a go, as anything that made her slightly less connected to reality was a blessing.

'And now a couple of tales from Tasmania with a sting in the tail,' said Sim.

Sarah braced herself as Sim began. 'In the land of Tasmania, good and evil had fought a constant battle over thousands of years. The good people of Tasmania lived together in harmony on the mountain while the low, hairy, vile people of the plains lurked at the forest edge, carrying off the occasional good person's daughter to ravish and take into slavery.

'One day the good people realised they only had one beautiful daughter left, the daughter of the chief, and they resolved, much as they hated fighting, to defend her to the last life. Sure enough the low hairy people ('Was Charlie one of them?' Sarah wanted to ask) crept to the village in the middle of the night and snatched the chief's beautiful daughter. The good people sprang from their beds and a great battle commenced until sure enough all the good people lay dead or dying and the chief of the low people carried away the sobbing daughter of the good chief. A tear fell on his neck as they ran and he changed in an instant into a snake and slithered away and that is how the Tasmanian Devil was born.'

Sim sat back with a smug look on his face.

'Hang on a sec,' said Charlie. 'The Tasmanian Devil's not a snake.'

'Whatever,' said Sim.

'Yeh, whatever,' said Charlie and handed Sarah a freshly rolled joint.

Sarah took a massive pull on it and nearly catapulted back through the wall.

'Christ Almighty, Flower,' she said hoarsely, 'that is some fucking blow, man.'

Flower, who was inured to its power and quite stoned, nodded absentmindedly and didn't think to try and contain this novice's intake. Sarah went remarkably quiet for about half an hour and when Flower asked her if she wanted herb tea, Sarah looked at her with an expression of pure malice and said, 'I am evil.'

'Oh dear,' said Flower, 'the double zero's got her.'

'Right,' said Sim, 'here's another really cool tale from Tasmania called "Why the Trees Don't Talk Any More".'

'I'm not Sarah any more,' said Sarah.

'Hey, chill babe,' said Sim. 'There might be something in this story for you.'

'Only my death would be any relief,' said Sarah.

'Fucking hell,' said Sim, looking worriedly at Flower and Charlie. ''Fraid I can't oblige you there, little princess.'

Then Sim, never one to be too concerned by the mental state of his audience – for if he had, he wouldn't have had an audience – ploughed on regardless.

'In Tasmania,' he said, 'the trees used to talk to each other, man.'

Sarah began to cry.

'Yeh, I know it's beautiful, babe,' he said.

Sarah snarled like a wolf and this sent an alarm signal to Flower who was pretty stoned so it was as if the cry for help came down a very long cottonwool tunnel. Then Sarah began to howl.

'Yeh, carry on, delightful lady,' said Sim, 'there was wolves on this island. Glad you're joining in. Anyway, to continue the story,' he said, 'the trees would make love with words and their green branches would swoosh with anticipation . . .'

'You want a story?' said Sarah. 'Here's one for you, you boring hippy twat. It's the story of a little girl born into the shitty world of an ex-prostitute who was knocked up by a client and got her dates wrong, so missed out on having a legal abortion by two weeks. The illegal one failed so the baby arrived into a nasty little flat in an evil town and the order of the day for that little girl was to shut the fuck up while Mum's at work so the neighbours don't ring the social. A selection of boyfriends passed through: some of them hit the girl, some of them touched her up and some of them, she had to suck off.'

Sim looked bemused and Flower and Charlie's middle-class sensitivity showed on their faces.

'Sarah,' said Flower gently, 'you don't have to do this.'

Sarah ignored her. '. . . And then when she grew up the girl got away and met someone really handsome and intelligent and breathed a sigh of relief, until one day he hit her . . .' Sarah buried her head in her hands and began to sob.

'So what poor slag's that about?' said the ever-prescient Sim.

For once Charlie was puncher not punchee.

Sim was reluctantly ushered out of the door protesting that his best story so far from Zimbabwe about the witch-doctor's chickens, had been left unaired.

Flower lay Sarah down on the makeshift bed, put a

blanket over her and hoped she'd have a good night free of demons.

In the morning the flat looked immaculate; the dope had obviously had a bit of an odd effect as Sarah had cleaned it from top to bottom, dropping unconscious at about six o'clock in the morning.

'I took an aspirin for my headache,' she explained and Charlie kept quiet.

No one had done anything sensible like check the weather for the demo, so Sarah's wailing 'I don't know what to wear,' made Flower even more irritable than she already was.

'It's not like a party or a wedding,' she told her. 'You can wear what you like – express yourself through colours and fabrics.'

'But I like to be told what to wear, so I know,' said Sarah, whose lack of structure and security as a child ensured she now imposed a rigid routine on all her domestic chores and a system of coding her clothes that would defeat the most anal of obsessive compulsives. In the end Flower chose the least formal things she could find in Sarah's suitcase, all of which had been painfully pressed and folded.

'Will I need an umbrella?' said Sarah.

'Only to thump a pig with,' said Charlie cheerfully.

'Are there going to be animals there, then?' said Sarah. Charlie gave up and decided to leave well alone in Sarah's mind which to him seemed to be a vacuum with the odd bit of celebrity knowledge floating about in it.

Sarah, Flower and Charlie caught a bus up to the City to the prearranged meeting place. The atmosphere was relaxed and unthreatening although Charlie immediately pinpointed the troublemakers who would doubtless produce some medieval instrument of torture from their rucksacks and continuously bang it on the heads of policemen until they flew off.

The demo was at the vague behest of an umbrella organisation which covered a loose federation of eco-friendly groups brought together by the internet and with their main aim to destroy global capitalism. Unfortunately, no one in any of the organisations had worked out how this could be done properly so the groups were forced to gather at centres of global capitalism like the City of London where they were today and shout abuse in the vain hope that all the City boys on the dealing floors would suddenly see sense, stop washing for a bit and join their ranks and curtail their evil operations. Except it was a Saturday and the place was deserted bar protesters and police.

There was music, a few stalls selling food, lots of singing and dancing, and for once Sarah felt attracted to this world she had looked at from the sidelines for the past week.

'So it's not just dirty dogs on a rope, is it?' she said to Flower.

'No, it's not,' said Flower, who felt under pressure for some reason she couldn't put her finger on.

Sarah had assumed that as Flower was trying to be a comedian she would be funny all the time at home but was shocked to discover the opposite: Flower was akin to a pressure cooker, letting out little bits of steam here and there and often on the point of exploding. Sarah knew all about Flower's legendary PMT and why Charlie didn't have a dog which he had always wanted. Flower had explained that she would only kick it every month when she was stressed, and when Charlie looked at the way Flower treated *him* monthly, he was pleased they didn't have a dog as its poor arse would by now be concave.

Charlie and Flower were chatting when Sarah said, 'Hey, isn't that Martha and Ted coming with, er, what is he called?'

'Don't know,' said Flower. 'Hey, Martha!'

Martha had seen something about the demo on the local news and felt sure Charlie and Flower would go along, taking poor Sarah with them. It would be an opportunity to tell them Jesus's new name. Ted agreed, but was along on sufferance and once he saw the array of raggle-taggle hippies everywhere, part of him, and he put it down to his age, felt rather sorry for the minibuses of young policemen spotty and raw who sat waiting for crusty Armageddon.

Martha, Sarah and Flower all kissed and hugged, because this was the first time for a while that they had all been together. The place was starting to get more crowded and bustling so the naming ritual had to be done while there was still room and they could all hear. Martha got the baby out of his buggy and held him up like a trophy, which he didn't much like and started to grizzle.

'As you know, everyone, we couldn't agree on a name,' said Martha. 'I wanted Jude, Ted wanted Melvin after his dad. So we've decided to compromise and we would like you to meet . . .' there was a short pause '. . . Jelvin!'

This was followed by a long silence in which the entire population of the demo seemed to stand in openmouthed horror.

Bloody hell, that's worse than Jesus, thought Sarah.

'Only kidding,' said Ted. 'It's John.'

A sigh of relief spread over the group. Flower was still worried Martha might have done something stupid, like given John the middle name of 'The Baptist', but no, it was just good old John. Nobody had broached the fact yet that Ted ran a lap-dancing club and Flower wondered whether she should mention it.

'What do you think?' she asked Sarah. 'Should I say something to clear the air?'

'What, you mean ask him for a job?' said Sarah. 'I might do too, I'm bored shitless in that call centre.'

Flower stared into the chasm that was the gap between her and Sarah socially, culturally and, well, in every way.

'No, I didn't mean that, Sarah. I meant how unacceptable it is as far as women are concerned for these clubs to exist.'

'Oh, lighten up,' said Sarah. 'People don't care about that sort of shit any more.'

Perhaps they don't care about domestic violence any more, either, thought Flower but said, 'Well, they bloody should and I'm sick of it.'

'Oi grumpy,' said Sarah.

'Sorry,' said Flower. 'Forget it.' And she kept her mouth

shut, because she didn't want to get into a row with Ted on today of all days, a lovely sunny one with a happy band of protesters.

Unfortunately this didn't last long.

As the group stood round chatting, a missile hit Flower on the back of the head, 'missile' being the euphemism used in these scenarios for anything bigger and heavier than a bar of chocolate.

'Ow,' said Flower and looked down to see what the missile was. It was a quarter of a brick and she marvelled that it hadn't knocked her out. It seemed to have come from the area where the police were.

'The police have started something!' she screamed at Charlie above the music.

'Right,' said Charlie, 'they're not getting away with this,' and he pushed his way through the crowd towards the straggly police line, as were many other men dressed in exactly the same uniform as Charlie.

'Don't do anything stupid,' shouted Flower at Charlie's retreating back, which was a bit like shouting after a cat, 'Leave those mice alone, now won't you.'

Ted suddenly realised that his baby and Martha were in the middle of a riot just about to go off and he said to Martha, 'We'd better get going,'

Martha, temporarily forgetting that she had given birth a few days ago, was quite keen to get stuck in, calling him a spoilsport.

'Come on, let's go,' said Ted.

It was too late. The unrest had spread quickly and there

was no way out as the police had surrounded what they thought was the biggest group of troublemakers and, like sheepdogs herding sheep, were trying to force them down a side street where they could control them better, rough them up a bit and drag out the ringleaders.

Martha saw a few people attack McDonald's. 'Look at those stupid bastards,' she said, 'and I'm bloody starving.'

'They're fighting the influence of global capitalism,' said Flower.

'Well, standards have dropped in there recently. Maybe they need a wakeup call,' said Sarah.

'Come on, Martha,' said Ted, and tried to push the opposite way to the crowd; as he was such a big bloke, it started to work. Martha, John, Flower and Sarah trailed in his wake and after much shoving and cursing, with their nostrils assailed by unwashedness and hippy perfume, they reached the edge.

'Let me out, mate,' said Ted to a copper on the edge. 'I've got my family here and I'm worried they'll get hurt.'

'Should have thought of that before you joined the troublemakers,' said the policeman. 'Stay where you are.'

'Oh come on,' said Ted. 'We're caught up in this totally innocently.'

'Let us out please,' said Martha. 'I'm dying for a pee and I feel faint.'

'Shut it, slag,' said the copper.

This was too much for Ted and with his clenched fist propelled at some speed, the policeman was soon sprawled on the ground with no helmet, looking very angry.

Chapter 30

Ted was immediately swarmed over by a group of policemen on a mission, the mission being to uphold the honour of their colleague who had, rather too easily some felt, plummeted to the deck at the lightest of touches. Still, however hard Ted's touch had been it didn't matter because one by one they took it in turns to kick him.

Martha was overcome with shock by this behaviour being practised so openly. Rather naively she had imagined that, at the very least, the police would make an effort to pretend they weren't a bunch of thugs, but they didn't seem too bothered.

At one point, as blows were flailing down upon him, Ted received a few curt words in his ear to the effect that he was under arrest and would be taken down to the police station and dealt with. Ted sighed, aware that his arrival at that particular venue would probably involve another flurry of blows from Her Majesty's finest.

Martha tried bravely to reason with the policemen who had arrested Ted but as they weren't the sort of men who would support the idea of paternity leave and this was Martha's starting point, it seemed highly unlikely they would let Ted go home on the basis of being the father of a newborn baby.

Sarah amazingly found herself outraged, too. Given that she had lived her life in a right-wing tabloid cocoon of sanctimony, she had, up until now, refused to admit that bad police behaviour existed. As for more subtle concepts, like class differences, a little clock ticking in her head had started to count down to enlightenment. Billy's words rang in her ears, the putdowns, the swearing, the threats – and suddenly she saw him as a very successful policeman. Perhaps she should suggest a career-change. He might hit others instead of her. She joined in Martha's pleading to no avail and found herself addressing the big policeman as 'a cunt', not something he liked to be called and certainly a word Sarah would never have imagined herself using a week or so ago, particularly to a policeman.

'Well done,' said Martha, patting her on the back and temporarily forgetting that her man was buried underneath a sea of serge and about to be removed.

Suddenly the police sprang into action, lifted Ted up as though he was a great big coffin and ran with him to a van and delivered him into the back as though he was a big sack of shit in a great big coffin.

Martha, whose hormones were continuing to race around her body at almost the same rate as they had when she gave birth, burst into tears as Flower ineffectually shouted, 'Die, you pigs,' to the backs of the policemen and Sarah joined in sounding awkward but with a fair degree of gusto.

Suddenly Charlie appeared from nowhere licking an iced lolly as if he was on a day out at the seaside. Everyone looked at him aghast and he returned their look with a benign perplexed face.

'What?' said Charlie, and then he realised that Martha was crying, Sarah was redfaced and looked like she wanted a fight and Flower had her usual demonstration expression on, a mixture of bemusement and aggression.

'For Christ's sake, Charlie,' she said irritatedly. 'You've missed everything. They've taken Ted away.'

'That proto-fascist,' said Charlie. 'What did he do? Beat up a woman?'

Martha stopped crying. 'Fuck off, Charlie,' she said. 'He may not have your Glastonbury credentials but at heart he's a decent man.'

'Tell that to the junkie women with AIDS he employs in his lap-dancing club,' said Charlie.

'Oh grow up,' said Martha. 'They're all posh students raking in a fucking fortune.'

'They're exploited, man,' said Charlie.

John started to cry.

'Right, I'm off,' said Martha. 'Suppose I'd better find out what's happening with Ted.'

'I'll come with you,' said Sarah. 'I might talk to you about getting a job with Ted.'

'Sarah,' said Flower, 'what the hell are you thinking of?'

'Well, I've got the figure,' said Sarah, 'and I bet it's a fuck of a sight better than my present shitty job. Anyway, do I always have to have a politically cracked reason for you?'

'It's "correct",' said Flower.

'What will Billy say?' said Martha, before she could stop herself.

'I don't care,' said Sarah. 'Billy and I aren't together any more.'

Flower and Martha clapped and danced up and down on the spot. Charlie looked pleased too.

'Come on then,' said Martha to Sarah and off they went.

Flower and Charlie watched them go and the crowd seemed to part for them. Charlie shook his head. 'Should we talk her out of it?' he said, unthinkingly lighting a joint.

'Nah,' said Flower. 'I don't think you could.'

Just then, a policeman flew almost horizontally through the air at Charlie, rugby-tackling him to the ground. And that was how Charlie and Ted ended up sharing a rather small cell at the local police station.

The cell was packed. It contained two pickpockets who'd taken advantage of the crowds to see what they could drum up, a mentally ill hippy whose care in the community wasn't being managed very well, since he tended to drift towards any trouble that was going on, a man who had hit his girlfriend during an argument, and two teenage boys who had stolen a car and driven it round the fringes of the demo aiming an air rifle at anyone they didn't like the look of.

Charlie and Ted got themselves into a corner and tried to avoid any involvement with the madness going on around them.

As there wasn't much else to do, Charlie cast himself in the role of the father of the bride, interviewing Ted as to his suitability as Martha's partner. It was natural that Charlie should launch straight into the subject of the club that Ted ran, as he had spent so much of his life railing against this industry that he felt it his duty to try and take it apart brick by metaphorical brick.

'Women are just treated like objects, man,' opined Charlie, 'and you're encouraging that.'

'Look mate,' said Ted, exasperated and bruised and unfamiliar with the inside of a cell, 'I'm not arguing with you and yes, that's the way our society is, but isn't it better that if these places have to exist, that they are run by someone like me who's kind to the girls and makes sure they're safe.'

'So you don't perv them up then?' asked Charlie.

'No, I don't "perv them up" as you so charmingly put it,' said Ted. 'Come down one night and see.'

'Flower would never allow it,' said Charlie, with a very slight trace of regret.

'Bring Flower too,' said Ted.

Charlie guffawed loudly at this suggestion and imagined himself asking Flower, particularly when she had PMT. He shuddered.

'Has someone just walked over your grave?' said Ted.

'No, but they fucking would do if I ever asked them down a lap-dancing club,' said Charlie.

Ted laughed. 'I'll have a word with her,' he said.

'I hope they let us out by tonight,' said Charlie. 'Flower's got a gig in Maidstone, and it's her last one before she does her first proper night at London's top comedy club tomorrow. I really want to go and support her.'

'You'll be lucky,' said Ted. 'I reckon we're due a night in the cells.'

Charlie realised that being with big ugly Ted was protecting him, the puny scruffy old hippy, and for the first time in ages, he felt quite secure. Ted only had to look at the other guys in the room to warn them off and his great big body acted as a solid reassuring barrier during the night.

Flower and Martha had tracked Charlie and Ted down to the same police station on Flower's mobile and were told they would probably be released sometime in the morning when they had been processed.

They're not lumps of cheese, thought Flower to herself, and was then reminded of Charlie's old sandals that she could not persuade him to throw away.

'Shit,' she said aloud. 'We'll have to go to Maidstone on our own.'

'Wish I could come,' said Martha. 'I'll have to wait at home with John in case his dad is let out.'

Flower and Sarah noticed that Martha had a little glow about her and a catch in her voice as she mentioned Ted.

'Are you and Ted going to stay together?' said Flower.

'I don't know,' said Martha, 'but we're getting on well at the moment and he is gorgeous, isn't he?'

Flower and Sarah examined her face to see if she was taking the piss.

She wasn't.

'Right, I suppose we'd better make a move,' said Sarah. 'Shall we go home and get ready for this gig then?' She felt really weird about seeing her mum after so long.

Martha was feeling regretful that she couldn't spend the evening with Sarah and Flower as they used to do in the old days and, as they prepared to part on the other side of the river and go their separate ways, she got a taste of the way that her life would change now she had a child. The flexibility she once took for granted would be eroded the more she became committed to John and possibly to Greasy Ted.

She thought briefly about leaving John with Junior's mum next door and having one last night out with her two best friends but, strangely, found she didn't want to. She had lived the life that she wanted to live, and was ready now to settle down. She had travelled geographically, sexually and emotionally through a life full of craziness, melodrama and really good friends and laughs, and that was important to her. So when Flower and Sarah looked at her with concern, she genuinely meant it when she said, 'Look, Flower and Sarah, you go, have a bloody good night out and have a laugh. I'll be quite happy at home in front of the telly or a book. In fact, to be honest with you, I can't wait to lie down in the flat and not have to be constantly wondering what I'm going to wear, where I'm going to go, am I going to meet someone, have I got decent enough pants on, does my breath smell, should I have had a bath and am I ever going to meet someone who isn't a complete fucking tosser who pisses off after three months or treats me like shit.'

'So Ted's the one, is he?' said Sarah, aghast. She thought having an ugly boyfriend was like having herpes – you never mentioned it to anyone in company but secretly people knew, discussed it and felt very sorry for you.

As Flower and Sarah headed home, Flower realised how worried she was about the gig at the Comedy Store and also about the Maidstone gig tonight. As she looked through her list of the new jokes she was going to try out, in her and Charlie's room, she wondered why she was feeling so edgy. She had an upset stomach which was never the best condition to have when you are doing a gig because the facilities in comedy clubs are not of the highest calibre, and worrying that you will shit yourself doesn't sit very well with the fact that you are metaphorically shitting yourself.

Sarah was perched on the rough old sofa in the sitting room thinking about Billy, from whom she hadn't heard since leaving the flat. Seven days had passed, and although she knew objectively that he was a violent man and that his violence was exclusively directed at her, the feelings of revulsion and fear had been diffused to such an extent that she missed him and even fancied having sex with him. She decided not to tell Flower this, because she knew how her friend would react with one of her lectures. It was all very well for Flower, thought Sarah, having a nice uncomplicated relationship with someone like Charlie, much harder for her, being in love with a man who was flawed.

'Are you ready?' said Flower, coming into the room with an air of doom and irritation.

'Yes,' said Sarah, sensing Flower's mood and wishing she felt jolly enough to uplift her, but having spent twenty minutes working herself up to the belief that she was still madly in love with Billy and that no one else would do, she didn't feel minded to be Flower's comforter.

'We'll get the train, shall we?' said Flower.

'OK,' said Sarah, feeling unreasonably pissed off that someone wasn't there to drive them and wishing she could just phone Billy and ask him. 'How will we get back?' she asked rather sulkily.

'Oh, we'll get a lift from one of the acts,' said Flower. 'There's always someone with a car who can sort us out.'

Sarah couldn't think of anything worse than coming back from a gig with a carful of wanky, arrogant comedians all talking rubbish and trying to outdo each other. Sarah didn't come from the school of women who love nothing better than being close to comedians and find them clever, charming and attractive. On the whole she thought they were knobheads who were full of themselves and tended to be surrounded by sycophantic women who laughed and waved their heads around as though they had some sort of neurological condition that prevented them from keeping still. But she would make the effort for Flower, who she could see was struggling, and she would put Billy to the back of her mind until another day.

Chapter 31

The train journey to the show wasn't the most pleasant or relaxing and, after running the gauntlet of some schoolboys at the station, hanging about shouting abuse at late-night travellers, Sarah and Flower spent a miserable hour staring out of the carriage window at what they could see of the countryside festering with commuter sprawl and much-abused grass. They stepped out at the station and headed, with the vague directions that Flower had gleaned from the promoter, towards the pub where the gig was being held.

When they arrived Flower realised with a sinking heart that there was no separate area in which the stand-up comedy would be performed and that the show had taken over the public bar of a pub, thereby giving themselves a headache as far as holding off all the regulars who wanted to cling to the bar and bore the arse off the barmaid.

Sarah looked at the pub and even she, pretty much a

comedy virgin who had only been able to get to the odd gig Flower had done because Billy wanted to do other things with her like languish in the pub or go to football, could see potential disaster looming

Flower said to Sarah, 'Will you be OK on your own if I go to the dressing-room?'

'Oh yes, I'll be fine,' said Sarah. 'I'll get as near the front as I can and cheer my head off. Don't worry it'll be great.'

'I hope so,' said Flower, wishing that they had the third member of their threesome there to bolster her confidence and shout abuse at any potential hecklers.

She made her way round the back to the makeshift dressing-room, a smallish box in which a couple of foldable chairs and a broken mirror on a ratchety table were the only concessions to showbusiness.

In the room were Mal Fogarty, the compère, a local guy who worked at the abattoir and whose scary Northern wife Glenys wouldn't let him go to comedy gigs very often, partly because it was 'a load of fookin' shite' but mainly because she was frightened that he'd give up his fulltime job and end up earning a pittance and then fail, leaving them all on the dole. Tonight, however, because he was near home, his wife had sanctioned his regular compèring slot and she was secretly delighted with the seventy quid he brought home every week, proudly telling anyone at work who'd listen that her husband was a stand-up comic.

Two other comics had travelled down from London, one of them called Terry Twat and the other, Jake Ashkenazy.

Both were totally different in style, Terry Twat emphasising his speech impediment and falling over a lot, whereas Jake Ashkenazy had a rather serious and clever political act which he feared would not be best suited to the good burghers of Maidstone. Unfortunately, it hadn't been best suited to the good burghers of anywhere – apart from a political benefit he had done to a group of seriously committed activists who had all but carried him out on their shoulders whilst wetting themselves with joy after his twenty-minute exposition on the recent troubles in the Middle East.

Flower had met Terry Twat, real name Joe Evans, on a number of occasions and always found him to be a nice bloke who was good fun, whereas Jake was rather distant and somewhat superior, a trait displayed by many left-wing comics whose socialist credentials don't quite extend to treating their fellow man with much respect. Jake was incredibly posh, which seemed strange to Flower, as he had eschewed all that to live on an estate in North London, and although a big part of her admired him for this, she also thought it made him a wanker as well. It was interesting to see him in a room with a real member of the working-class like Mal because Jake didn't have a lot to say to him apart from seeming embarrassed to be in his company. Terry Twat chatted away easily and asked Flower how her comedy life was going.

'Not too bad,' said Flower, her stomach churning at the prospect of the night's proceedings. 'I've got my first gig tomorrow at the Comedy Store, but I've had this odd heckler wandering around at my gigs and just fucking things up for me.'

'What, like a stalker?' said Jake.

'I wouldn't quite say that,' said Flower, 'but he's appeared more times than I feel comfortable with.'

'I'm surprised Charlie's not here tonight,' said Terry. 'I would have thought he'd want to protect you.'

'He's in prison,' said Flower, 'for causing some trouble at a demo.'

Jake Ashkenazy visibly perked up. 'Oh, do tell me he hit a fucking fascist, darling girl,' he said.

'No, he was caught smoking a joint,' said Flower. 'I'm sure they'll let him out soon.'

'Wow,' said Jake. 'Was he at the demo earlier today?'

'Yes,' said Flower. 'So was I.'

'Fucking great, wasn't it?' said Jake. 'We showed those pigs a thing or two. I got a couple of digs in at them.'

'You twatted a copper?' said Mal.

Jake noticed that the muscles on Mal's neck were slightly strained and his face had taken on a bull-like quality that wasn't there before he mentioned hitting a policeman. He backtracked and laughed in an embarrassed fashion.

'Not really hit him, man,' he said. 'Shouted at him – you know.'

'Well, I hope you didn't hit a copper, because I might have to hit *you*,' said Mal.

Jake quivered and looked at the floor. Mal winked at Flower. The landlord stuck his head round the door. 'I think we're ready, mate,' he told Mal. 'The natives are getting restless.'

'Right you are,' said Mal.

It had been decided that Jake would go on first, Flower in the middle and Terry Twat at the end to balance the show properly. Flower wished she could go on first, so there was a good excuse for dying on her arse and she could get home and see whether they'd let Charlie out.

Jake went on first and his heart sank as he saw he was faced with a whole cohort of the working classes, many red-faced blokes on their way home from Saturday shiftwork who had stopped in for a pint and were hoping for a lot of sexism, a touch of racism and plenty of filth served up for their delectation; Jake Ashkenazy was certainly not what they wanted.

'Hello brothers,' he began.

'I'm not your fucking brother, you cunt,' said one of the red-faced drinkers. 'I wouldn't have a brother who sounded like he'd been born with a silver spoon in his gob. Gonna tell us what's wrong with our lives and how you're gonna put it all right for us, are you?'

That was exactly what Jake had been intending to do. He wondered whether to persevere and desperately hoped a lot of knob jokes would come to mind. Unfortunately they didn't and after a brief struggle, Jake Ashkenazy was strangled at the birth of his act and resolved immediately to do a tour of arts centres in the hope that he would only encounter the middle classes who loved being told they were working class and wouldn't dream of aiming the 'C' word at him.

Jake slunk back into the dressing-room as the red-faced

drinkers claimed their first victim. They had left Mal Fogarty well alone because they liked him and he was one of their own, but these posh wankers from London were a different matter.

Sarah had been a bemused spectator when all this was going on and felt sorry for Jake Ashkenazy because he was good-looking, although of the few minutes he actually had managed to perform before he left the stage, not a word had she understood. Mal Fogarty, on the other hand, she immediately warmed to because he reminded her of the men who had surrounded her mother while she was growing up. Her mother had been the only negative part of the equation, being grasping, spiteful and unfriendly to a series of men who loved her to distraction for her wild looks and quick humour, something that sadly, Sarah hadn't inherited.

She was just thinking what a pain in the arse her mother was when there was a tap on her shoulder.

'Long time no see, Sez! How you doing, gel?' followed by an unmistakable high-pitched laugh.

'Mum, It's great to see you,' said Sarah, wondering if it was.

'Well, I couldn't pass up the chance to see you and your big-nosed hippy friend, could I?' said Connie McBride. 'And hey presto, here you are. Besides, I quite fancy the MC.'

'Mum,' said Sarah wearily, 'he's married. Leave him alone, will you.'

'All's fair in love and war, Sez,' replied Connie sagely.

'Can I get you a drink, love? Anyway I'm bored shitless with Philip – he's getting right on my tits.'

Philip was Connie's longterm and longsuffering boyfriend, a mild-mannered, slightly hirsute bank manager in his early sixties who couldn't believe his luck when Connie had dragged him into her bed and done things he had never been allowed to even think about with his wife.

'How's that gorgeous Billy?' demanded Connie, who had heard about him from her daughter during one of their rare phone conversations. Sarah wasn't sure whether to tell her mother what had happened for fear she might jump on a train to South London and try to bed him, as she had always flirted relentlessly with any of Sarah's boyfriends whenever they had come down to see her.

Sarah asked her mother for a vodka and tonic and Connie went to the bit of the bar where Mal was standing and leaned against him as much as she could without becoming a surrogate Siamese twin. The landlord had called a bar break in between each act as he thought it would drive the normal punters mad if they had to wait until a proper interval. Connie had been in the pub for some time, apparently, and had managed to get herself quite pissed.

'When's your mate on?' she enquired genially, leaving Sarah to hope that when Flower came on, Connie wouldn't feel the need to converse with her.

'She's on now,' said Sarah, as Mal introduced Flower who had been shaking just behind the thin curtain that separated them, the stars, from the riff-raff.

Flower walked up to the microphone. 'Good evening,'

she said. 'I was at the demo up in the City today. Hit a few crusties, caused a bit of mayhem.'

The audience looked bemused.

'Still,' said Flower, 'it's a great life being a fucking copper.'

Big laugh.

'Sarah never told me you was a copper,' came a voice from the front row where Connie had deposited herself to gaze adoringly upon the portly physique of Mal.

'Bloody hell,' said Flower, 'I didn't realise that Camilla Parker Bowles moonlighted as a stripper in Maidstone.'

There was a huge roar of laughter from the crowd. Flower felt exhilarated and really mean all in one go.

'Fuck off,' said Connie, rather hurt.

'I hope you don't use that sort of language round Highgrove,' said Flower.

The crowd loved this and continued to play along as Flower got stuck into Connie, feeling rather guilty about her being Sarah's mum but convincing herself it was fair because Connie had started it.

It was going very well when suddenly a familiar voice cut through the laughter.

'What are you being so fucking nosy for?' said the voice. 'I suppose with that conk you can't avoid it.'

It was at this point that Flower learned that even though you may have the love of an entire audience floating around you like honey, they are never a guaranteed support and a split second can turn them into your greatest enemy.

The crowd laughed loud and long at this intervention

and Flower froze; all the joie de vivre she had garnered bantering with Connie flew away and she was struck dumb. She prepared for battle, but it didn't come. Just the one heckle and whoever he was melted back into the audience.

Flower stayed and struggled on for long enough to earn her money and then she came off. 'Sorry, Connie,' she said to Sarah's mum.

'Soyoushouldbe,' said Connie, who by now was running every other word together.

'Well, you started it,' said Flower.

'No, I fucking didn't,' Connie objected.

'You did,' said Flower.

'Look, you silly little cow,' said Connie, 'you were crap and you know it and if I hadn't been there helping you out you would have had a terrible time.'

'Don't make me laugh,' said Flower.

'You certainly didn't make *me* laugh,' retorted Connie, quite cleverly for one so drunk.

At this point they turned to Sarah, who had spent the evening so far blissfully unaware of the proceedings and just thinking about Billy.

'Oh, I don't fucking know,' she said and walked out.

Once outside the pub and having walked fast for five minutes, Sarah found herself on a semi-rural badly lit road and in that sort of reckless bolshy mood you get when you've just split with someone, which allows you to walk home alone through graveyards, swear at policemen or approach strangers and speak to them in a very aggressive way. She decided to head for town and was nearly within range of some dull orange light when a hand came from behind and clamped itself round her throat.

Chapter 32

Flower was a bit worried when Sarah didn't reappear that night but just presumed that she had ended up going back to Connie's to kip down. Not having Connie's number she didn't bother to phone her; Sarah was bound to turn up at some point during the next day.

Sarah eventually phoned late Sunday morning.

'Hi Flower, it's me,' she said with a strange strangled cheerfulness.

'Down at your mum's?' said Flower.

Sarah didn't answer this question.

'I'm not coming back to yours,' she said. 'But I'm really grateful for everything.'

'Staying at Connie's for a bit?' said Flower. 'Are you sure that's wise?'

There was a long silence.

'I'm back with Billy,' said Sarah.

'Fuck, shit, wank, what did you do that for?' said Flower, unable to pretend she was pleased.

'He came to Maidstone to find me last night,' said Sarah. 'I met him on the road when I walked out. He pretended to attack me. It was so sweet.'

'Why fucking pretend? He doesn't normally,' Flower nearly said, but kept her mouth shut.

'I've really missed him and he'll try hard to change,' said Sarah, unaware that she was repeating the most clichéd line in the domestic-violence script one more time. 'Look, I can't stop. I've got to go – see you soon.'

'Yeh, see you soon,' said Flower, depressed, hung-over and very pissed off about the night before after the journey home with Twat and Ashkenazy had turned into a noisy argument about her doing the Comedy Store gig tonight and being accused of selling out.

She wished Charlie was there and at that very moment, the front door opened and a rather smelly, exhausted Charlie dragged himself inside and collapsed on the battered settee.

'Sarah's back with Billy,' said Flower.

'Oh yeh?' said Charlie, totally disinterested.

'Don't you fucking care?' shouted Flower.

'Don't you?' shouted Charlie. 'I've been in a police cell all night with Mr Fucking Pretty Boy Heffner! You could at least ask how *I* am.'

'Yeh, but you haven't been beaten on a regular basis by your boyfriend,' said Flower, annoyed by this appeal from Charlie to put enquiries about his health first.

'No, but I have been shagged up the arse by a troupe of Peruvian nose flautists,' said Charlie.

'Oh shut up,' said Flower. 'I'm going to see Martha.'

It felt really good to get out of the house, where Flower was feeling decidedly claustrophobic. For some reason it seemed dirty and small and she didn't want to be there any more. She hated Charlie and she hated her lot in life.

'Fuck a duck,' said Martha, when she heard about Billy and Sarah.

Ted was lying on the settee looking pained as if he had been anally penetrated by some nasal flautists too and he gave the same weary 'Oh it's a girl thing' look to Martha when she expressed surprise about the reunion of Sarah and Billy.

'Don't try and talk her out of it,' said Ted. 'Ultimately people only do what they want to do so there's no point in looking for hidden motives or any of that shit. She'll stay with him until the arsehole kills her.'

'Thank you for that,' said Martha. 'Ever thought of being an agony aunt?'

Ted went back to sleep.

'What are we going to do about bloody Sarah?' said Flower.

'Don't we just have to let her get on with it?' said Martha.

'You've changed your tune,' said Flower. 'You were all for intervening a little while ago.'

'I know, I'm sorry,' said Martha. 'It all seemed so much more important when I was on my own but now to be honest I've got stuff to be getting on with.'

'Oh thanks,' said Flower. 'That makes me feel really good. So I'm the saddo without a life, am I?'

'I know it sounded like that,' said Martha, 'and I'm really sorry.'

'I'm sorry too. It's just that I've been feeling so irritable and scared lately. That weird heckler was there again last night and just as I felt on top of my game and ready to tackle him, he disappeared. But I'm worried he'll come round again and Charlie keeps not getting to the gigs and I'm frightened,' said Flower shakily.

'Just shoot the bastard,' said Martha cheerily. 'You've got a gun, Calamity Jane.' Flower put her finger to her lips. She didn't want Ted to know. He actually might suggest something sensible, like handing it in to the police.

'Anyway,' said Flower, 'enough of that now – are you coming to my big debut at the Comedy Store tonight?'

'Oh, I wish I could,' said Martha, 'but it's just not possible with John. I feel I can't leave him.'

Flower thought with such a straight name as John, the poor kid was really going to get bullied in a playground full of Feargals and Jacks.

'What about Junior's mum?' said Flower. 'Go on, Martha, it's really important to me. I'm haemorrhaging support as it is.'

'I did think of her and asked actually, but she's going to be out,' said Martha. 'I'm really sorry but I wouldn't trust anyone else.'

'OK,' said Flower dejectedly. 'I don't suppose that Sarah will come either, now she's back with Billy.'

'Sorry,' said Martha. 'I know it means a lot to you. Perhaps we could bring John with us. I'm sure it'll be OK for one night.'

'Martha,' said Flower, 'there's nothing worse than a baby at a comedy gig. It's like a hypomanic at a funeral.'

'I don't really understand that reference,' said Martha, 'but that joke might come in handy if you're ever performing at the Royal College of Psychiatrists' summer ball.'

'That's my problem,' said Flower. 'Too intelligent for the masses.'

John, who had been dozing on Ted's lap, woke up and started to cry so Martha picked him up and began feeding him.

There was a sharp, unChristian knock on the door.

'I'll get it,' Flower offered.

It was the Rev Brian and Pat, Martha's sister Mary and her incredibly shrunken, bony husband Derek.

'Hello,' said Flower, 'come in.'

The quartet were ushered into the sitting room where Martha had very quickly roused Ted who was trying to smooth his hair, flatten his erection and sort out the drool that had dribbled down onto his shirt during the snooze.

'Christ, you pick your moments,' said Martha. 'Why don't you ever phone?'

'Because you'd tell us not to come,' said Pat.

Derek the skull sniggered and wheezed at this and wrinkled his nose as if there was an unpleasant smell in the flat. There was – John had just produced one.

'And what brings you up to this charming area?' said

Martha. 'Bit of sightseeing round the estate or an attempted conversion on the teenage murder squad?'

'Don't be sarcastic, dear,' said the Rev Brian. 'You're a mother now and you have to grow up a bit.'

'Bollocks,' said Martha and her father shuddered as if he had been stabbed.

'Let's not get off on the wrong foot,' said Pat mildly.

'Sorry,' said Martha. 'All right, I'll put the kettle on. Here you are.' She handed John over to her mother.

'I'll come with you,' said Mary.

Mary and Martha had never liked each other much, but in the kitchen as Martha made a big tray of tea, things were surprisingly friendly and they found themselves having a laugh about their respective men.

'We could go to fancy dress with them as Laurel and Hardy,' said Martha and got a laugh out of Mary.

'Look,' said Mary, 'I know I haven't been much of a sister.'

'Stop right there,' said Martha. 'Let's not do the happy families thing quite yet.'

'Wait till I have mine,' said Mary, 'then we will.'

'God, you're not pregnant, are you?' said Martha.

Mary nodded. Martha gave her a hug.

'We wanted to tell you all together. Mum and Dad are staying for the weekend.'

Martha felt slightly overwhelmed by all this family closeness. 'Are you going back tonight?' she said.

'Well,' said Mary, 'we were thinking, me and Derek, about staying in a hotel.'

'I don't suppose . . .' said Martha. 'You see, there's something really important I have to do tonight but I wouldn't trust anyone to babysit but you. I'll only be gone a few hours.'

'Express some milk,' said Mary. 'I'll give it to him in a cup.'

Mary made it sound easy but Martha knew she faced three-quarters of an hour tethered to a sadistic bit of plastic pumping away with all the dignity of a regimented Jersey milker to produce two teaspoons of the bloody stuff.

Pat and Brian were chatting in the sitting room with Ted whose job they hadn't been told about yet and so were fondly imagining that this big ugly bear of a man did something reassuringly dull, like working for the council.

Martha decided that bridge could be crossed at a later date and then scolded herself for not immediately telling her father and getting some pleasure out of it.

Flower was pleased to see Martha's highly dysfunctional family all together in one place and getting on reasonably well for a change. She felt the weight of the show that evening hanging over her like a big black sponge preventing her from concentrating on anything else, from relaxing or from having a normal day in any form at all. Martha through all the fug of family and John recognised this and said to Flower, 'Why don't you just go home, have a really long hot bath, relax and take it easy before tonight.'

'Yes, I think I will,' said Flower and headed off. She switched her phone back on. There were three messages from Charlie apologising, which just got on her nerves.

The afternoon seemed to last a couple of days and by six o'clock Flower felt insane with nervous tension. She was also tired and had a headache – not the perfect condition, it has to be said, for doing your best gig.

She wondered whether she should medicate herself with something from Charlie's medicine box, a cornucopia of homoeopathic cures for anything you cared to name. Flower never took anything for anxiety but today felt that she needed a calming influence to cocoon her from the worst excesses of the show.

'Take the little yellow tablet,' said Charlie, 'in the smallest Russian doll in the medicine box,' for he had an odd, yet reasonably well organised system. 'I got that from some bloke last Saturday. He says it's a German homoeopathic cure for stress. That should do you.'

Flower located it and popped it in her mouth. It wasn't a homoeopathic cure for stress, but a very strong amphetamine that the joker had given to Charlie in the hope that he would take it and a comedy situation might develop. Within minutes her extremities started to burn.

Flower's mobile rang. It was Sarah.

'Hi,' she said. 'Your big night – can we come? I really want to support you but I can't very well tell Billy to stay at home.'

Great, thought Flower, her mind changing course unpredictably, more fucking stress. Why can't all the bastards stay at home and let me go and die a little death then forget about comedy and go back to my job.

Before leaving, she bathed and changed into something

very neutral so she wouldn't have to consider if what she wore had any effect on the reaction she got.

The gun was in one of her bags, wrapped up in an innocuous-looking piece of material. Flower, who unwittingly was heading up the scale of arousal by the second, looked at it and put it in her pocket which already contained her set list. She then remembered she'd forgotten to put her lucky pants on, located them annoyingly in the washing basket after the Maidstone gig and sprayed them with a squirt of sandalwood in a gesture Martha would have been proud of, then slipped them on.

Charlie kept quiet and very much in the background. He knew the score before these shows: Flower could be really vicious when in a pre-performance paddy.

They arrived at the Comedy Store at eleven; the show was due to start at twelve. Flower managed to get Charlie, Martha and Ted, and Billy and Sarah in for free. She felt decidedly odd and said to Charlie, 'Are you sure that stuff that guy gave you is OK?'

'Of course,' said Charlie, whose network of mates/ suppliers extended through squats up and down the country. 'It could be the four cans of lager you had at home.'

'This is going to be awful,' said Flower, but in some ways because she was out of her head she felt quite elated and excited, as if that night was finally going to sort her out and show everyone she could do comedy.

The audience was also excited and some were quite pissed, while the old troupers who had done this gig many times sat dejectedly in the dressing-room . . . just another day at work for them. Flower's nervousness injected a sense of foreboding into them though.

The compère was Adrian Mole, his real name, a sweet-tempered rather bumbling Lincolnshire-born computer programmer whom everyone loved.

At one point Flower found herself alone in the dressing-room with Dick Knob. She hadn't seen him since that awful gig at the college which prompted her to go with him and get the gun.

Dick Knob always stormed it in the late show.

'Take the gun on as a joke,' he said, 'and wave it if someone heckles.'

'I haven't got it with me,' said Flower.

Dick Knob threw her a look which said, 'I don't believe you.'

The unreconstructed Australian comic Pat Denny was pacing up and down and wondering whether to try out a joke about Australian women looking like horses' arses. He felt safer in London but had been followed round half of Australia by a small coterie of feminist students who had made his life a misery by turning up at his gigs and shouting words like 'Rapist' at him, which didn't exactly improve his reception.

Jake Ashkenazy turned up, looking sheepish after his diatribe to Flower about selling out the night before. Another comic had fallen by the wayside and he'd been offered a slot. He was lathering himself with false hope again.

Double act, The Fuckwits, were playing cards and drinking beers.

Adrian went on and tried to calm the audience down. That night it consisted of a few stag-night groups of City boys whose sole aim was to get alcohol down and up again as quickly as possible and were foolishly going to see a stripper after the comedy show, by which point their genitals would be in no fit state to respond. There were also lots of tourists who'd been in the West End all night and so were quite drunk, and many groups of friends from out of town on a special night out.

Flower was on last and had two hours to wait. She watched the progress of the other performers on the small monitor in the dressing-room.

Meanwhile, up at the bar Charlie, Billy, Sarah, Ted and Martha could not be said to be getting on like a house on fire. Ted and Billy were niggling at each other because Ted could somehow sense that Billy had some hold over Martha and resented this enormously. Martha had discovered the incredible elastic noose of motherhood was trying to catapult her back to the flat and John, but she kept telling herself to be strong and at least give Flower the support she deserved on her first big night. She too felt a sense of foreboding and wondered if Flower had the gun but was too scared to ask as she seemed jittery and unpredictable.

Martha looked from the handsome Billy to old horse-face Ted and was genuinely glad that she was with Ted. Also, of course, she was still relishing telling the Reverend Brian about the lap-dancing club and awaiting his reaction which she predicted would be nuclear, particularly if Ted was her husband by that point too.

Jake Ashkenazy's name was announced by Adrian the
compère, who looked towards the door onto the stage, which
stayed resolutely closed.

'Jake Ashkenazy!' he said again, rather desperately.

'Oh, the poor git's bottled it,' said Ted and the action of
the comedy faded into the background as they started
talking again.

Martha wondered whether she should phone Mary and
Derek to see if John was all right. Ted advised against it –
he was having too good a time. This was lucky as John had
been screaming his head off since Ted and Martha left and
had sprayed Derek's velour-look maroon jumper with a
particularly pungent strain of baby vomit. He had refused
the bottle and both Derek and Mary had separately felt that
Mary's pregnancy might have been a very serious mistake.

Sarah and Charlie both seemed nervous and slightly
jumpy for their own reasons. Billy looked pleased with
himself though and was basking in the relief of Sarah having
stayed with him, his resolve to change strengthened and
his proposal of marriage just a couple of hours away from
making the transition from thought to speech.

The stage-manager of the Comedy Store, after Jake
Ashkenazy's untimely exit, had told all the acts to do a bit
longer while he combed the audience for any comics who
might agree to do Jake's slot.

Dick Knob stormed the show, of course.

Pat Denny started very mildly with some stuff about
being an Australian in London and then moved to the heart
of his act.

'Most girls in Australia look like horses, arses,' he said, to the delight of the stag-night groups who whooped and cheered and shouted, 'So do they here, mate!'

'Really?' said Pat, surprised to be getting such an easy ride. And then he got an even bigger surprise as a lump of horse manure hit him full in the face. This serendipitously appropriate faecal heckle was the work of a Central London women's group who had been phoned by the Australian students and purely by chance had planned to go to the Comedy Store on the day one member's dad had had a delivery of manure for his roses and just on the off-chance she'd popped some in her handbag.

Pat Denny couldn't come back from that and left. It was looking like a short show.

However, The Fuckwits could always be relied upon to save the day. Working on the premise that one in two people love jokes about snot and farting, they produced a tour de force of bodily effluence which the stag-night groups would remember for the rest of their lives.

Eventually, and she thought it would never happen, Flower's name was announced and she went on to a pissed, tired, but essentially cheerful crowd.

There was some immediate barracking which usually met the arrival of a woman onstage and extended through the continuum of their suitability as a sexual partner to some serious misogyny, which always came from at least five or so member of the audience. The one consolation was that they all shouted together so no individual piece of abuse could be heard, apart from a continuous stream of low-level heckling from a familiar voice in the front row. Flower could see nothing, nor could she bear to dip down beneath the spotlight and see exactly who her tormentor of the past few weeks had been. She thought the voice sounded a bit like Charlie's.

In a split second she elected to throw away her prepared material and in her amphetamine-befuddled brain decided she could just surf.

'How many of you blokes in the audience beat their partners?' she asked. There was a ripple of puzzled surprise and she added, 'And I don't mean at pool last week.'

People laughed as their tension eased slightly, even though the joke wasn't very good.

'My friend's boyfriend hits her,' said Flower, 'and sometimes she doesn't even deserve it because the dinner's quite nice. Fair enough if the gravy's lumpy, eh?'

Confusion was the main effect of this statement on the audience although the stag-night group continued to cheer.

'The funny thing is,' said Flower, 'we – that is, my friend Martha and I – thought the best way to deal with it might be to kill him.' The audience laughed cheerily and then laughed harder as Flower pulled out her gun.

'I know you think this is a replica,' she said, 'but look.' She pointed the gun at the ceiling and fired and some plaster exploded and crashed down. A low murmur heralded the beginnings of audience panic.

Flower realised that Billy, Ted, Martha, Sarah and Charlie were in front of her, looking constipated facially, but their body language conveyed the message they might be incontinent at any time.

'Come on,' said Charlie, in the tones of a hostage negotiator. 'Give us the gun. You're off your face, love.'

'No, you get up here, Charlie,' said Flower, pointing the gun right at him. 'I want to talk to you ... and the others too.' She motioned to Martha, Ted, Billy and Sarah to join Charlie and they shuffled up, hearts beating fast. The audience members couldn't quite make up their minds whether to rush out in a panic, screaming their heads off in case this disturbed hippy shot them, or stay and watch what was essentially the fascinating dénouement of a friendship crisis. Flower wasn't bothered either way. Her intention was to resolve her life, not keep an audience watching her only because of the threat of a bullet through the head. Consequently, the nervous ones dropped to their hands and knees and made their way quietly out of the door at the back, several of them choosing to phone newspapers and TV stations on the way and all of them forgetting that the police might be more appropriate.

Luckily, the manager of the club had walked to the office and called the police who began to put together an operation that would maybe have flushed out some IRA terrorists but was slightly over the top for a pissed-up hippy woman full of amphetamine.

'Right,' said Flower, her words being picked up by some floor microphones which were used for the improvisation show on a Wednesday night. 'Seeing as we're all here, we might as well sort out a few things and then we can all go home and get on with our lives. *Comprende?*'

Charlie winced. Flower would never use a word like that if she was sober.

'Flower,' he started.

'Shut up!' shouted Flower. 'You're always . . .' she searched for the right word '. . . heckling me. In a nice way, sure, but it amounts to the same thing. I never get to say what I want. I don't want you to interfere. I need to sort this out my own way. Keep it shut, will you?'

Charlie nodded.

'Are you the one who keeps following me around heckling me?' said Flower, staring at him very hard and holding the gun surprisingly steadily for a person who had consumed a pillful of consciousness-altering chemicals.

'You're fucking joking, aren't you?' said Charlie. 'Surely—'

'Just say yes or no,' said Flower.

'No, of course not! You've got to trust me,' said Charlie.

'And do you trust me?' said Flower.

Charlie hesitated for a split second.

'You see!' shouted Flower. 'You don't, you never have and I know you're a nice bloke and all that, but you're driving me mad with your suspicion and twenty-four-hour surveillance. I can't relax.'

Charlie was wondering whether to make a grab for the gun. He couldn't believe that this mild-mannered, sweet woman had turned into a gun-toting tower of unpredictability. This was several big steps up from the kitten-kicking diva of PMT fame.

Perhaps Sim will make a story out of this one day, he thought, and it will be a fuck of a sight more interesting than any of the bollocks he normally comes out with. It also occurred to him that one's thinking really clears in circumstances such as these.

Flower noticed someone in the front row had their hand up.

'Yes?' she said.

'Can I go to the toilet, please?' said the young man, a sweat breaking out as he tensely tried to avoid her eyes. Flower was shocked at the degree of deference he was demonstrating, even through the fog of her altered perception.

'Go on,' she said tersely, and he scuttled off as if he was under fire.

This awareness of her own power gave Flower the push she needed to turn the gun towards Billy. The audience gasped.

'Well?' she said.

'Well, what?' he answered nervously, having shrunk in stature, his usual cockiness missing.

'Let's hear from you about your behaviour over the last few months, shall we?'

The audience strained forward. They were almost enjoying themselves.

'Look, Flower,' said Billy, 'I know you and Martha hate my guts and I don't blame you. I realise I've been a right little shit all my life really and I've got away with it 'cause I always picked on people who were scared of me.'

'Go on,' said Flower.

'I can't,' said Billy. 'I don't know what else to say.'

'You can tell us why you've been hitting Sarah for a start,' said Flower.

'Yes,' murmured the audience: a surreal soap opera had sprung to life in front of their eyes.

'I don't know,' said Billy. 'She just gets on my tits sometimes. Women do.'

'Why, what do we do that's so irritating?' said Flower, enunciating every word slowly and sarcastically.

'Shall I be really honest?' said Billy.

'Yes,' said all the women in the room under their breath.

'You're all too vulnerable, smarmy and clinging sometimes . . . and like a dog I want to kick,' he said. 'Sometimes I can't stand the condition of being loved by a woman. It chokes me.'

This was the most insightful and possibly the most intelligent thing Billy had ever said in his life and it left him with a very surprised look on his face.

'All?' said Sarah and Martha together.

'Yup, pretty much, eventually,' said Billy, 'and I don't mean it in a bad way. It's just the way I feel.'

'So why are you like it?' said Sarah, throwing a glance across at Flower to check it was all right to take questions from the floor.

'I don't know,' said Billy. 'I was just brought up that way, I suppose, and I've never even thought about it.'

'Well, maybe you should if other people are getting it in the neck,' said Martha.

'I grew up with it,' said Billy wearily, as though he had told this story a hundred times before when in fact it was the first time.

He continued: 'I watched my father treat my mother like shit for all of my childhood and I suppose I just absorbed it. I didn't like the way my dad treated her and it made me angry, but look at me now – I'm almost a carbon copy of my old man. Perhaps it's unavoidable.'

Martha shuddered. Was she a carbon copy of the Rev Brian?

'And even when my mum was being treated really badly, I remember feeling guilty for thinking she was so pathetic. My dad had her in such a state that he just had to look at her in a certain way or make her jump by dropping something and she'd do what she was told. She started to have this expression on her face constantly as if she'd been hit, even when she hadn't, and I found it repulsive and wished she'd sort herself out.'

'Not your dad, then?' said Flower.

'Eh?' said Billy.

'Why should your mum have had to sort herself out?' said Flower. 'It was your dad who was the problem.'

'S'pose,' said Billy, hanging his head and looking like this initial foray into self-analysis had killed off half his brain cells, including the ones that controlled his neck muscles.

'You're a bully,' said Flower, 'and you rely on your physical strength to intimidate people. It's just not fucking fair.'

'I know,' said Billy. 'I'm not proud of it, you know.'

'Are you not?' said Martha, trying inappropriately to get a one-liner in. Everyone ignored her.

'It's partly my fault, you know,' said Sarah.

Flower cackled, a very high-pitched sound she had not heard herself emit before and it quite unsettled her. To Charlie it signified that she was well on the way to being completely out of control.

'Oh, don't make me laugh,' said Flower. 'You're not going to do that old talking doormat "I deserved it" bollocks, are you, Sar?'

'Look, Flower, we're not all bloody lesbians, you know,' said Sarah.

'I presume that's your way of saying we're not all left-wing separatist feminists, is it?' said Flower.

'Maybe,' said Sarah, continuing, 'and we're not all going out with Harry the Fucking Hippy either. What I mean is that I have sat there and taken it over the months and surely that's given him' (she pointed at Billy as if he was a road sign) 'the message that it's all right. I should've left ages ago, but I stupidly thought if he really liked me he wouldn't hit me.'

'Fair enough assumption,' said Ted, who had been quiet up until this point.

'Look, Flower,' said Charlie, 'I'm not being annoying, but I suggest we wrap this up fairly soon because some of these punters must've told the Old Bill you're on one in here. Surely it's only a matter of time before they send a sniper in.'

This had the opposite effect from what Charlie intended.

Flower, losing what composure she had left, screamed at Charlie to shut up with such a degree of vehemence that the audience became rather frightened and all looked at the floor lest they incur Flower's wrath.

'Look, I just want to sort Billy out and find out who heckled me,' said Flower, 'then we can all go home.'

'Billy doesn't need you to sort him out,' said Sarah. 'He'll do it himself.'

'Well, he hasn't looked much like doing that so far,' said Flower.

'Come on, you two, don't fall out,' said Martha. 'Us girls have got to stick together.'

'What, even when you've fucked my boyfriend?' said Sarah.

Ears pricked again in the audience, bowels loosened inside Martha. She was too shocked to construct an argument against this statement so just looked sheepishly at the ground and said, 'How did you know?'

''Cause it was bloody obvious,' said Sarah. 'What else could have happened? You look guilty as hell every time I see you and you talk rubbish every time we mention that night.'

'So why didn't you come round and slap me about a bit?' said Martha, realising as the words came out of her mouth that this wasn't the most tactful thing to say, given the circumstances.

'Because,' said Sarah, 'I suppose I was hoping that if I just ignored it, it would all go away and that Bill and I could get back on an even keel again and that we would never need to bring it up.'

'So why have you?' said Martha.

''Cause I'm bloody livid,' said Sarah.

'Me too,' said Ted.

'Excuse me,' said Flower, waving the gun about as if it was a wilting bunch of flowers, 'but I think you'll all find this is my fucking crisis and I'm in charge. Now let's sort the heckler business out. Was it you, Billy?' She turned the gun back to him.

'No, I swear on my mother's grave it wasn't,' said Billy.

'Fucking drama queen,' mumbled Ted under his breath, having developed a recent desire to punch Billy in the face.

Sarah added, 'I thought you could only say that if your mother was actually dead.'

'I believe you, Billy,' said Flower.

'Perhaps it's a stranger, and he's gone home and you'll never find out,' said Ted.

'Shit,' said Flower. 'That kid that just went to the toilet – do you think—?'

'No,' said Charlie. 'Couldn't be.'

'Are you *sure* it's not you, Charlie?' said Flower.

'Oh, for Christ's sake,' said Charlie, 'why would I, someone who loves you to bits, follow you round heckling you? We're not all like Billy, you know.'

'That was below the belt,' said Billy.

'So hit me then,' said Charlie. 'Everyone else does.'

For once a fist did not visit Charlie's face, nor a boot his bollocks. This caused him to launch into a speech he had been planning to make for some time, and now seemed a perfect opportunity.

'Look, Flower,' he said, 'I can't tell you how hard it's been to see you dragging yourself round this godforsaken comedy circuit trying to get laughs, not to mention finding that bloody heckler. In fact, I know you'll be angry, but one night I did come to see you and heard the guy. I tried to get across the audience to see who it was but by the time I'd got there, I couldn't find him. Please stop putting yourself through this, will you? You're too nice for all this. It's more Martha's sort of thing.'

'Oh cheers,' said Martha.

'Give up and come home. I'll really make an effort not to be so possessive and all that shit, I promise,' continued Charlie.

A tear rolled down Flower's face. She knew Charlie was right and that she wasn't any good. In fact, on the rare occasions Martha had been to a club she'd always come out with far funnier things from her seat in the audience.

'Come on, Flower, give us the gun,' said Charlie. 'Let's go.'

Flower drooped. She lowered the gun and began to walk towards Charlie. The dressing-room door opened and Dick Knob, who had been watching the whole thing on the CCTV in there, sauntered past.

'Great piece of entertainment,' he said. 'Right beautiful.'

A massive firework went off in Flower's memory as neurones began firing to tell her that the word 'beautiful' held the clue to the identity of the heckler.

'Fuck me, it was you!' she shouted, wheeling round to

face Dick Knob and retaining the steadiness of hand that had surprisingly characterised her gun-use all evening.

'Me what, Princess?' he said, feigning casual.

'You who's been heckling me,' said Flower.

'Nah, you've got the wrong geezer, Flower. I'd never do that to you,' said Dick. 'I love you. Don't you know that? Oh shit, what am I saying? I know the heckling was a fucking weird thing to do but I didn't want you to leave the circuit and I thought you were about to, so I was doing my best to harden you up, to give you that extra shell you need to cope. Christ, if you think you've had it bad so far, just wait till your career progresses and the critics start on you. They're far worse than any pissed-up old cunt in the audience, I'm telling you. No one survives them, even the ones who seem the hardest. That hairy wanker's right, you are too nice. So I was just trying to prepare you for the sort of shit you're bound to get if you stay around in this job because fuck it, Flower sweetheart, you're bloody gorgeous and I adore you. Shoot me now if you want.'

Dick started to get a hard-on at the very thought of being shot down on the stage of the Comedy Store by the woman he loved.

Even though he looked so greasily forensic Martha found herself slightly jealous at this disturbed declaration of love and looked towards Ted for one to equal it. Unfortunately Ted was still coping with the idea of Billy entering her flat that night . . . and her, of course. Charlie had a fist raised.

'Calm down, Charlie,' said Flower. 'There's no need for that. He loves me – you don't have to hit him for that.'

'Do you love him?' said Charlie.

'Of course not,' said Flower and then, seeing how crest-fallen Dick looked, wished she'd left out the 'of course'.

'Is it 'cause I'm ugly?' said Dick.

'You're not ugly,' said Flower.

'Oh yes he is!' tried a few wags in the audience.

'Don't listen to them,' said Flower.

'Bollocks,' said Ted, who'd barely said a word all night. ''Course he's plug ugly and so am I, and it's something you have to learn to live with. Not for me the romantic gesture coupled with a granite jaw and steely good looks framed with wild black curly hair. Oh no, just an overweight victim of acne whose limbs appear to have been designed for someone three times my age and whose hair has the texture of greasy spaghetti. I've been laughed at, spat on, sneered at, avoided, put down, ignored, kicked, beaten up, used as a trampoline and left on the pavement in a very ugly heap so many times I've lost count, but I've had to put up with it.'

'What about surgery?' said Sarah, the queen of tactful interjection.

Martha drew in a sharp breath at this innocently cruel remark, but Ted just laughed.

'Christ no,' he said. 'I just went into a job that suited my face. Everyone expects me to be a pervert, so why disappoint them? Confound them from inside the job, that's what I plan to do. I run my club well, I'm kind and I pay good money. And it's as a result of that club that I've met the most disturbed, unpredictable, silly, petty, messy, stubborn, most gorgeous woman in the world, we've got a son and that's me sorted. You'll just have to keep looking, Dick old son.'

'Yeh,' said Dick, still reeling from the response of Flower to his secret, the one he had nursed for two years. He couldn't believe his chance of happiness had been trashed so decisively and so quickly.

Martha beamed a broad grin. 'I always wanted an ugly one,' she said, 'so no one would try and nick him off me and I've hit the bloody jackpot with Ted.' Ted started to laugh.

Martha continued, 'Reluctant as I am to join amateur psychology hour, Flower and I just wanted Billy to stop hitting Sarah, whether they sorted things out with each other or not. Sarah and Ted, I am so sorry I ended up sleeping with Billy. I'm not going to come up with any excuses but my raging hormones and drink contributed. It will never happen again and I'm sorry if I've hurt anyone. In a weird way I suppose I thought Sarah might leave Billy if he was unfaithful and that would sort the situation out.'

'Did you really think that?' said Ted.

'No,' said Martha, 'but I refuse to accept I am quite such a moral bankrupt.'

'I'm not sure I can forgive you,' said Sarah.

'Oh dear,' said Martha.

'But I'll have a good go,' said Sarah.

'Fucking great,' said Dick Knob, 'so everyone's happy except me, then?'

They all nodded solemnly and the audience clapped.

Dick Knob strolled dejectedly past the audience and up the stairs.

'Hang on,' said Martha. 'Flower, didn't we say the only way to absolutely guarantee that Billy is sorted out is to threaten to shoot his testicles off if he ever touches Sarah again?'

Billy instinctively covered his bollocks, having found it difficult to decide whether Martha was joking or not.

'Yes, it's a joke,' she said.

Dick Knob appeared again, at the back of the room.

'There's fucking loads of police out there,' he screamed.

'Well, I suggest,' said Flower, picking up the microphone out of its stand, 'that you, the audience, file out in an orderly fashion with your hands up and we'll all come out at the end and explain ourselves. But hang on one little minute, I haven't finished my set yet. Down you all sit.'

'Flower,' said Charlie, exasperated.

'Well, fuck it,' said Flower, 'I haven't shot anyone. At least let me do a couple of jokes. And they are the last ones I'll ever do.'

A beleaguered police Inspector with a loudhailer and two vanloads of policepersons who could shoot in a straight line shook his head and turned in a puzzled fashion to his colleague.

'They're all killing themselves laughing down there now,' he said.

'As long as they're not killing each other with that gun,' replied his colleague.

'You should be a fucking comedian,' replied the Inspector.

You can buy any of these other **Review** titles from your bookshop or *direct from the publisher*.

FREE P&P AND UK DELIVERY
(Overseas and Ireland £3.50 per book)

Green Grass	Raffaella Barker	£6.99
Cuban Heels	Emily Barr	£6.99
Jaded	Lucy Hawking	£6.99
Pure Fiction	Julie Highmore	£6.99
The World Unseen	Shamim Sarif	£6.99
Blackthorn Winter	Sarah Challis	£6.99
Spit Against the Wind	Anna Smith	£6.99
Dancing In a Distant Place	Isla Dewar	£6.99
Dad's Life	Dave Hill	£6.99
Magpie Bridge	Liu Hong	£6.99
My Lover's Lover	Maggie O'Farrell	£6.99
Ghost Music	Candida Clark	£6.99
The Water's Edge	Louise Tondeur	£6.99

TO ORDER SIMPLY CALL THIS NUMBER

01235 400 414

or visit our website: www.madaboutbooks.com